Its touch brought glory or death!

"Die, swine!" cried the rebel. The man's sword rose and fell. Blood spattered from the constable's wound. The remaining constable proved easy prey. The six who survived the ambush stood over the bodies, gloating. Again Vered tried to attack, and again his blade passed through his target as if traveling through smoke.

Vered jumped back to reassess his actions. The rebels paid him no heed. It was as if he did not exist for them. But he *saw* and *heard* so clearly!

Movement behind drew him around. He faced the leader of this small group. He *felt* power exuding from this man.

The wizard halted and cocked his head to one side. He yelled, "Search the area! There is another lurking nearby! Another wizard!"

Vered spun and used his *sight* to look for the other wizard. He *saw* no one. It took several seconds for him to realize that this sorcerer did not mean another. He meant Vered.

THE GLASS WARRIOR
Book I of the DEMON CROWN TRILOGY

ROBERT E. VARDEMAN

BOOK I OF THE DEMON CROWN TRILOGY

THE GLASS WARRIOR

A TOM DOHERTY ASSOCIATES BOOK
NEW YORK

THE GLASS WARRIOR

Copyright © 1989 by Robert E. Vardeman

A TOR Book
Published by Tom Doherty Associates, Inc.
49 West 24 Street
New York, NY 10010

Cover art by Don Brautigam

ISBN: 0-812-55704-2   Can. ISBN: 0-812-55705-6

Library of Congress Catalog Card Number: 88-51001

First edition: January 1989

Printed in the United States of America

0 9 8 7 6 5 4 3 2 1

CASTLE OF THE WINDS

YORRAL MOUNTAINS

TUNNEL

CLAYMORE PASS

UVAIN PLATEAU

FRON

N

RIVER TY

CASTLE POROTANE

IRON RANGE

SWAMP

CITY OF STOLEN DREAMS

THE KINGDOM of POROTANE

50 MILES

CHAPTER ONE

"Betrayed! Lord Dews, we've been betrayed! Everywhere! Their soldiers surround us!"

"Calm yourself, Jiskko. They come to join us, not to fight us." Dews Gaemock leaned back, feeling the bones in his spine separate. Jabs of pain made him think for the hundredth time this day that he had grown too old for insurrection. No matter that the rulers in Porotane were despots and that the royal line had died with King Lamost. Gaemock slowly straightened a war-weary arm. More joints cracked, like corn thrown into a campfire.

"But Lord, look at them! They do not carry the black and gold banner of Ionia's ruffians. The only war pennants in sight are pure green."

Gaemock forced himself upright, then got to his feet. It took him only seconds to see that his adviser had spoken the truth. "Whose banners are those?" he demanded. His dark eyes scanned the circle of his silent commanders. They shook their heads and averted their eyes.

Again, his intelligence had failed, perhaps fatally. Gaemock cursed. "This never happened when Efran rode at my side."

1

"Lord," said Jiskko, "your brother is long the traitor."

"Never say that!" raged Gaemock. His dark eyes burned like coals. Jiskko wilted under the look. "My brother is no traitor. He has chosen to support the royals. That is all."

"But Lord, we *fight* the royals. We march on Porotane to take it from Duke Freow and his sycophant dogs."

Dews Gaemock forced down his seething anger. His younger brother had always acted independently. Sometimes Efran had been independent of good sense, but Gaemock could not fault him for that. Sometimes *he* acted stupidly.

As he did now. The green banners were not those of Lady Ionia, his temporary ally in this siege of Porotane's castle. Had she betrayed him already? Ionia was a treacherous bitch, and he had allowed Jiskko and the others to convince him against his instincts that alliance with her would prove the turning point in the civil war. Too long they had battled, faction against faction, brother against brother, Gaemock thought bitterly. If only King Lamost had not died so suddenly. Assassinated some said.

The cause of the king's death mattered little. The kidnapping of his twin children, Lokenna and Lorens, did. Without a successor to ascend the throne, without a true heir to don the Demon Crown, the entire kingdom had disintegrated over the past twenty sorrow-and-death-filled years. Duke Freow claimed to hunt for the children. Gaemock could not believe it. Even if the duke's claim that Lorens and lovely little Lokenna had been stolen away by a wizard were true, some trace of them would have been found over *twenty* years.

"Sire," called Jiskko. "A runner from the front lines." Gaemock's adviser motioned. A youngling, hardly more than eight summers, dashed up and fell to his knees, head bowed.

"What have you seen, son?" asked Gaemock, holding back the tears as he spoke. So young. The boy was so young. His spies had been reduced to children. Not two years ago his intelligence network had been the strongest in all Porotane. Not even Duke Freow matched it. But that had been before Efran left to side with the royals. Gaemock hoped that the duke appreciated his brother's tactical brilliance and unerringly strategic instincts.

"Lord Dews, they are commanded by a wizard. I was unable to learn his name."

"That is all right. Wizards are not known for their loquacity when it comes to naming themselves in public."

"Lord, I was close enough!" the boy cried. "If I had learned his name, I could have slain him!"

"The wizard's name means little. Another trader in magicks entering the battle does not matter. We have many who chevy our steps for their own gain. What did you see of their battle strength? This is of true importance."

"Lord, I believe the wizard entered into treacherous alliance with the Lady Ionia. He mentioned her often, laughing as he did so. At his command are a full five hundred armed soldiers. They have fanned out along the valley to our right flank, and move steadily forward to put themselves between Porotane's castle and our escape route."

Gaemock nodded. "Continue your report, son." The boy rattled on but Gaemock did not listen. His mind worked over the tactical considerations of continuing the siege against Duke Freow and the castle of Porotane. He had to consider that Ionia had either been destroyed or had betrayed him. Gaemock's eyes rose and scanned the two hills his troops occupied—and the valley below. If he ordered the attack on Porotane's castle, the wizard would be in good position to push through that valley and cut Gaemock's rebel forces in half.

If he did not advance, Gaemock controlled the high ground and might be able to trap the other's forces should the wizard prove impatient.

"Lord, we should retreat. Leave Porotane for another day. Without Ionia's assistance, we stand little chance for success in battle." Jiskko shifted nervously from foot to foot, his fingers drumming on his sword hilt.

"The River Ty," said Gaemock. "Have our sappers readied the dams?"

Another commander spoke to this. "Lord, they are ready. The flow can be diverted in less than an hour, leaving the castle without water."

Gaemock brushed this aside. "That is of no consequence now. Freow has cisterns filled with water. He has tuns in the cellars of the castle, enough to supply his defenders for a month or more. When we planned this attack, we saw it as a lengthy siege. We would cut off their water, burn their fields, and force as many to take shelter within the castle walls as possible."

"Lord, the wizard's troops begin to advance," said Jiskko, his attention focused on a semaphore signaler on a distant hill. Even as he watched, the signalman burst into flame.

"The wizard's doing," Gaemock said tiredly. "I can fight with sword and bow, but not their demon-damned magic! How I hate them all!" Dews Gaemock waved his fist at the sky, cursing all sorcerers.

The earliest battles in the civil war had been feeble when compared with more recent ones. Only a month previous, Gaemock had seen an entire field ripped asunder by a wizard's lightning bolt. Not only the crops in the field but a score of peasant farmers had perished. The wizard had misdirected his blast and missed the rebel soldiers.

Seldom did such wanton and senseless killing occur when sword was in hand. The warrior's code held, even among the fighting segments of Porotane, and only those armed and in battle were slain. Surrender might come too slow, but was observed more often than not when soldiers could fight no more. Gaemock had gained his most valued commanders through surrender. Jiskko had roamed the countryside with his own band of mercenaries for over three years before meeting Gaemock's forces and being vanquished.

Jiskko had given his solemn oath of allegiance, and Gaemock valued him above all others on his small staff. And never had Jiskko given him reason to doubt that loyalty.

But wizards? Gaemock scoffed at them and openly shouted obscenities when he saw one. They had no honor. Random slaughter meant nothing to them. A field filled with peasant farmers, women, and children? The wizard had no doubt felt only passing scorn for them. Perhaps anger at his intended victims for not being where he directed his magical blast, but remorse for the innocent dead? Never.

How the wizard he now faced had subverted Ionia, he couldn't say. The woman had given her word, but Gaemock had extracted it from her under less than honorable circumstances. A smile slipped across his lips, vanishing as quickly as it had appeared. The night in Ionia's camp had been interesting. Seldom had Gaemock found a bed companion as skilled and exciting. She had vowed her undying love for him. This Gaemock had thought exaggeration generated by the throes of passion, but she had also pledged support for his thrust into Porotane's belly.

"Damn her, too," he said.

"Lord?"

"Nothing, Jiskko. You are correct in your appraisal. We cannot attack the castle successfully. Not now, not with a rival force in the field threatening us."

"We do not believe Freow will sally forth from the castle," said another commander. "We can deal with this wizard and . . ."

Gaemock shook his head. The commander's voice trailed off when he saw the disapproval on his leader's face. "No," said Gaemock, "this battle must wait for another day. We seek only escape now, escape with as little damage done to our soldiers as possible."

"Lord!" protested Jiskko. "We have spent vast sums on this attack. To stop now, why, that would set us back six months or longer. We could not hope to mount another force before autumn, if then."

"I will not see my brave fighters killed senselessly," Gaemock said firmly. "There will be more gold." He laughed harshly. "We have lived as brigands for years. Another few months should do nothing but enhance our cutthroat reputation."

"I'll order the sappers to destroy the dikes, Lord," said the commander of the battle engineers.

"No!"

"But why not? Diverting the River Ty was intended to break the spirit of the castle's defenders. Why—"

"No. Bring me a map and I'll show you what I have in mind."

The boy dashed away, returning in a few minutes with a large parchment scroll. Gaemock took it and spread out the illuminated map, ignoring the dragons and other wivern frolicking around the borders. Gaemock stared at the map, then thrust his finger onto it.

"Here. This is the point where the sappers have prepared the temporary dams. If they move them less than a hundred paces upstream and place them thusly, the Ty will flow past our position. Otherwise, the river is diverted into the southern swamps past the castle."

"The valley between our forces will be flooded if they move upstream," said Jiskko. "But such a move is not possible without an additional week of hard work. The sappers sought only to divert the river from supplying the castle, not bring its course down this valley."

"A pity, isn't it?" mused Gaemock. "We need the valley flooded, if we are to rout the other forces."

"That prevents the wizard from attacking," said Jiskko. "But even if such a flooding were possible, his purpose is still served. Our strength will be halved. He can choose which side to attack and we shall be unable to reinforce because of the river."

Gaemock nodded, a lock of lank black hair falling forward to dangle before his eyes. "It would appear so, wouldn't it?" He smiled broadly. "We shall have a surprise for our backstabbing wizard."

"And Ionia?" urged Jiskko. He alone had cautioned Gaemock repeatedly against any alliance with the woman.

"We might seek her out at leisure, after our troops are secure. I would have words with her. Curt ones." Gaemock moved his finger on the map around the sappers' position, then stabbed down hard. "Abandon the dikes along the Ty. Since the engineers cannot serve us in time, remove them immediately. We will need them in the autumn for our new campaign."

"As my lord commands," said Jiskko.

Dews Gaemock dismissed his commanders to begin their new assignments, turning attention from the Porotane castle to the wizard's forces. He reached out and collared the boy who had acted as messenger.

"A word with you," Gaemock said.

The boy dropped again to his knees, head bowed. "I am yours to command, Lord Dews."

"Rubbish. Stand up straight, proud. Why do you think we fight?"

"To gain power over all Porotane."

"And then?" Gaemock prompted. "What do we do then, once we have won this war?"

"Why, you become king. I do not understand what you seek of me, Lord." The confusion on the boy's face showed that he had no firm knowledge of why Gaemock fought this bloody war. But then, the boy was only eight years of age. How many of Gaemock's adult advisers understood the purpose? Simple power? To throw Duke Freow out and sit upon the throne in his stead?

"I fight for freedom, son. I do not wish to replace the regent only to rule. I wish to restore order, to give Porotane a sense of security. Without any of royal blood on the throne, without the Demon Crown on the head of the true ruler, upstarts like Baron Theoll will force brutal laws on all our heads. I do not wish to overthrow royal authority, I fight to restore it—with freedom."

"But there are many others besides the baron," protested the boy.

"Most roam the countryside, setting up their own fiefdoms, enslaving rather than freeing. Yes, I know, oh, how I know. I fight them, also. That makes the war all the more brutal. Not only do I fight those who have usurped the throne, I fight those who *want* to usurp it."

The boy grinned shyly. "I never thought Duke Freow was a bad man."

"He isn't. But he is old and infirm and has been unable to restore either Lorens or Lokenna to the throne."

"Have you worn the Demon Crown?" asked the boy.

"No, and if I should triumph against the duke, I would not. Although royal blood flows in my veins, there is not enough to protect me against the ill effects of its magic. The crown is a symbol; it is also a two-edged weapon. It can be used for good, as King Lamost used it. It can also slay mercilessly, both the wearer and those unfortunate enough to reside within its range."

"Does the duke wear the Demon Crown?"

Gaemock shook his head. He had no idea what had become of the fabled, demon-given circlet. Duke Freow had never worn it in public. Spies told of Baron Theoll's attempts to steal it—and his failures to find it. Duke Freow had been a resourceful, if flawed regent. He had not kept order in the kingdom, but neither had he allowed ambitious men such as Theoll of Brandon to take full control.

"When we depose the duke and the baron and the others now in the castle, we will not wear the Demon Crown. That is only for full-blooded royalty. Unlike Freow, we will find the twins and place one on the throne."

"Which one, Lord Dews?"

"I cannot say. Either will do, if the kingdom can be united."

Gaemock shook himself free of the daydreaming. His power waxed and waned. He must now retreat and conserve his strength, prepare to again launch a siege of the castle. In the autumn, next spring, sometime. To do that, he must win free this day.

"I am entrusting you with a singular mission, son. You will run as fast as you can and tell the old woman who lives at the edge of the river that I need her immediately."

"But Lord, there are so many old women living on the River Ty. Which shall I fetch?"

Gaemock laughed. "You go. Which old woman I want will become apparent to you. And you shall not fetch her. You will be polite, do as she says, and make it plain to her that I am in dire need of her skills. If she will not aid me, get her to tell you outright and return immediately with the message. Do you understand?"

"No," the boy said slowly. "I might choose the wrong woman. Please, Lord Dews, describe her to me more fully."

"Trust me in this. You won't miss her. And I cannot tell you what she looks like, because her appearance changes often. Go now. Be swift of foot. She must respond before the sun sets this evening or half my troops will be lost."

The child bowed deeply, backed off a pair of steps, then turned and ran, his bare, callused feet pounding hard on the grassy slopes. Gaemock watched the boy leave and wondered if this fight was worth the death and suffering it caused. The boy obeyed so eagerly, not knowing his errand would mean the deaths of dozens or even scores of valiant men. Or perhaps the boy *did* know and that added speed to his step.

That thought appalled Dews Gaemock. The young learning the ways of death and dying and reveling in it. And why not? For an entire generation, war had been a constant, unvarying companion.

"The war," he wondered aloud. "Do I seek to overthrow Freow for good reasons or foul?" He shook his head. Gaemock knew he did not want to rule. He wanted only to install a rightful heir on the throne. Let another carry the heavy burden of the Demon Crown. But one of the royal blood would rule! He would see that the duke and his followers were deposed! The fight was worth it, if only to stop the tyranny that had grown, if only to put to rest the Inquisition that Archbishop Nosto fostered in Freow's name.

"Lord, the signals have been sent, but already the enemy marches on our position." Jiskko shook him gently, bringing him out of the latest round of endless worry about the righteousness of this war.

"Sorry, Jiskko. You say they have us boxed already?"

"Split, Lord. Each band can flee."

"Can we lure them into pursuit of one group, then attack their rear?" Even as he spoke, Gaemock saw that this would not be possible. The wizard they opposed might be venal and conniving, but he was no fool. The magical ward spells would alert him to any such plan in time to break off the engagement and retreat up the valley.

"If the wizard retreats, can we reform in the valley and pursue?" Gaemock asked.

"Yes, of course, but the wizard must know this. He will have prepared a surprise for us, I am sure."

"I am, also, Jiskko. Just a thought, not an order. Continue. Let the wizard divide our forces. But also alert each band to the chance to drive the swine's troops back into the valley. We do hold the high ground."

Gaemock's eyes turned toward the castle. It pained him to put away the siege until another day, but survival demanded this course. Duke Freow could not maintain his flimsy grip on Porotane forever. If Gaemock failed to dislodge the regent today, then autumn would see another attack. Let that fail, and another could be mounted in a year's time. Eventually the defenders had to tire and relent.

"They attack, Lord!" cried Jiskko.

"So I see." Gaemock watched as a thready line of his troops began falling back under the uphill charge on the far side of the valley. The range proved too much for the archers arrayed around him, but those on the other hill took a fearsome toll on the enemy.

"They waste lives with their attack. Their commander throws troops against the strongest parts of our line." Jiskko shook his head.

"They die, yes," said Gaemock, "but they have diverted us from Porotane's castle. No matter the outcome this day, Duke Freow has won a small victory."

"And Lady Ionia," Jiskko said bitterly.

"And lovely Ionia," agreed Gaemock. He settled down on his haunches to watch the progress of the battle. When the wizard's troops reached a spot two-thirds of the way up the hill, the boy Gaemock had sent as messenger came back, breathless from the long run.

"Quick, boy. Did you find her?"

"Yes!" The boy's eyes opened wider than saucers. "It was as you said. I had no trouble locating the old woman. I gave her your orders—"

"My *suggestions*." corrected Gaemock. "I do not order one such as she." He had not wanted to use the witch at all, but now he was obligated to her. So be it.

"Aye, that I found, Lord Dews." The boy swallowed hard. "In spite of my error, she has agreed."

"Good!" Gaemock rose and motioned. The signaler to his right passed the message across the field. The distant troops mounted a savage counterattack that drove the wizard's fighters back toward the valley floor. In concert, Gaemock ordered those arrayed around him to plunge downward, down into the valley, down to attack the enemy's rear.

The response from the enemy's line, although

expected, still stunned Gaemock and sent him
reeling. The wizard had placed more than a simple
ward spell along the bottom of the valley. Huge
sheets of flame rose more than a hundred feet into
the air to cut off any possible attack.

"We can't fight this!" cried Jiskko.

"We won't have to," said Gaemock, recovering. The heat boiling up from below made him
think he stared into the opened gate of hell. "The
wizard is not powerful enough to maintain this
spell for more than a few seconds." Even as he
spoke, Gaemock worried. The flames continued to
rage long past the point where a sorcerer should
have collapsed in exhaustion. A well-trained warri-
or might march all day and fight for an hour before
tiring to the point of insensibility. Gaemock had
never encountered a wizard able to maintain a
potent spell for more than a minute.

But still the flames clawed upward, preventing
him from reinforcing his troops on the other
hillside.

"Lord," said the boy suddenly. "Mayhap we
face more than one sorcerer."

"The boy speaks the truth," said Jiskko. "We
need more information about who oppose us."

"The only possibility is that Duke Freow has
formed an alliance with several wandering wizards. I do not believe this is possible. We would
have heard of the duke's intent to recruit. No, we
face only one wizard. He will tire."

Gaemock smiled when he saw the outer
fringes of the flame wall begin to cool. The sheets
of fire flickered, died, and soon only charred land
remained—land and more than a few skeletons of
those unfortunate enough to be caught in the
blaze.

"Are those ours or the wizard's?" asked Gaemock of his adviser.

Jiskko said, "Evenly divided, I fear, Lord. We took as good as we gave."

"Signal the assault on the other hill," said Gaemock. The sight of the burned bones of valiant soldiers sickened him. Damn all wizards!

"Should I also order your personal troops to retreat?"

"Yes. Do it now. The enemy will remain in confusion for a few minutes due to the wizard's spell. He did not warn them before casting. I can see the signs of their disarray."

Dews Gaemock watched as his tactic unfolded. The soldiers who had borne the brunt of conflict thus far responded well, driving the wizard's troops back to the valley floor. Only when the enemy began retreating up the valley did Gaemock signal for full attack. His two halves met, then pursued.

"Jiskko!" called Gaemock after they had gone less than a hundred paces after the fleeing enemy. "To the high ground. Both sides of the valley. Signal it now. Break off pursuit and run for the high ground!"

"But Lord, why?"

"Do it, damn your miserable hide!"

Jiskko ordered the signalers, but the formation proved too drawn out for effective communication. Two trumpeters came to the fore, their mournful blasts producing instant obedience by Gaemock's troops. None had the heart for this battle. They all sought the downfall of Duke Freow, not some wandering wizard intent on looting and random destruction.

The soldiers racing for the high ground

brought a change in the enemy troops. They wheeled and attacked.

The pounding of their horses' hooves, the triumphant shouts of their pikemen and bowmen drowned out the deep, resonant sounds from high up the valley.

"Keep the trumpeters a-blowing," ordered Gaemock. "Get the troops to even higher ground."

"The sound, Lord," murmured the boy. "It . . . it's a flood!"

Before the words had blossomed from his lips, the ten-foot-high wall of water swept through the valley, caught up horses and soldiers and rocks and trees, and carried them away. The roar of the watery battering ram silenced the trumpets, and a sheet of spray blasted into the air higher than the flame wall the wizard had constructed.

Gaemock leaned against a tree, his arms circling it. He watched the carnage below. The old woman might be a minor sorceress, scorned by those more powerful, but she controlled the dikes along the River Ty with her petty spells. A simple pass of her hand had opened flood gates and washed away all challenge to Gaemock's army.

And now he owed her. Damn!

"Get the semaphores working, Jiskko. Signal the far side of the valley. Rendezvous in one week at our training site."

"We abandon the siege of the castle?"

"For now Duke Freow and Porotane are safe from us. But only for the moment," said Gaemock. "I will not stop until the kingdom is wrested from him." With that Dews Gaemock spun and stalked off. The attack had been blunted by that meddling wizard, but his forces remained intact. For that, he gave thanks.

But so many deaths this day. And for what?

The only thing sadder than not knowing the name of the wizard he had slain this day was not caring.

CHAPTER TWO

The black cloak whispered softly around the man's small, wiry frame as he pulled it closer about his shoulders. With the cloak in place, he vanished from sight in deep shadows. Softer than the shadows he mimicked, he drifted down the castle's main corridors, found secondary routes, stopped to look to see if anyone followed, then reached out and tugged at a rocky protrusion high on the wall. Silently, a section of wall slid back. The ebony-cloaked man entered. The door closed behind and plunged the secret passage into utter darkness save for seven tiny pinpoints of light in the distance.

On feet quieter than velvet moving over velvet, he went to the first spyhole and peered into the room beyond. Nothing. The next afforded a sight hardly more interesting. Two serving wenches sat about gossiping. Their wild rumors and obscene comments about the lords in the castle of Porotane might have interested him at another time. Not now. He drifted on, choosing the fifth spyhole.

Eye pressed hard against the hole, he looked into lavishly appointed sleeping chambers. Tiny moans of pleasure came to his straining ears. He turned until he saw the large bed piled with silks and furs. Atop the bed lay a nude couple, their bodies intricately intertwined in the passion of lovemaking.

He held down his own excitement as he watched the act proceed as surely as any play in the castle's yearly drama pageant. Licking dried lips, he moved away, then placed his other eye to the spyhole. His right had become blurred from the tension of the position.

If he had designed these secret ways, the spyholes would have been placed lower to better accommodate one of his stature.

"Oh, Johanna," came the soft cries from the room. The watching man smiled. This confirmed all he had heard. Lady Johanna and the lieutenant of the night guard. For this dalliance the guard could be put to death. His post was along the castle battlements watching for rebel attacks, not locked in the passionate arms of a noble lady.

"Seen enough, Baron?" came a low voice. The dark-clad figure sprang from the spyhole, his hand flashing to a dagger sheathed at his belt. He blinked rapidly, trying to readjust his eyes from the light of the sleeping chamber and the amorously locked pair to the inky darkness of the passageway.

"Who's there?" Baron Theoll demanded. "Speak or I'll slice your tongue from your head!"

"It is a sin to spy on others," came the disembodied voice. Although Theoll could not see his accuser, he recognized the voice now.

"Archbishop Nosto, you startled me. I only spied on those disloyal to the throne."

"You get strange pleasure from this act of 'patriotism,' Baron. It is not natural. Is the scrying power granted by the Demon Crown the reason you desire it so?"

"Do not think to anger me, Nosto," snapped Theoll. He sheathed his dagger. His eyes had found the dim figure of the prelate. The floppy headgear, the tight-fitting red suit of a cleric, the tall, thin body, all these identified Archbishop Nosto.

The Archbishop brushed past Theoll and peered through the spyhole, then pulled away. Theoll saw the cleric shaking his head in bewilderment. What did a cleric know of intelligence-gathering? The entire castle ran rampant with plots, allegiances forming and disintegrating hour to hour, second to second. Without such current information, how was Theoll to survive?

How was he to ever find the accursed Demon Crown? And don it?

"Let us adjourn to my chambers, Archbishop. It is quieter there." The crescendo of sobs and moans from Lady Johanna's chambers emphasized the baron's words.

They walked down the secret passageway and out into a main castle corridor. At this late hour, no one stirred in these halls. Baron Theoll made an impatient gesture to the cleric and strode off, his short legs trying and failing to outdistance the taller man's. Theoll stopped in front of the door leading to his quarters, glanced along the corridor in both directions, and then entered.

"Always so suspicious, Baron. You should learn to trust those within the castle. We all oppose the rebel forces."

"That is true," said Theoll, "but it does not mean that we do not also oppose each other. Enemy of my enemy does not make my friend."

Archbishop Nosto settled onto a simple footstool and looked up at the baron. The man's quick movements betrayed nervousness. Or excitement?

Had he been so stimulated by spying on the Lady Johanna? Nosto shook his head sadly. For all the instruction he had given Theoll, this seemed one lesson that had been ignored. Privacy meant nothing to the Baron of Brandon—except his own, which he guarded with a jealousy approaching fanaticism.

"The Demon Crown is once more within the castle walls," Theoll said. "That fool Freow has sent for it. I must obtain it! I must!"

"What is the source of this information?" asked Archbishop Nosto. "No one has come forward and told me."

"You mean you haven't been able to torture the information from anyone," Theoll said, sneering. "You prattle on about me peering through a spyhole at traitors while you break bones and burn out eyes in the name of the Inquisition. Which method obtains the better intelligence?"

"I do not enjoy my work as Inquisitor," said the cleric. He sighed. "But sinfulness is everywhere. So many stray from the True Path." He straightened on the stool, his face almost glowing with his righteousness. "The tortures are not to squeeze out information but to instill godliness in the miscreants."

"It's fortuitous that your heretics and my enemies happen to be in league," said Baron Theoll.

"Who can say where a lamb blunders when it leaves the True Path?"

Theoll laughed harshly. "This lamb will never stray, will it, Nosto? I see that it won't." Theoll settled into the heavily padded chair on a dais. From this vantage, he towered over anyone who sought an audience with him. Theoll had long since stopped noticing that the Archbishop always sat on this footstool to maintain a "proper" elevation. They needed one another, the baron and archbishop, and neither fully admitted it.

"You have sought the Demon Crown since King Lamost died. Why do you think the duke has become so careless to reveal it to you now? Although he is gravely ill, Freow retains much of his former cunning."

Theoll smirked. Direct assassination had proven impossible with the regent, unlike the unlamented King Lamost. Duke Freow had deftly avoided every attempt. Even the judicious use of wizardry had proven ineffective. But Theoll had found the way through Freow's defenses. For over a year he had been slowly poisoning the duke with a potion prepared by a sorcerer sequestered in the upper reaches of the Yorral Mountains. Not magical in nature, the potion worked by accumulation over the years. Theoll often waited weeks or even months before adding new doses of the potion to the duke's food. Even a taster with a sensitive palate could not detect the poison in such small amounts.

"Now that the duke lies near death, he has summoned the keeper of the Demon Crown."

"Have you learned who this mysterious keeper is?" asked Archbishop Nosto. "I have heard only rumors."

"We thrive on rumors in Porotane," said Theoll. "I *know* the keeper." He paused to build the proper amount of anticipation in the cleric. Nosto enjoyed these revelations and Theoll delivered the words dramatically and well. "It is the Glass Warrior."

Archbishop Nosto made a rude noise and

waved his hand, as if dismissing the baron. "Do not waste my time, Theoll. She is legend and nothing more. The Glass Warrior." He snorted and pushed to his feet. Even with Theoll's raised chair, Nosto stared directly into the baron's cold eyes.

"I do not jest," snapped Theoll. "She exists. She has been entrusted with the Demon Crown until the twins are found."

"Does that search progress any better than your other schemes?"

"Duke Freow has not pressed the search; he has enjoyed rule in Porotane for too long."

"And you seek out Lokenna and Lorens to slay them, to establish yourself as heir to the throne."

"Would such an occurence displease my lord archbishop?"

"The twins have been missing for too long. What would they know of ruling a kingdom the size of Porotane? I feel you are a better choice, Baron. You know that."

"They would certainly never honor the leading cleric in the realm as I would, I who know your true merit," taunted Theoll.

"If you seize the Demon Crown from this mythical warrior woman, what would you do with it first?"

Theoll studied the tall, thin man intently. The question seemed innocuous. Theoll knew otherwise. "There are two problems of paramount importance to unifying Porotane," he replied. "The Inquisition must be brought to an end by the elimination of the heretics, and the rebels must be routed. Dews Gaemock and his ruffians must not continue to rob and pillage as the duke has allowed for too long." Theoll saw the fervor return to

Archbishop Nosto's face. The death of all heretics lay near to the cleric's heart. For all his protests, Nosto enjoyed the sight of tortured bodies as much as Theoll enjoyed the stolen sight of women with their lovers.

"After these matters are resolved," Theoll continued, "I would don the Demon Crown and seek out Lokenna and Lorens."

"They are of the blood. They are the true heirs," pointed out Nosto.

"I would take care in how I eliminated them." Theoll smiled wickedly. "Perhaps the sight granted by the Demon Crown would show that the children have become heretics."

This line of thinking appealed to Archbishop Nosto. He nodded. "They have been gone from the grace of my services for almost twenty years."

"They were stolen away the year following King Lamost's death."

"Nineteen years then," mused Nosto. "A time long enough to be seduced from the True Path."

"They would be of twenty-four summers now," said Theoll.

"If they live."

Baron Theoll said nothing. As he had learned that the Glass Warrior had been entrusted with the Demon Crown, so had he learned that both twins survived. All that he needed was to locate the pair.

Locate and kill the offspring of Lamost—and take the Demon Crown for his own. Success that had stretched out of reach for years now dropped into his lap.

The jester shook his head and sent his lank dark hair flying in wild disarray around his face, turning him into something less than human. Harhar bounced up and down on legs that seemed to have steel springs instead of flesh and blood muscle, then he slipped and fell heavily to the floor.

Sheepishly, the jester looked up and smiled weakly. He rubbed himself where he had fallen. Those he tried to entertain ignored him. Their full attention focused on Duke Freow, lying pale and emaciated on his bed.

"Has she come yet? I must see her," the ancient duke said.

"Please," said the court physician. "Rest. Do not speak, my duke. You are too weak."

"Let me tell a joke. Let me make him better." Harhar bounced up and perched on the end of the duke's bed. "O Mighty Duke, once there was a sweet young lass of sixteen summers who—"

Harhar crashed to the floor when the physician cuffed him. "Leave us, fool. The duke requires rest, not your madness."

"No, wait," said Freow, a skeletal hand clutching at the physician's sleeve. "Let Harhar stay. He . . . he amuses me."

With ill grace, the physician nodded. The jester moved to a corner of the room and stood quietly, ebony eyes darting around, seeking out any opportunity to amuse the failing monarch.

"I must see the Glass Warrior," said Freow. "Bring her to me at once."

"Sire, she was summoned. She travels as she pleases. The messenger told her that you . . . that the matter was of utmost urgency."

"I have been so selfish," moaned Duke Freow. "So selfish. I thought to rule Porotane."

"You tire yourself, Duke," said the physician.

"You have done what you thought best for the kingdom. None fault you for that."

The old man made a gesture. The physician said nothing. The duke was dying by slow inches and he had been unable to discover the reason. The best wizards had checked for ensorcellments and found naught. Physically, the duke seemed healthy. But he died, slowly, painfully. The physician guessed at a slow poison, but had been unable to detect it.

The physician cursed his own failure to discover the reason for the infirmity even as he secretly considered the potential of the poison. To possess this for his own use would enhance his power in the court a hundredfold!

"Leave me for the moment," ordered Freow. "No, Harhar can stay. He still amuses me."

The physician left the jester to do what he could to brighten the old man's flagging spirits. It seemed little enough for a man who might not see another sunrise.

The castle walls rose into the darkness of the night until they blocked even the stars. The snow-white-haired woman walked her steed at the base of those walls until the postern gate appeared behind a tall, leafy shrub of indeterminate variety. The Glass Warrior drew her strangely shining blade and slowly pushed away the bush. No trip wires had been attached since last she entered the castle of Porotane.

Careful examination of the door lock betrayed no bright, recent scratches. She drew a key of glass from a pouch and inserted it in the lock. A quick twist and the narrow, low door opened. She hurried down the long, dark passageway between the walls and emerged to glance about the deserted courtyard beyond, then ducked back to tie her horse to the bush.

"I'll return before dawn," she said, patting the animal on its powerful neck. The mare nickered and tried to pull away. The Glass Warrior stayed until the horse quieted. Only then did she slip back into the castle and make her way through silent passages to the uppermost levels of the castle where Duke Freow lay dying.

Tall, confident, she walked along the deserted halls of power. Only when she reached the branching, empty corridor leading to Duke Freow's bed chambers did she pause. A frown marred the perfection of her ageless face. She took off her cape and wrapped it around her left arm. A guard always stood at this juncture.

The lack of a guard meant danger.

She sucked in a deep breath, settled herself, and drew her sword. The faint light from candles along the corridor caught the glass blade and reflected rainbows. Along the back side of the blade gleamed a thin tube of purplish liquid. The Glass Warrior adjusted the tube in such a fashion that it would not break if she slashed or thrust with the blade. Only then did she advance.

Her quick gray eyes darted back and forth, studying every entryway. But only her quick reflexes saved her from the attack from above. A dark clad assassin dropped from a niche in the roof.

He shrieked in pain and death as she took a quick step away and dropped to brace the sword hilt against the floor. The falling killer impaled himself on her blade. She rolled him over and carefully drew the now-bloody blade from his chest. His open eyes stared sightlessly at the ceiling from which he had jumped.

She spun in time to meet the silent, vicious attack of another. Her glass blade deflected shining steel. A quick whipping motion brought her cape around and tangled the man's feet. The Glass Warrior jerked hard, sending him to his back. He hit hard, rolled, and tried to escape her vengeance. She lunged, the tip of the long glass sword driving through his back and penetrating his heart.

She swung about and faced a third assassin. The Glass Warrior deflected the first thrust with her cape. She flicked her sword wrist in a curious fashion. The action forced the thin-walled tube of liquid along the back blood gutter and to the tip of her sword. She danced away from the wall, parried, backed, then riposted. The tube broke and liquid sprayed forth.

The soul-tearing scream torn from the assassin as the burning acid melted his face died when she lunged and drove the tip of her blade into his throat. Coughs, gurgles, thwarted shrieks of pain, then silence. The final assassin lay at her feet.

The Glass Warrior flicked her wrist once more, sending the now-empty tube to the floor. She drew another tube of the purplish acid from the hilt of her sword and fitted it carefully onto the tip of her blade. If three had ventured out to kill her this night, more might await her.

Armed and ready for any new ambush, she went to the door of the duke's chamber and pressed her ear against the heavy wood panels. From inside came muffled words and a weak chuckle. She opened the door a fraction and

peered in. She smiled. Harhar entertained his
dying master.

"Duke?" she called softly. "I have come, as
you commanded."

The jester swung about, eyes narrowed, hand
clutching his rattle as if it were a weapon.

"Harhar, no!" cried the duke. "She is a
friend."

The Glass Warrior bowed deeply. "And I will
always remain a friend to whoever attempts to
restore King Lamost's line to the throne of
Porotane."

She stiffened when she saw tears forming in
the old man's eyes. How he had aged in the four
years since last she had seen him. It might have
been a hundred passing for all the ravages time
had brought to him.

"I am unworthy of such loyal followers," the
old man sobbed.

"You have done well, my duke."

"No!" he protested. He reached out his bony
hand and clutched at her cape, drawing her closer.
"I have not. I have betrayed the trust placed in me
by Lamost."

"How is this? Have you not sought out
Lokenna and Lorens? Have you not given into my
protection the birthright of the Porotane rulers?"
His stricken look put her on guard.

He shook his head and cried openly now. "I
have made no such attempt to find Lamost's kidnapped children. I have done nothing! I sought
only to rule Porotane myself. The power, oh, how I
loved the power!"

"But, my duke, you could not love only power.
Why entrust me with the Demon Crown when
wearing it would allow you the ultimate power in

the kingdom? No place would be closed to you, no action hidden, no thought too well guarded."

"You know of the crown's power," Freow said, his voice faltering. Both the Glass Warrior and Harhar moved closer. She reached out and squeezed the jester's arm to reassure him.

"I do," she said.

"Then you know that, when the last demon bestowed it as tribute and reparation on the rulers of Porotane, a condition went with it."

"Yes, only those of the blood royal may wear it. But Freow, you are a *duke*. You are Lamost's brother."

The wizened old man shook his head. The tears pouring from his eyes soaked the bedclothes. "I am a pretender, a fraud. Harhar is more a duke than I."

"You are a changeling? But Lamost—"

"Lamost never knew. The true Duke Freow ruled the lands along the sea. None in the castle had seen him in many years."

"There had been some dispute between Lamost and you."

"Between Lamost and his true brother. When the king was assassinated, Freow began a solitary journey of penitence and mourning. I . . . I slew him on the road and assumed his role."

"You are not of the royal line," said the Glass Warrior. "You cannot wear the Demon Crown!"

"Nor could I relinquish the power I found following the king's death. I was weak. Never had I seen such wealth, such riches. Freow was a cruel lord. I considered this a way of regaining what had been taken from me."

Harhar moved about nervously, looking from the frail old man to the Glass Warrior.

"You also killed the duchess when she came to Porotane," accused the woman.

"I did. She would have exposed me. I was so weak, so weak." The man's voice told of weakness beyond that of morality.

"You have ruled well, however," the Glass Warrior said. "And you did entrust the Demon Crown to me when others might have destroyed it."

"Again, weakness. I sought only to keep it from those with true claim to the throne. But now I am dying."

The Glass Warrior stared at him. Her emotions raged. She had believed Freow—the man posing as Duke Freow—to be honorable and honest. Now she discovered his venality overshadowed even that of Baron Theoll. Did this erase all the good he *had* done? She needed time to consider.

"Please, I wish to repent my sins. You have the Demon Crown?"

Silently, the Glass Warrior pushed back her cape and pulled forth a small backpack of the purest midnight velvet. She opened it. Within rode a crystalline box. Within the box rested a plain circlet of gold. A few runes crossed the brow. Other than this, the crown lacked ornamentation of any kind.

"So simple-looking, yet so powerful a tool for good or evil," Freow said.

"You wish to don it?" She thrust the glass box toward the man. He recoiled.

"No! I wished only to gaze upon what can never be mine."

"Why did you summon me?" The Glass Warrior wondered if Freow had sent the assassins after her. She doubted it. Whatever troubled the old man, it was not her caretaking of the Demon Crown. He had only to ask for it without baring his soul.

"I want you to perform the task I should have carried out nineteen years ago. After Lamost died, I was appointed regent for the twins."

"Did you have them kidnapped?" demanded the woman. Dying or not, he would suffer the dire consequences if he had made craven war on young children.

"No, not I. A wizard. Never have I learned his name."

"How will I locate the heirs?" she asked.

"Never have I revealed this to another. The wizard responsible for Lamost's death is Tahir d'mar. Seek him out. He knows what has become of Lorens and Lokenna. He must!"

The Glass Warrior frowned. Tahir had vanished long ago. She had never suspected him of complicity in King Lamost's death, but then she avoided political intrigues and idle speculation on them.

"Tahir acted on orders from another. Who, I have never learned. Baron Theoll of Brandon perhaps. Almost certainly," the old man said. "But he is both cautious and powerful, and I have never openly challenged him."

The Glass Warrior wondered how many assassination attempts had been made. This man who posed as Duke Freow might be of common birth but he possessed a royal's knack for court machinations.

"Go, find the children, restore one to the throne—it matters little which one. Let one wear

the Demon Crown and end the war wracking
Porotane. I want the kingdom to find the peace I so
ardently seek for myself."

Harhar tugged on the woman's cape. "He
fades quickly."

"Yes, he does, but within is a core of steel.
Duke Freow might recover enough to maintain
order until I have completed the mission he has
given me."

"But he isn't—" The Glass Warrior's hand
covered the jester's mouth and silenced him.

"You are not to repeat this to anyone. Do you
understand?" He bobbed his head in assent.
"Good. Look after him as if he were the true duke.
Keep his spirits up with your antics."

"And you'll return with a new king or queen?"
The jester's eagerness amused her.

"I will try. Finding Tahir after so many years
will be difficult. He might have had nothing to do
with the kidnapping." She abruptly cut off her flow
of words.

"I will find the true heirs and give them their
heritage."

The Glass Warrior held the crystalline box
containing the Demon Crown at arm's length, as if
it contained only death and destruction.

CHAPTER THREE

Baron Theoll drifted along the castle corridors like a phantom, his dark cape making the only sound as he moved. He stood stock still when he saw the first assassin laying face down in the hall. Burning eyes lifted and found the second killer. Theoll knew that the third assassin had also been slain. Although the trio had not been his best, they represented a new school of mercenaries in whom he had placed great trust.

They had not proven adequate for the task of slaying a lone woman.

Theoll experienced a polar chill racing up his back at the thought of the Glass Warrior. For so many years he had tried to kill her. Each attempt had been thwarted. Theoll had no evidence that he had done more than irritate her. Never had even one of his carefully trained assassins seriously wounded her. Theoll worried that she had not even been bloodied.

He paid no heed to the corpses. He rushed to a panel in the hall and ran his nimble fingers along the horns of a ram trapped forever in the ornately carved hunting scene. The secret door swung inward. Theoll paused for a moment before entering. He controlled so little in this portion of the castle. High risk meant more than mere discovery. If Duke Freow caught him, no amount of influence-bartering would save him from the castle executioner.

Theoll closed the secret panel and moved quickly along the narrow passageway, climbed a short flight of stone steps, and then crawled on his belly for another fifty feet. The spyhole into the duke's chambers had been drilled at the juncture between ceiling and wall. The view was obstructed by furniture in the room and overhearing what transpired within proved impossible. But any knowledge gained might mean his salvation.

Theoll squinted and scooted closer, his eye hurting as he strained to see through solid furniture and the gauzy curtains veiling the duke's deathbed.

He saw only the duke's feeble hand—and the Demon Crown beside the duke on the bed.

Theoll caught his breath and held it. The Glass Warrior had brought the Demon Crown to Freow!

The baron almost turned and wiggled back to summon a full platoon of his guards. Seizing the Demon Crown now might allow him to assume the throne. Then reason settled and he continued his uneasy vigil.

The Glass Warrior might be capable of fighting even a brigade of his best soldiers. She was rumored to be a sorceress, a fighter second to none, a phantom returned to the world, a goddess. The first might be possible, the second had proven true on many occasions, and the other two rumors Theoll doubted. But capable of defending Freow she was—at least long enough for those still loyal to the failing duke to aid him.

". . . entrust you with this mission," Theoll heard Duke Freow say. Moving about, almost injuring his eye, Theoll spotted the Glass Warrior. She stood quietly beside the bed, hand resting on the hilt of her glass sword.

The woman's words rang clearer than the dying duke's. "You may depend on me, Duke."

Theoll saw the Demon Crown vanish from the bed. A sharp click as of a latch closing echoed through the silent chamber. Two quick, hollow bootsteps and the sound of the door closing.

The Glass Warrior had departed!

Theoll knew he could never get back to the corridor in time to stop her. The coldness he had experienced on realizing that she had slain three of his better assassins poured like cold water over him once more. His fighting prowess on a good day equaled that of many in Porotane. But those that he could consistently best were few. To attempt to stop the Glass Warrior alone would be suicidal.

He watched as the jester cavorted about, uttering silly noises, trying to make the dying duke's last minutes less painful. Theoll wished that he could poison both duke and jester. Harhar always made him the butt of his cruel jokes, but who could discipline a lowly jester? To do so would show weakness that others vying for power in the castle might exploit.

When he became king of Porotane the jester's ugly head would grace a pike outside the gates.

Theoll worked his way backward in the tight crawl space and descended the stairs. He pressed his ear against the secret panel leading into the corridor, listening intently for a hint that the Glass Warrior lay in wait for him. Theoll finally opened the panel a fraction of an inch and peered out. He saw only one corpse. Slipping out, he glanced back and forth.

As he had thought, the woman had not lingered. Freow had given her a mission, and the baron had a good idea what it might be. For almost twenty years Duke Freow had told the council of nobles that he sought the heirs to the throne of Porotane. Theoll knew that he lied. No emissaries visited neighboring lands to inquire of the missing twins. No soldiers scoured the countryside, save to do war against the rebel bands. No wizards cast scrying spells. The duke ruled and did not want to find the children.

Until now. Until he felt the life holding him to this world slipping from weak, poisoned fingers. He had dispatched the Glass Warrior, with the Demon Crown, to find Lokenna or Lorens.

The baron threw caution to the winds as he raced along the deserted corridors. His heavy bootsteps echoed until the sound threatened to deafen him. He skidded on the slick floor and spun about to enter a tiny dormitory on the level below his own quarters.

A dozen men slept on pallets. His entry brought them awake, daggers in hand. Theoll paused to smile at their alertness. They would need that and all the training he had lavished on them for the past two years to equal the Glass Warrior.

And equal her—best her!—they must.

"You, you, you," Baron Theoll barked, pointing out the soldiers he wanted. "Come with me immediately. The rest of you, prepare to ride at the first light of dawn."

He stood by impatiently as the trio donned

their uniforms and settled their sword belts around their waists.

The baron spun and hurried from the barracks room, the three following close behind. He hastened to the battlements and studied the stars above. The constellations twisted in preparation for sliding below the curtain of blue that drew across when the dawn broke. The Box of Gems had closed for the night and the Thief's grasping hand had almost vanished, too. There would be enough time for his soldiers to pursue the Glass Warrior, Theoll decided. The darkness would hinder her.

"Scan the countryside for a lone rider," he ordered. These three had the sharpest night vision of any in his small platoon. "Be alert for any glint of light off a glass weapon."

"Glass?" asked one. "The only one carrying a glass sword is—"

"Look!" snapped Theoll. "You need not make comments."

The trio began their scrutiny of shadows and movement across the broad fields surrounding the castle of Porotane's ruler. Theoll paced along the battlements, hands clasped behind his back, a dark scowl marring his regular features. As he walked, he thought hard of what must be done. The duke's condition worsened daily. It was only a matter of time—perhaps hours—before the potion worked its fatal duty and left Porotane without a ruler.

Duke Freow was only regent for the twins, or so went the thread of law. Freow had ruled in their stead, but the children were children no longer, if they lived. The Glass Warrior had been sent to locate Lokenna and Lorens. It took only one twin to don the Demon Crown and become undisputed ruler of Porotane.

The baron growled deep in his throat. A soldier looked fearfully at him, then turned back to his duty of searching for traces of the Glass Warrior. Possession of the Demon Crown was pivotal to ruling Porotane. With it on his head, Theoll could project his image anywhere in the realm. His phantom image might spy on enemies in their most secret councils, no matter how near or distant. Theoll's fists closed so tightly that his fingernails cut into his flesh. How he needed the Demon Crown now with everyone possessing even a drop of royal blood in their veins conspiring to succeed Freow!

The Demon Crown would allow him to root out Dews Gaemock and the other rebel bands. No one would dare stand against him within the castle walls—or without. He would rule with an iron hand because he would know his enemies' cleverest schemes!

The baron pondered Freow's failure to use the Demon Crown. It had to be for a reason other than the fiction that the Demon Crown rested only on the brow of Porotane's rightful ruler. Theoll *knew* Freow had not pursued the search for the twins. Why had the duke not used the Demon Crown to cement his power over the years? That failure had plunged the kingdom into civil war. A wise man, even one truly acting only as regent for one awaiting majority to assume the throne, would have used the Demon Crown to quell the rebellious factions.

Theoll knew that the Demon Crown tried to possess the wearer, but the knowing of its evil kept the wearer pure. Theoll did not foresee any possibility of being seduced by the power of that crown.

Why had Duke Freow chosen not to wear it during his two decades of rule?

The secret lay with the Glass Warrior. Theoll's curiosity on this point was great, but not as great as the need to possess the Demon Crown for his own.

"There, Baron, there. See?" The soldier who had gone to the north side of the castle battlements called. Theoll raced to his side. "Beyond the line of trees. A spot of darkness against darkness."

Starlight flashed against a glass sword, or so Theoll imagined.

"Yes!" he cried. "She rides north to the Uvain Plateau!" Theoll rested his hands against the cold stone walls. But why? How did the Glass Warrior know where the twins would be, if they still lived? The Uvain Plateau seemed a poor choice, too.

"She might turn to the east, Baron," said the sharp-eyed soldier. "The River Ty affords access to many points in the kingdom to the northeast."

"She might think to confuse pursuit," said another.

"Mark that spot," ordered Theoll. "Mark it well. You will lead the others after her at first light."

"Do we follow only or should we slay, Baron Theoll?" asked the third soldier, just arriving from his position along the western castle wall.

Theoll considered. All twelve would ride after the Glass Warrior. She had bested three hidden assassins. How would she fare against a dozen making no secret of their pursuit?

He came to a decision quickly. For all the information carried within the warrior woman's head, he desired above all else what she carried in trust for Duke Freow. "Kill her. And bring me everything in her possession."

"The Demon Crown?"

Theoll sucked in his breath. Secrets were difficult to keep in Porotane. Everyone bartered information for gain. "For a commoner to don the crown means instant death," he said. "Do not think to gain advantage for yourself or any of the others with you. Only through me can you prosper."

"That is why you chose our platoon so carefully," said the guardsman.

Theoll laughed harshly. "I know your pedigrees and talents better than you know them yourself. You are all of the basest peasant stock. Nary a drop of royal blood flows through your scurvy veins. Touch the Demon Crown and you will have visited upon you the full wrath of the last demon to walk this world."

"Only nobles of royal blood can wear the Demon Crown," muttered one.

"Aye, only nobles. Such as the Baron of Brandon." Theoll executed a mocking bow. "Bring me the Demon Crown and each of you will be rewarded beyond your wildest imaginings." Theoll let their avarice run unchecked. He smiled sardonically. He had chosen them well, and trained them well, too. They would not betray him.

They would not dare.

"Off with you. Rouse the others, mount, and ride after the Glass Warrior." They rushed to obey.

Baron Theoll leaned against the wall and peered into the false dawn beginning to turn the night sky into a glowing pearl. What information drove the Glass Warrior toward the Uvain Plateau? Or did she seek passage on the River Ty? Theoll had been careful in his quest for supreme power in Porotane, but a nagging thought returned to bother him. Should he have pursued the search for the twins when it became apparent so many years ago that Duke Freow had not?

To *know* they were dead would let him rest easier.

Theoll had been engaged in constant intrigue to maintain his position in Porotane. He had done all he could. The time to act was now.

Resolution surging through him, the small man straightened and turned. The barely audible scrape of boot leather against stone gave him scant warning. Thoughts flashed through his head. His men had left. They would not return until they had the Demon Crown. The guard officer posted on the walls this night had been locked in the Lady Johanna's arms. His sentries had no doubt drifted off to sleep in some warm corner. Who walked the battlements?

Theoll threw himself forward as a small missile sang a deadly song and smashed into the wall. The stone's passage had ripped a piece of scalp and hair from his head. Theoll landed heavily, rolled and came to his knees, dagger in hand.

A second stone whistled through the gathering light of dawn, catching him in the upper arm. He yelped in pain. His dagger fell from a numbed hand. Theoll fought to get to his feet. He opened his mouth to cry out, to alert the sleeping guard, to get his personal guardsmen to return.

A heavy stone caught him squarely in the center of the chest. He felt himself lifted up and thrown backward over the battlement. Dazed, he lay on his back, staring up at the stars fading in the new light of day.

Strong hands grabbed his ankles and heaved. Theoll threw out his arms as he fell through the air, his cape trailing like the broken wings of a bat. He tried to scream but the stone's impact had driven the air from his lungs.

The baron plunged toward the ground from the highest point of the castle's battlements.

CHAPTER FOUR

Baron Theoll gasped for air as he turned slowly in midair. For a brief instant, his head spun about so that he could see where he fell. He saw only death rushing up at him, but the stone had driven the wind from his lungs and he could not scream in fear.

He crashed into the ground—hard. The pink and gray blossoms of dawn vanished in a blackness filled with pain.

Theoll groaned when he felt hands on his shoulders, lifting, shaking, bruising his already battered body. His eyes popped open and a cry of surprise escaped his lips.

"I still live!" He fought to get free of the clutching hands and look around.

"Quiet, Baron. You are sorely injured."

"I'm still alive, damn your eyes! What happened?"

"You fell from the battlements."

"I know that, fool. What saved me?" Theoll forced his head up and got a chance to look around. He had crashed through the thatched roof of a chicken coop. The slender poles supporting the roof had taken the force from his fall; landing in the soft muck on the floor had also cushioned his landing. Everywhere he looked he saw frightened chickens, feathers suspended in the air, and a uniform grime of chicken shit. Theoll tried to pull entirely free of the hands supporting him.

He failed. To his horror, he found that his legs refused to obey his wishes. He tried to reach down and lift them. His right hand twitched weakly. His left gave only throbbing pain.

"Baron, you are severely injured. I have called the court physician, but he can only tell you what I already have. Both your legs are broken, as is your left arm. If you have no other injuries, count yourself as fortunate. Few survive such clumsiness."

"Clumsy!" Theoll bellowed. The air came smoothly to his lungs now. His legs and arms might be fractured but he felt nothing but power within his chest and loins.

For an instant, he wondered at this. Death had been close and now he felt . . . aroused.

"How else could you fall from behind such tall battlements?" demanded his benefactor.

"I was thrown over the wall!"

No answer came. The man dressed in the dingy, tattered clothing was obviously a peasant. Equally as obvious was his disbelief that such a thing might happen in Porotane. In his tiny world only carelessness produced such unfortunate results.

In Theoll's world, the carelessness lay in not completing an assassination. Someone had foolishly allowed him to live. He would discover the villain's identity—and he would not be as inept with his swift, killing blade.

Pain began to mount within his small frame, driving knives of agony into his brain from all quarters. He allowed the shock to take him to a land unvisited by the red-hot pain.

"Your personal saint watches over you well, Baron," said Archbishop Nosto. The tall man stood over Theoll's bed, staring down at him. Theoll tried to guess at the thoughts within the cleric's mind. He failed. Theoll saw no hint that Nosto had been the one trying to kill him, although the idea had certain merit.

"For that I give thanks," said Theoll. "My legs were unbroken, for all the damage they sustained."

"But your left arm is definitely broken." Nosto stared openly at it, his face curious. "It does not appear that you will have the use of it again."

"The physician claims it will not heal properly. Although it might be bent permanently, I will have some use of it." Theoll flexed his right hand. The only damage he had sustained to his right side had been the stone striking the fleshy portion of his upper arm. The large bruise remained tender to the touch, but Theoll was in no condition to be stroking it.

"The saints are bountiful indeed. You are beloved by all, Baron," intoned Archbishop Nosto.

"All save one of this world," Theoll said bitterly. "I will find the person responsible for throwing me over the wall, Archbishop. And when I do . . ." Theoll's right hand gripped down so hard on the edge of the bed that mattress stuffing escaped through the rents he opened.

"I have made discreet inquiries but have found no one willing to accept blame for this."

"Had they killed me, no one would," said the baron. "They maneuver into position, waiting for

Duke Freow to die. They all realize I am the leading contender for the throne when he dies. Remove me before his death and it does not appear to be a self-serving assassination."

"Your mind walks curious paths," said Archbishop Nosto.

"I sinned, Nosto. I had the sin of pride thinking none would harm me because of my power in Porotane. I see the error of such pride. They would harm me *because of* that power."

"This is the reason for the armed guards outside your chambers?"

"It is. While I lie abed, my agents circulate throughout the castle hunting those responsible. If they tried to kill me, they might be bold enough to injure the duke—or even you, my dear Archbishop." The expression on the cleric's face told Theoll nothing. Nosto appeared startled at this notion of being harmed for some abstract, secular gain, yet Theoll knew that the cleric played the power game as well as anyone in Porotane.

"You should forgive the person responsible, and apply your energies toward the betterment of Porotane. The civil war rages on."

"You refer to Gaemock's attempted siege?"

"Only a wandering wizard more interested in booty saved the castle from this siege," said Archbishop Nosto. "Gaemock had to decide between holding position or retreating in the face of this new menace. He retreated."

"For the time, yes," said Theoll. His mind raced. Could Dews Gaemock have sent the assassin to remove the true power within the castle? Theoll decided that Gaemock had worries other than assassination. Also, it behooved a lord bringing a castle to siege to allow the leaders to surrender.

Assassination created turmoil, not opportunity from without.

"Only from within," Theoll said aloud.

"How is this, Baron?"

"Nothing, Archbishop. I require your cooperation in finding the assassin."

"But, Baron, I have told you that my inquiries have proven fruitless. There is nothing more that I can do."

"I need the power of the Inquisition to—"

"No!" The answer came sharp and emphatic. "The Inquisition is not a political tool. It is a religious quest to find and remove heretics from our midst."

Theoll saw no difference. Any opposing him had to be a heretic. But Archbishop Nosto saw his holy tortures in a different light. Theoll shifted in bed and raised himself slightly on his good arm. The time had come to firm the tenuous alliance with the archbishop.

"Nosto, I *must* move against those opposing me."

"Do so," the archbishop said primly. "But do not think your affairs are those of a cleric."

"Our interests cross. The heretics are responsible for my condition."

Archbishop Nosto's skepticism did not have to be put into words. His thin face radiated doubt and even contempt that Theoll stooped so low in his accusations.

"I have not spoken of this before. I am compelled to do so now."

"Of what?"

"I trust you, Nosto. You will not reveal what I say to anyone, will you?" He peered at the tall man and read only confusion on the cleric's face.

"I cannot make such a promise, Theoll. If this matter is of importance to the Inquisition, it is my sworn duty to reveal it."

The baron nodded solemnly. "I understand this. I leave it to you to decide if this is truly a matter for Church investigation."

"Speak."

Theoll forced away the grin of triumph. The archbishop had taken the bait and now found himself trapped with a cage of words. Not until Theoll had finished would Nosto be released.

"There are those in the castle who summon a demon for counsel."

"Impossible!"

"So I thought, but with my own eyes I have witnessed such a meeting of supernatural with . . . those of this world."

"Who? I demand that you reveal their names. Such obscene and blasphemous congress is forbidden!"

Archbishop Nosto calmed himself and continued in a quieter voice. "There can be no such congress. The Demon Crown is proof of that. Kalob, the last demon to walk this world, made reparation for the misery it had caused. The crown given to Porotane's ruler signified total demonic surrender."

"So I thought. Perhaps the Demon Crown remains as a gateway for the demons' return," said Theoll, playing on a theme that unnerved Nosto. "Or perhaps there is more to the pact than we have been told. So much of the gift of the Demon Crown is shrouded in mystery."

"There has been no demon in the land for over three hundred years."

"Yet the Inquisition finds traces of demonic influence," said Theoll. "Why else seek those who have strayed from the True Path?"

"You make light of the testing," accused Archbishop Nosto.

"No! Not I!" protested Theoll. The baron pulled himself to a sitting position. "I tell you that I have witnessed a meeting between a guard officer and a demon."

"Before the Inquisition you would swear to this?"

"Archbishop, I am sorely wounded. Better that a cleric—such as yourself—also witness it and assess the truth or falsity of my claim. You are trained in such matters. I might have been an unwilling dupe, though I doubt it. On my soul and the blessing of my personal saint, I so swear."

"I can witness a meeting of mortal and demon? When? Where?"

The baron could not hold back the smile twisting the corners of his lips. How the cleric believed!

"This very night. Do you know the unused pantry behind the castle kitchens? You do? If you enter through the kitchen and hide behind the furniture stored there, you will see a meeting such as I have described."

"Who is the heretic?"

"Archbishop Nosto," Theoll said seriously. "I may have erred. See for yourself if this guard lieutenant is not also a traitor and heretic."

"Yes, yes, I will."

"At midnight, Nosto. The demon will come at midnight."

The archbishop left Theoll's chambers, muttering to himself and invoking the succor of a dozen different saints. Theoll sagged, the strain of the meeting wearing on him. Still, he called out.

A guard appeared instantly, hand on sword. "How may I serve you, Baron?" the guard asked. His quick eyes circled the room to check for danger, then returned to lock boldly with Theoll's.

"The jester. Harhar. Bring him. I feel the need of amusement."

"The physician has ordered rest."

"Damn the physician! Obey me! I need the jester's wit. Fetch him immediately."

The guard saluted and left. Theoll let the grin spread broadly now. Victory edged ever closer. He had no idea who had tried to kill him on the battlements, but with Archbishop Nosto's unwitting help, he would remove one cabal plotting against him. If they were not responsible for the assassination attempt, at least the effort would not be wasted on hapless innocents.

As if anyone in the castle of Porotane was truly innocent. All had blood on their hands from a score of years under Duke Freow.

"Baron?" came a tremulous voice.

Theoll jerked around to see Harhar standing in the doorway, a rattle in one hand and a battered rag cap in the other. The sudden movement sent waves of pain throughout Theoll's body. He fought to keep from fainting.

"If you wish, Baron, I will leave. The guard said . . ."

Theoll gestured the fool to silence. "I require your services, Harhar. Will you perform for me?"

"Baron, yes!" Harhar stuck the cap on his head and put the rattle in his mouth. With an agility that defied joints and muscles, Harhar began a series of leaps and aerial twists. Each movement allowed him to snap his head about, causing the rattle to whine and purr and whistle and produce sounds Theoll could not identify.

"Harhar, wait, stop. No more. You make me tired watching this display."

"It does not please you, Baron?" Harhar sank to the floor, his forehead on the rug beside the baron's bed. "A joke?" the jester asked hopefully.

"No, no, not here, not now. But a joke, yes. A fine jest. The best you have ever done. Will you do this for me?"

"Oh, Baron, yes, of course!" The jester's eagerness to perform disgusted Theoll, but he needed this simpleminded acquiescence to his scheme. For over a fortnight he had prepared the pantry for Archbishop Nosto. He had intended to be the primary actor in the drama but his condition prevented it now. Letting Harhar perform struck Theoll as ironic and appropriate retribution for Nosto's pomposity.

"You will be costumed by the guard who will accompany us."

"Us? But Baron Theoll, your condition!"

"That is not your concern, fool," he snapped. "You will dress and speak loudly the words I whisper in your ear. Is that understood?"

A frown crossed Harhar's handsome face.

"You will repeat what I tell you," Theoll explained, impatient with the jester's lack of understanding. "If you please me, I shall give you a gold coin. Displease me and I shall see you whipped through the streets like a dog!"

The jester cringed again, head banging on the rug. "I will please you, Baron, I will, I will!"

Theoll summoned the guard to aid him. Although fully three hours remained until midnight, Theoll thought the journey to the pantry would prove slow and tedious. He endured the pain, but had to stop even more often than anticipated. A scant hour remained by the time the trio—baron, jester, and guard—reached the deserted pantry.

"Guard, remain hidden in the kitchens. No matter what you see or hear, do not reveal your presence. Only on my command will you attend me. Do you understand?"

The guard nodded. To Harhar, Theoll said, "Help me into the pantry storage room."

The jester helped the disabled noble. Theoll pointed out a hidden panel. "There. We go in there."

"Why, it is like a small stage," marveled Harhar. "The door closes, but a window opens to reveal us."

"To reveal you," corrected Theoll. "Put on this costume. Can you use makeup?" He drew forth a large box of paints and colored greases.

"It is second nature to me, Baron. But what character do I perform this night? Punctilious? Or perhaps Wobbles?"

"Nothing of the sort. No characters from a children's play. A demon. You must look like a demon." Theoll snorted in disgust when the jester cringed away. The baron grabbed the fool's collar and dragged him into the small box built into the wall. He settled down on the floor. Harhar had to stand with legs spread to avoid stepping on the noble. When the window in the secret door opened, Harhar would be visible only from the waist up, allowing Theoll to remain seated and coach him. The baron saw that this might prove more difficult than he had thought because of the fool's reaction.

"Put on this snakeskin jerkin." Theoll watched as Harhar stripped off his rags and donned the sleek, gleaming garment that transformed a human into a reptilian creature. The baron guided Harhar in applying the makeup. In less than twenty minutes, the jester had become a convincing serpentlike demon.

"Do I please you, Baron?" asked Harhar.

"Even this close, you look the part," said Theoll. "From the room, you will seem to *be* a demon."

Harhar stirred uneasily at the notion but said nothing. Theoll painfully worked his way into the secret box again and motioned for Harhar to enter also.

"Stand and wait. Do not open the window until I order you to do so."

Theoll drew a dagger and bored a small spyhole with the tip so that he could peer out into the dusty pantry. He had intended to look through a crack between window and shade but his injuries changed that plan. He looked at Harhar and decided that this might be even better. Nosto would never believe the jester capable of such perfidy.

"What do I say, Baron?"

"Remain silent. I shall whisper to you. Repeat exactly what I say or I will cut out your tongue."

The jester bobbed his head like a crane fishing in shallow waters but said nothing. Harhar entered the box on the baron's order and closed the secret panel. Within the box it was dark, stuffy, and for the jester, terrifying. For the baron, it proved only cramped and increasingly painful. He used his

spyhole to look out into the pantry. He hoped that
Archbishop Nosto proved prompt. It had to be
within a few minutes of midnight.

"Baron!" cried Harhar. "Someone is coming!"

"Silence, fool!"

Theoll squinted hard at the spyhole, a rising
excitement within his breast. He needed Archbishop Nosto's influence if he was to stop the Lady
Johanna in her drive to depose him. Whether she
had been responsible for his brush with death,
Theoll neither knew nor cared. Eliminating her
from power within the castle meant one less
opponent when the ancient duke finally succumbed.

"Good," murmured Theoll. "That's the way,
Nosto. Hide there. Yes, yes!" To Harhar he said,
"Scream as loudly as you can. I want his heart to
explode with fear."

Harhar responded. Even expecting it, Theoll
started. He smiled. Harhar was beginning to enjoy
his role and it showed.

Theoll began feeding the lines to his willing
fool.

"Archbishop Nosto," called Harhar. "You are
not the one I chose to meet this evening. Come
forth!"

Theoll watched as Nosto crept from hiding.
The baron reached up and opened the curtain.
Harhar, in his demon's colored makeup, was dimly
revealed to the cleric. Theoll had tested this effect;
it appeared as if the demon was inside the solid
wall, making it all the more frightening.

Archbishop Nosto made protective signs in
the air in front of him. "What demon are you?" he
demanded.

"You do not fear me?" Harhar asked, on Theoll's prompting.

"The saints protect me from all evil."

Theoll had to admire the cleric's courage—or his fanaticism.

"You would serve me as the lieutenant of the guard does?" asked Harhar, his voice rumbling in a deep bass.

"What guardsman is this who strays from the True Path?"

"You know the one," said Harhar. "The Lady Johanna fornicates with him nightly. You know the one. I have given him the object of his lusty desires because of his faithful service."

"Lieutenant Oprezzi?"

"That is his mortal name," agreed Harhar. The jester chanced to look down as Theoll worked on a candle. The baron motioned him back to the task. Archbishop Nosto must not suspect trickery.

"You are not a demon. The last demon was banished more than three hundred years ago."

"Aye," said Harhar. "When Kalob the Fierce made reparation to you puny humans, he left the trinket you call the Demon Crown. Kalob was banished, but others of considerably more power have returned. Oprezzi and those of his ilk appease us with their bodies and souls. They do our bidding. We will triumph over you, Archbishop Nosto. Demonic power returns to this world!"

To emphasize the words, Theoll lit the candle and cupped his hands about the flame to focus the light upward. From the pantry, it appeared as if the disembodied demon had opened a trapdoor to hell and the hellfire shone upward on his face.

Archbishop Nosto made another ward gesture.

"You will aid me, Archbishop?" demanded Harhar.

"I order you back to the depths of the hell from which you come!"

"You cannot order me. Not when there are those among you who do my bidding!"

"Then they shall be put to the Question. They shall never stray from the True Path!"

Harhar laughed until his voice began to turn hoarse. Theoll snuffed out the candle flame, almost choking on the sudden plume of smoke rising from the wick. He turned back to the spyhole and peered at Nosto. The cleric turned and bolted from the room.

Baron Theoll wanted to laugh and cry out loud at his victory. Nosto would not stop with his Inquisition of Oprezzi until the feckless lieutenant confessed everything—truth or not. And through the guardsman, Nosto had to come to the Lady Johanna.

Theoll did not care if Nosto put her to the Question. The cleric's suspicion would keep the woman busy and allow Theoll a free hand in his own dealings.

Duke Freow would die soon. Theoll would see to that. And when the duke passed on, the power would come to Baron Theoll of Brandon.

CHAPTER FIVE

The Glass Warrior rode slowly from the castle, knowing that she had seen Duke Freow for the last time. Success or failure, her mission marked the ruler's last significant command.

She reined in and looked at the dawn-lit castle walls. She shook her head, soft white hair floating like a nimbus around her face. It seemed an eternity since Freow—or the man posing as King Lamost's reclusive brother for all these years— had entrusted her with the Demon Crown. She reached behind, her fingers lightly touching the velvet sack in which rested the magical crown. As always, a tiny thrill passed through her. Although she had no royal blood and could never don the crown without risking instant and total madness, some of its magic inspired her.

"To rule all this," she said, her keen gray eyes looking around the farms surrounding the castle. Good land, rich and productive. And the workers strove to bring in bountiful harvests. "A shame the wars have raged so long. What might Porotane have accomplished as a whole instead of fractured into a dozen warring pieces?"

Again she shook her head. She tried to stay above politics, to remain aloof from the machinations of those in the Porotane court. But as long as she held the Demon Crown, she knew she would be the center of a vortex of death and intrigue.

"The scurvy son of a bitch wasn't even Lamost's kin," she said aloud. Freow had completely fooled her. She had believed him an honorable, decent fellow intent only on locating the twins and returning them to power. For almost twenty years she had believed this. It was for the best that she had not partaken of the feuds and power games being played out in Porotane. She was too easily duped.

But the man who had assumed Freow's identity had chosen her with uncanny skill. For twenty years she had fought off legions of thieves, both lowborn and noble, seeking to steal the Demon Crown. She had kept the crown as a trust for Lokenna and Lorens and never thought for an instant of betraying it.

The Glass Warrior stretched, her joints popping. She was no longer the young warrior woman who had accepted this task. It was for the good of all that she now do what Freow had promised for so many years. She had done her duty in protecting the crown for the twins. Now she must find them to hand over their heritage.

"Mayhap then I can rest," she said, patting her horse on the neck. The mare whinnied and tried to rear. "Whoa, now. What's the trouble? Do we have company on our ride this fine morning?"

The horse bobbed her head up and down, as if she understood. Sometimes, it seemed to the woman, the horse truly foresaw the future and tried to tell of it.

The Glass Warrior reached into her pouch and pulled out a short string of wildcat gut with a small cut-glass spike tied to it. She held it at arm's length and closed her eyes. Soft chants rose from her lips, the weak magic turning the glass into something more than a convenient device for finding her way. Vibrations from the crystal raced up the gut string and into her fingers, down her arm and into her shoulder.

Her entire body began to quiver under the impact of her scrying spell. A darkness fell over her mind as if a box of purest ebony encased her. With sight went sound and smell. She floated in the magical void, the only sense being the shivering gut string in her fingers.

"Come," she coaxed. "Show me who follows."

A vivid picture formed, as if before her eyes. But the Glass Warrior's eyes were screwed shut in concentration. The image came magically and from a distance beyond sight.

Twelve riders rode from the Porotane castle, circled to where she had tied her mare, then followed her spoor with uncanny skill.

The image intensified. She now heard the leader speaking. "I sighted her along the trail. Make good speed, men, for we ride under the baron's strictest orders."

"The baron," she murmured. "Baron Theoll. Who else could command such resources within Porotane?"

The riders galloped along her trail. She watched and listened magically until their leader reined in and slowed his band of fighters with their clanking swords and rattling armor. "Here," he said. "Here is where I sighted her. Dismount and find the trail. We must not lose her—or the Demon Crown!"

The Glass Warrior's concentration began to

slip. The pure blackness of the box in which her senses were encased developed cracks. Wind blew across her face, carrying soft scents and the promise of rain before nightfall. The light of a new day pried its way under her lids and she saw instead of *saw*. The chirping of a songbird broke the spell completely, and she again saw only the world around her. Her fingers tightened on the gut string and she drew the glass crystal into her hand. She squeezed so tightly that blood dripped onto it, renewing its power for her next use.

"So, Baron, you think it this easy to steal the crown?" The Glass Warrior threw back her head and laughed, her mockery of the diminutive noble frightening the wildlife into silence. She controlled her scorn, and slowly the birds again sang and the crepuscular animals moved through the low brush around the trail.

She put her heels to the mare's flanks and started off at a good pace. Let her pursuers tire their steeds. She had an unknown distance to travel before she found the heirs to the throne— and she had all day in which to lay a false trail for the baron's men.

They were soldiers, fighters trained in the ways of killing. She knew the forests and plains and all the ways of eluding pursuers.

The Glass Warrior used her full knowledge. By midday, another scrying showed the soldiers racing directly north to the Uvain Plateau. She turned east and then south, circling wide around the castle, and by late afternoon, was heading in the opposite direction from her pursuers.

The small cooking fire drove back the dampness of the night. The Glass Warrior hunched forward to warm her hands. The rabbit she had hunted and eaten for dinner had been too small, its taste doing little more than supplementing the dry trail rations she carried. But the tiny fire did more to raise her spirits than anything else. She could stare for long hours into the dancing orange and blue flames, studying the ever-changing patterns and trying to impose sense on them.

One childhood story she remembered well was that fire had been given to mankind by a demon repentant for all the woe it had visited on the world. The Glass Warrior smiled wanly. So many myths sounded similar. The Demon Crown had been given to King Waellkin by the demon Kalob in reparation for the destruction brought by demonic acts. It mattered little to her. The sight of fire carried its own magic, soothing and warming.

Her hand flashed to her dagger when distant clanking echoed through the copse where she camped for the night. She strained, listening intently. Then she dropped to the ground, pressing her ear into the dirt. She straightened quickly. The ground had been soaked by the afternoon rains and carried sound poorly.

The sound of a wagon grew louder. She sighed and stood, buckling the sword belt around her trim waist. Returning her glass dagger to its sheath, she drew her sword. In the firelight, its glass surface reflected rainbows. Moving like the wind, she vanished into the thicket around her campfire and crouched, waiting.

Those in the wagon made no attempt to hide their arrival. Boisterous shouts, curses, and laughter preceded the pair.

"I tell you, Vered, you cannot hope to escape the wheel if you keep doing such things."

"You're getting old, Santon, old and frightened!"

"Courage has nothing to do with it. You stole from the village elder."

"He was the only one with money. Why bother picking empty purses? Hot air I can get from you. Gold I get only from the rich!"

The one called Santon grabbed his companion's sleeve when he spotted the campfire. "Looks as if we've another traveler along the road this evening, Vered. But where has he gotten off to?"

"Your odor sends even the strong-stomached running. If my nose wasn't clogged constantly, I couldn't stand you either."

"Bathing gives me the vapors. I need all my strength."

"Not of smell, Santon, not of smell." Vered made a gagging noise. The sound of a strong blow silenced his antics.

"That's better," came Santon's words. "Since our fellow traveler has seen fit to rush off, mayhap a quick examination is in order. Just to be sure that nothing untoward has happened, mind you."

"And you declare me to be a ruthless, impatient thief. Ha!" The wagon came to a clanking, creaking halt and the pair dismounted.

From her hiding spot in the bushes, the Glass Warrior saw two tall men of good build separate and advance cautiously on the campfire from different directions. The one named Vered was young, hardly twenty summers, and carried himself with the assurance and arrogance of youth. From his quick movements and easy way of handling his sword, she thought him a dangerous adversary. But the other, Santon, held her attention. Older by ten or more summers, he carried the scars of devastating warfare. His left hand clutched powerfully around the handle of a battle-ax; his right arm dangled helplessly, a withered remnant of former strength. He moved like a soldier, his eyes seeing more than the superficial.

It took Santon only seconds to find the trail she had left in leaving the camp. The Glass Warrior rose and walked into the light of her campfire when Santon peered at the very bush behind which she had tried to hide.

"Good evening, sirs," she said.

"And to you, fair lady," answered the brasher Vered. Santon took a step to the side, his heavy ax held away from his body and ready for action.

"There is no need to rob me," she said. "I have little worthy of your attention."

"Rob?" protested Vered. "Gracious one, how can you think such a nasty thing of us? We are but traveling jugglers."

Her quick glance at Santon's crippled arm brought a laugh from Vered. The young man said, "*I* juggle for coins. My dear friend only assists, sometimes acting the fool."

"Quiet, Vered. She knows your honeyed lies for what they are."

"Lies? Really, Santon, we—" The man reached out, as if to protest. But as quick as he was in bringing up his sword, the Glass Warrior proved faster. She caught the edge of his steel blade and deflected it with her glass one. Vered recovered swiftly and tried to lunge, to drive the razor tip of his sword past her guard and cut a hamstring.

She stepped into the thrust, disengaged, and spiraled around his blade. She took it from his hand and sent the weapon flying into the night. Before Vered could recover, the glass point rested at the hollow of his throat.

"Stay your blade, dear lady. I meant nothing! Honest!"

"I doubt you've ever been honest in your life. Is this not true, warrior?" she asked of Santon. From behind she saw the man beginning to come at her. This pair worked well together, for all their insults and bickering.

"If his lips are moving, you can be sure Vered is lying."

"A vile canard!" cried Vered. He did not seem to notice the point menacing his throat. The Glass Warrior had to admire his courage. She lowered her blade and stepped away so that she could see them both.

"We've met our match," said Santon. "Can we call a truce? Or do you wish us to travel on?"

"Travel in this miserable, inky night?" protested Vered. "We'll become irretrievably lost. None will find us for a hundred years! Our bones will be gnawed by wild animals, then bleach in the sun for the rest of eternity. We—"

"Quiet, Vered. Do you not recognize her?"

Vered fell silent as he studied the Glass Warrior more carefully. "She is truly beautiful. Never have I seen such lovely hair and so fine a figure. And she is adept with her sword. A peculiar brand of weapon it is, too. Glass? Yes, I thought so. I've never seen one, though I've heard the legends."

"He thinks you a legend, Lady," said Santon.

"No legend," she assured him.

Vered frowned. "I do not understand." He brightened. "I do understand that we have been incredibly rude. Allow me to introduce ourselves.

I am Vered, and my friend who cannot juggle is Birtle Santon. We are—"

"Traveling entertainers," she finished, with a laugh. "Traveling thieves appears to be a better description."

"And you, dear lady, who are you?"

"She's the Glass Warrior, Vered," said Birtle Santon.

"That's ridiculous. She's only a legend." Vered's words trailed off as he looked at the glass sword held so easily in her hand and at the glass dagger sheathed at her belt.

"The cape is spun from glass, also," she said, seeing his interest. "I seldom wear it unless I require protection. Your dagger. Draw it and try to thrust through the cape." She spun about, sending the cape swinging from her body. She held out an arm and let the cape dangle.

Vered whipped out his slim-bladed dagger and slashed with all the power locked within his strong arm. The tip danced along the cape and skittered away.

"It can be cut, but it requires luck as well as skill and a sharp dagger," she told him. "Go retrieve your sword. You look lost without it."

"What would I do with it?" Vered asked, making a helpless gesture. "Never have I found a cape that resists my sharpest blade." He backed away, then went in search of his lost sword.

She turned to Santon and motioned for him to sit by the fire. "It is not much, but it helps hold back some of the night's chill."

"Vered can get more wood," said Santon. He settled down warily.

"No." The Glass Warrior's order came out sharper than she had wanted.

"So you are followed," mused Santon. "No, let me guess. I have heard the legends, but the reality must be something less. No woman, even one as handsome as you, could live up to the tales told over a tankard or two of ale."

He poked at the fire and urged the flames higher. "Do not worry," he said. "The flames are hidden and the smoke can't be seen. Vered and I both keep a sharp watch. We were almost upon you before we saw the fire."

"You run, too?" she asked.

"Let's say that we've had our share of disagreement," said Vered, returning with his sword. He dropped to the ground, legs thrust out and propping himself up on one elbow. In the firelight his brown eyes danced with mischief.

"Thieves," she said.

"Some have called us that," admitted Birtle Santon. "We think of ourselves as two lost souls seeking a bit of adventure wherever we can."

"Thieves."

"Yes," said Vered. "But you. What of you? We are an ex-soldier and a youngling unable to cope with a bad case of wanderlust. You are a legend."

"You flatter me, but I see that is part of your charm. Flattery and a quick slice with the knife to remove the money pouch."

"You have nothing to worry from us," said Santon.

"No," agreed Vered. "We can see by the way your pouch swings that it is as empty as ours." He reached out with the tip of his sword and bounced her money pouch. "I am more interested in how your blade survives real combat. Steel against glass? Surely, the glass must shatter."

"I am skilled at its preparation. At times, I wish it to shatter. At others, it is stronger than your blade."

They traded banter and odd stories for a time, edging around one another while they decided if trust was merited. The Glass Warrior decided long before either Santon or Vered.

"You are not actively sought by the authorities?" she asked. Their expressions, guarded though they were, showed that they were. "That is no concern of mine. What is of importance is a sacred vow I have taken."

"Sacred vows tend to be written in blood—others' blood," said Santon.

"You have seen combat too often. You grow cynical," she accused.

"I have, and that is a fact. For long years I rode Porotane trying to maintain order. Too many demon-damned brigands for that. Kill one and two spring up. I decided to make a path for myself through the world."

"Would you see an end to the civil war?" she asked.

"Who wouldn't? But the duke is too feeble. The others in the castle . . . by the saints, I wouldn't trust a one of them!" declared Santon.

"You would support a true king or queen?"

"One of royal blood?" asked Vered. He shrugged. "For all my life, there's been naught on the throne but Duke Freow. Santon remembers old King Lamost."

"Aye, and his children," said Santon, almost dreamily. "They'd be older than young Vered by now, had they lived."

Both men stiffened when Santon uttered

those words. Santon paused for a moment, studying the Glass Warrior's face, then asked, "They are dead, aren't they? It's been too many years for them to still live."

"This I do not know," said the Glass Warrior. "But Duke Freow has entrusted me with the task of finding Lokenna and Lorens. He is dying. One twin must assume the throne soon or Porotane's wars will intensify and permanently divide the kingdom."

"Where there's strife, there's opportunity," quoted Vered.

"For the likes of us, aye," said Santon. "For the likes of Baron Theoll, too."

The Glass Warrior saw the men's dislike for the small baron. "I seek the twins. I hope to find both, but either will be able to succeed to the throne. We must hurry, though. Freow is dying and the baron is becoming bolder."

"We? You think to count us into this madness? Oh, no, dear lady, not us. No," said Vered. "We're honest thieves, not heroes bent on dying nobly."

"He has a good point. This is not our worry. Theoll is a swine, but the likes of Dews Gaemock oppose him, not that he is that much better. I say, any who seek the throne should be denied it."

"Spoken like a former soldier," she said. "But I do need help. The baron has sent a squad after me. No, do not fear. I have eluded them for the moment, but they are determined. His threats drive them faster than any promise of reward."

"We want nothing to do with it," said Vered, his tone firm and his gaze unswerving.

"And you?" she asked of Birtle Santon. "What of you?"

"Vered's right. We have no stake in this.

Gaemock would make no different a ruler than Theoll—or either of the twins."

"You are wrong. There is good reason for once more seating royalty on the throne. Too few follow Gaemock or any of the hundred other would-be rulers of Porotane who are little more than brigands. No one wants Theoll on the throne. No one, I assure you."

"No," said Santon.

"I cannot coerce you," she said. "Come morning, we'll ride our separate ways."

Santon nodded, then asked, "Would you like a small drink of brandy? I've saved it for a special occasion. Meeting the famed Glass Warrior on a mission for the duke is as special as I'm likely to find."

"I'd be pleased."

Santon fetched the bottle and two battered metal cups. He poured her some and took one for himself. "What of Vered?" she asked. The young man had already drawn his cloak tightly around himself and lay sleeping by the low fire.

"Vered doesn't drink such swill. Slows the reflexes, he says. Burns out the brain, he says. He drinks only the finest of wines from the Uvain Plateau wineries."

"In that, he may be right."

"He is," said Santon. "It burns out both brain and memory. It's the only relief I get from the past." He tossed back the full cup, coughed, then poured himself another.

The Glass Warrior sipped slowly and considered the two men carefully. "I am sorry you will not aid me," she said.

"If it's true you're a wizard you might put a spell on us," suggested Santon.

"I command a few spells," she admitted. "But I would not force you to help. Such would only work against me."

The Glass Warrior took a long drink from the cup, the brandy burning her gullet and belly. She put the cup down and said, "You know that a wizard seldom reveals a personal name."

"The name can be used against them in spells and in battle," said Santon.

"It is a sign of trust."

Their eyes locked.

"My name is Alarice," the Glass Warrior said.

CHAPTER SIX

Vered stirred and turned, wrapping himself so tightly in his cloak that his arms tingled from lack of circulation. He sneezed, his nose clogged. Still more asleep than awake, he opened one eye and tried to remember his dreams.

Pleasant ones, he knew. The saucy wench chasing him had been gorgeous. And the commotion when she insisted that they . . .

Vered sneezed again and came fully awake, the dream remnant finally fleeing from conscious thought. He sat up and looked around. The fire lay cold and black between him and Birtle Santon. For a few seconds, Vered puzzled over the curious lump where his friend lay.

Vered then realized that Santon had not slept alone this past night. The Glass Warrior had curled up close by, whether to share only warmth or more, Vered didn't know or really care. She was an attractive one, he thought, but not his type. More Santon's, with her sturdy build and obvious fighting prowess. Vered preferred his women less combative and more curvaceous. Like the one in his dimly remembered dreams.

He shook free of his cloak and stood, stretch-

ing. The cold morning air caused his breath to
come out in silvery plumes, but it invigorated him
and convinced him that this day might be better
than the last. He strolled off into the bushes to
relieve himself, then returned to the cold camp-
site.

Santon and the Glass Warrior lay spoon-
fashion, sleeping deeply. It might be another hour
before they roused. What harm could there be in
aiding this handsome woman by giving her some
of his expertise in packing? She carried a lush-
looking knapsack, but the lumpiness must tax her
sorely, Vered thought. The harsh edges of whatever lay within had to cut into her softer curves as
she walked.

Fingers nimble from practice, Vered opened
the ties on the black velvet knapsack. The only
sounds were those of the forest animals and wind
blowing softly through the spring leaves. The
sounds of velvet slipping across velvet were
drowned out even by the distant brook burbling on
its way to the River Ty.

He drew forth a crystal box and ran his fingers
along the edges, seeking a possible trap. Some of
the less enlightened booby-trapped their prize
possessions with poisoned needles that leapt out at
the wrong touch. Vered had even found one or two
who installed spring-driven catapults within to kill
the unwary.

No such trap had been laid by the Glass
Warrior. He held the box at arm's length and
peered through its crystalline sides. A simple gold
circlet rested within.

"Not worth more than a few days' lodging in a
good city," he decided aloud. He looked at the
sleeping pair. Santon stirred now, unconsciously

considering rising. In another few minutes, he would awaken.

Vered knew that it would be a churlish thing to do to steal this simple gold ornament from a woman who might have been Santon's lover the past night. He knew it. Still, he opened the crystalline lid and withdrew the circlet.

A tingling passed through him, electric and startling. Vered rocked back on his heels and laid the crown on the ground until he regained his senses.

"Too little food," he decided. "Weak from starvation. Imagine me, master thief the length and breadth of Porotane, being unable to lift a light gold circlet without fainting dead away! A travesty of honorable thievery!"

On feet quieter than a stalking cat, Vered went to the wagon and searched through the littered interior until he found a coil of wire. He balanced out an amount equal in weight to the gold circlet and placed the wire into the crystal box. The tricks light played as it went through the cut glass box walls made it appear as if he had left the circlet untouched. Pleased with his petty deception, Vered took the box with its wire crown back to the velvet knapsack. With care equal to that he had shown in removing the box, he replaced it and retied the velvet bindings, duplicating the Glass Warrior's simple knots.

Birtle Santon made an inarticulate sound that Vered knew to mean that his friend awoke.

"Good morning, Santon," Vered greeted brightly. "And how did you sleep? Better than I, from all appearances." He inclined his head in the direction of the still-sleeping Glass Warrior.

"Aye, for once you've hit on the truth of the

matter." Santon disengaged himself from the woman's arms and stood.

"What do we do about her?" asked Vered. "I have no desire to be broken on the wheel because of her mission for the duke."

"Nor I, but she pleads her case well."

"How well?" asked Vered, a grin on his face.

Santon grunted and threw a stone at him. Vered dodged easily. "We can let her ride along with us for a time," said Vered. He smoothed out his rumpled clothing and ran his fingers through light brown hair hanging in greasy strings. "If she can stand the odor, that is."

"You worry too much about appearances. You should consider the inner soul, that which cannot be scrubbed clean with only soap and water."

"And you, Santon, worry too much about your soul and not enough about how you smell!"

Alarice rolled over, awakened by their banter. Her eyes blinked open, gray orbs holding Santon and Vered pinned as firmly as if she had driven pins through them.

"Good morning, Lady," said Vered.

"It is, isn't it?" she said.

"And it will be even more of a good morning when we've eaten. I could eat a horse."

"Touch that nag pulling our wagon and I'll cut off your ears," growled Santon. To Alarice he said, "His belly often gets the better of him. No discipline."

"Santon wants us to march on no rations for a month, though he is a less than harsh taskmaster at times," said Vered. "He might let me drink a thimbleful of water once a week." The younger man began preparing a cooking fire, then jumped up when he saw Santon heading toward their dilapidated wagon.

"Here, Santon, you do the fire. I'll get the rations." He pushed past his friend and blocked the view into the wagon. He had forgotten to hide the pilfered circlet properly. Deft movements drew forth small portions of their food and hid the gold band where neither Santon nor the Glass Warrior was likely to see it without much searching.

"You hate to cook," said Santon. "Why the change of heart?"

"There is no constant in the world but change. Perhaps I've tired of your flavorless, tough concoctions. Perhaps I seek a cook who washes his hands."

"Perhaps I can get some peace," grumbled Birtle Santon.

Vered worked quickly and well to fix breakfast. The trio ate in silence, cleaned their plates, and stared challengingly at one another, almost daring the other to speak first. Vered broke the deadlock.

"I'll tend to the wagon. We can be on our way in an hour or less."

"May I have a word with you, Birtle?" asked the Glass Warrior.

"Let's walk," Santon said. He heaved his bulk up and forward and got his feet under him. His immensely powerful left arm showed no strain when he helped Alarice to her feet. Together, they vanished into the dense undergrowth.

This suited Vered. He hastily packed their equipment, tended the swayback horse, and then climbed into the wagon, its rear door slightly ajar

so that he could keep watch for the Glass Warrior's
return.

He reached under the sacks where he had
hidden the gold circlet. He drew it forth and stared
at it.

The electric tingle returned and set his heart
racing faster. Hands trembling slightly, Vered
lifted the Demon Crown and placed it upon his
head.

Santon and Alarice found a small game trail
and followed it until they came to the brook
wending its way into larger waters. Santon paused
and stared at the churning surface, then picked up
a stone and dropped it into the stream. The rapid
current robbed him of the pleasure of seeing
ripples expand outward.

"Have you come to a conclusion, Birtle?"
Alarice asked. "This is not something to be taken
lightly. The fate of Porotane rests on your decision."

"What can I do to help? Or Vered and me?
We're not soldiers. We're certainly no heroes."

"You are adept with a blade and, in spite of all
you say, I see the goodness within you both. And
courage. More than you think."

He stared into her slate gray eyes and felt as if
he fell a hundred miles. More stirred within this
woman than he could guess. So like the stream she
was! The surface carried one message, while
others lurked beneath frothy waters. Santon felt as
if he would step into her eyes and vanish forever
into a world beyond his wildest imagining.

"We cannot. Despite all that you say, this isn't
our fight."

"I understand," she said. "But I had hoped for

more from you. It was wrong of me to impose, even asking this of you. Duke Freow has given me the mission and no one else. I sought only to lighten my burden."

"Alarice," he began. He bit back words ill considered. Santon almost agreed to abandon Vered and travel with her.

"Friendships are precious," she said, supplying him with an excuse.

"Vered and I have traveled far," Santon said. "He's saved my life well nigh as many times as I have saved his." He smiled as he remembered. "We met on the coast. I had been mustered out of the King's Guard over fifteen years when I came on this ruffian trying to steal from a sailor. The old salt had caught him and wanted to cut off Vered's ears. The boy lacked a summer of being fifteen."

"You rescued him?"

"Of course. I pretended to buy him from the sailor. I paid five gold pieces. Oh, that Vered's quick on the uptake. He saw what I did. He had the sailor's money pouch long before I grabbed him by the ear and led him from the tavern. He tried to rob me when we got free! After we settled that, we got along well. His skills are great."

"As are yours," Alarice said, her fingers moving along the sinews on Santon's powerful arm. "I remember last night."

"It's been a long time," he said, embarrassed.

"For me, too. Perhaps that made it the sweeter. I choose to think otherwise."

"We can't go with you. There's too many on our trail," Santon said, coming to a firm conclusion now. "We would only hold you back from wherever you go."

"I seek the wizard Tahir d'mar."

"A wizard, is it? That's too risky for the likes of a pair of sneak thieves. Neither Vered nor I are adept at even simple fire spells."

"I feel more in Vered," she said. "Are you sure he is not hiding spell-casting abilities from you?"

"We've been together five years. He's a sly one, but not even Vered could pretend for that length of time. He's as lacking in magic skills as I."

Santon stared at her and said, "I wish it could be otherwise, Alarice. If for nothing more than to guard your back."

"Companions can mean life or death." She saw the conflict still raging within his mind, but Birtle Santon had decided. The Glass Warrior would not ask him to recant. "Let's return to camp. I . . . I have an uneasy feeling."

"Theoll's men?" he asked.

"No, something . . . more."

Alarice spun and started back to camp at a pace Santon worked hard to equal.

Vered lowered the crown, then jerked back when biting sparks exploded from the circlet and burned his scalp. But the Demon Crown remained on his head—and he *saw*.

He had always thought his vision good and his hearing acute. Vered knew the truth now. He had been as one aged and infirm, seeing half the world and hearing nothing. But no longer! The world sharpened and brightened and the sounds blasted into his ears.

He saw the songbird in the tree a mile distant, heard the faint quavers in its mating call, understood all, and found the golden bird's mate four miles away. Vered listened to her answer, saw her take wing and fly directly toward the tree branch.

A shiver possessed him. His *sight* extended farther along the road he and Santon had traveled. His hand flashed for his sword when he *saw* the rebel band stalking the four local constables. Vered did not know which side he should support with his fighting prowess.

He had no love for the constables; they insisted on foolishly enforcing laws that Vered chose to break or ignore. But the rebels! These were of a band led by a minor wizard. How Vered knew this, he could not say.

He knew. He *knew*!

The rebels ambushed the four constables, killing two instantly. The two survivors stood back to back to defend themselves. Vered chose. He rushed forward to aid them against the rebels. Politics meant nothing to him. Helping those against whom the odds fell appealed to him. For all his life, he had been the longshot, the poor bet, the one no one expected to survive.

Vered rushed forward, sword swinging. The blade drove down on a carelessly exposed wrist . . . and passed through.

He gasped and stared in disbelief at his blade. Every detail of the blade was his to examine minutely. The tiny nicks he thought he had honed out, the imperfections in the metal, small islands of carbon in the steel, Vered *saw* all this and more.

"Die, swine!" cried a rebel. The man's sword rose and fell. Blood spattered from the constable's wound. A second slash ended the man's life. The remaining constable proved easy prey for the rebel band. The six who survived the ambush stood over the bodies, gloating openly. Again Vered tried to attack and again his blade passed through his target as if traveling through smoke.

Vered jumped back to reassess his actions. The rebels paid him no heed. It was as if he did not exist for them. But he *saw* and *heard* so clearly!

Movement behind drew him around. He faced the leader of this small group. He *felt* power exuding from this man.

The wizard halted and cocked his head to one side. He yelled, "Search the area! There is another lurking nearby. Another wizard!"

Vered spun and used his *sight* to look for this other wizard. He *saw* no one. It took several seconds for him to realize that this sorcerer did not mean another. He meant Vered.

The thief blinked and moved away from the wizard. The speed of retreat took away his breath. Never in his life had he run this fast. Vered *looked* beyond the rebel wizard and saw other men and women, in a village, beyond the village, beyond the River Ty, all the way to Porotane's castle.

And within the strong stone walls stirred hundreds of people. Vered found it increasingly easy to follow an individual. Freow lay dying. The court jester, called Harhar by a nobleman, cavorted and pranced and tried to cheer the duke.

Vered's head spun. Dizziness assailed him. He *saw* even farther away than the castle, to the coast, to a swamp, to the Yorral Mountains, across the Uvain Plateau. The world swung in wide circles, twisting him around, turning him inside out, forcing sensations on him he could not put into words.

Vered cried out for Santon to help him, but no words formed. He spun and gyrated and tumbled and surged endlessly. Trapped. Unable to right himself. Trapped and helpless. Helpless. Helpless!

CHAPTER SEVEN

Vered tried to cry out in panic. The words clogged in his throat—but he *heard* them. He *heard* everything. The pounding of his own heart, the sweat breaking out from his skin, the creaking as his hair grew, the rush of blood through his veins, everything.

He *heard*!

He gagged when a heavy fist drove into his gut. Vered tried to double over and vomit. The Demon Crown held him in thrall. The more he struggled, the worse became his disorientation. Spinning colors filled his eyes. He *saw* too much. His eyes refused to separate the details, the riot of hues, the lightning-intense blasts that seared his brain.

Again came the blow. He tried to reach out to defend himself. He failed. No matter what course of action he tried, he failed. The blows increased in severity until he thought a giant wielding a sledgehammer was breaking his bones.

Vered felt himself rising up, even as the kaleidoscope around him robbed his senses of direction. The impact as he struck the ground stunned him—and the senses-wrecking assault stopped.

Gasping for breath, unable to move, he stared up from the ground at Birtle Santon. The man towered over him, his single arm bulging from the exertion of lifting his friend into the air and then flinging him down.

"You?" asked Vered, the air painful in his lungs. He choked. A gentler hand slapped him on the back to help him regain control. He looked over his shoulder and saw the Glass Warrior, concern etched on her fine face.

"Who else would save you from yourself, you stupid lout," grumbled Santon.

"What happened? I . . . I remember what I experienced, but what was it? I mean, my head, oh, it feels like some vile forge and a smithy is banging away at his anvil—my head!"

"You are adept at thievery," said Alarice. "I never noticed that you had stolen the crown."

"Crown? Ah, the gold circlet, that paltry bauble of insignificant value. There it is." Vered reached out to recapture the fallen crown. He yelped in pain. The Glass Warrior's boot crushed his hand into the dirt, preventing him from again touching the Demon Crown.

"It will kill if you touch it again."

"That?" Vered's amazement was echoed by Birtle Santon.

"What manner of magical device is this?" Santon asked, peering at the fallen crown. "It seems no different than any other crown for a minor noble."

Alarice said, "You forget the legend. How Kalob gave over the Demon Crown as a token of restitution, how only those of royal blood can wear the crown."

"That's the Demon Crown?" asked Vered, his eyes widening.

"What of your parents?" Alarice asked. "What can you tell me of them?"

"Nothing. I am an orphan. The unrest after King Lamost died caused many such as me. My entire village died as rebels pillaged and burned. Or so I was led to believe."

"Royal blood runs in your veins," Alarice said. "To touch the Demon Crown without that blood means instant death."

"I felt as if I had died. But not at first. On fitting the crown to my head—ouch!" Vered had touched his brow. A charred band of flesh circled his skull. He touched the burn gingerly. "The Demon Crown did *that*?"

"And more, unless they have lied to me about its effects," said the Glass Warrior. "Your vision became perfect, and not only for things within normal sight. You saw events at a great distance, as if you stood nearby."

"I did," Vered said, his fingers still probing the extent of his physical injuries.

"All your senses became heightened. You saw, you heard, you felt—"

"Wait! No, I did not experience anything of the sort." He sneezed. "And my sense of smell did not improve. I am still cursed with nose drip."

"The blood in your veins is not pure enough," said Alarice. "You have some touch of royal blood, but not enough, not enough." She sighed. "If you had donned the crown and controlled it, there would have been no need to find Lorens or Lokenna."

"You would have installed Vered as ruler of Porotane?" Santon made a rude noise.

"Why not? As it turns out, he is not pure enough of the blood. My guess is that his mother might have been raped by a soldier carrying as much as one-eighth royalty in his veins. Many pretenders to the throne existed at the beginning of the war. Time and intentional extermination have eliminated most over the past years."

"That makes me one-sixteenth noble," said Vered. He made a face. "I do not like the idea. I wish to be nothing more than a mongrel. Like Santon."

"You've had your taste of power, Vered. How did you like it?" Alarice asked.

"I didn't," he admitted. "Can you tend my wound? It is beginning to burn."

"First, a favor of you," said the Glass Warrior. "Pick up the crown and replace it in the crystal box. No, it won't kill you if your fingers move swiftly enough."

Vered moved the Demon Crown from where it had fallen back into the glass box Alarice carried inside the velvet bag.

"See how the metal glows a dull green?" she asked. "The crown would have blazed with blinding light had he been of pure blood."

"My blood's pure, as is my heart," said Vered. "It's just not pure royal blood."

"The crown's back in place," said Santon. "What do you need to tend his wound?"

"Very little. The wound, although magical in origin, is only physical. There might be a scar but it does not extend down into his brain." The Glass Warrior began working on the deep burn on the man's scalp.

"What happened to me?" asked Vered. "I wore the crown and found myself spinning out of control. How did I chance to again return to this fine world?"

"Santon's doing," said Alarice. "I ordered him to get the Demon Crown from your brow without touching it. He hit you in the belly several times. Now *there* will be a bruise, on the soft part of your stomach."

"Soft part!" protested Vered.

"Birtle forced you to bend over. The crown fell from your head and the spell it cast on you was broken. For either Birtle or me to have removed the crown in any other way would have meant both our deaths."

"But you're a sorceress. Surely, a spell or—"

"Only in this way. Kalob's coronet possesses a magic far beyond my control." Alarice finished doctoring Vered and stepped back to survey her handiwork. The bulky white bandages made him appear to carry a cloud for a hat.

"What was it like?" asked Santon. "To be a king, if only for a few minutes?"

"Santon, you can't believe what I saw. How I saw! Every detail of my blade, of a songbird miles distant, of a quartet of constables ambushed by a rebel band led by a wizard. I saw it all. No, I *saw* it. Description of the experience is beyond my powers."

"Speechless," muttered Santon. "For the first time, he's speechless. It must be magic."

"A moment," cut in Alarice. "A wizard? Where? Did he sense your presence?"

"He ordered his troops to seek out another wizard, but I *saw* no one else in the area." Vered's face went slack with shock. "He meant me!"

"He sensed the Demon Crown. We should leave immediately. The value of so much power to a wizard would be incalculable. Vered, direct us away from this wizard and his armed men."

"Why, I saw them over . . ." Vered's words trailed off as he stood and turned in a full circle. "I saw them, but I cannot say where. My head spun so that I've become confused. One instant I looked at the haze-purpled peaks of the Yorral Mountains, and the next I saw only the dusty flatness of Uvain Plateau."

"We were proceeding to the south," said Santon. "Let's continue in that direction. We stand as good a chance of avoiding this marauding sorcerer by this tactic as by trying to scout him out."

"I agree," said Alarice. "Staying here only invites disaster." She looked at Santon for a moment, then said, "May I accompany you? Our paths need not continue together, but for now it might be for the best."

"Is Vered in any danger?"

Alarice laughed. "He's in constant danger— from his thieving impulses. The crown has done all it can, unless he wears it once more. Are you willing to do this, Vered? To don the Demon Crown again?"

"No!"

"So I thought. There is no permanent harm. Even the burns will heal without scarring."

"Let's be on our way. We've let that worthless swayback nag of ours rest long enough. It's time to be a-pulling, beast," called out Santon. He hitched the balky horse to their wagon and climbed into the wagon box. Vered pulled himself up beside his friend and waved to the Glass Warrior.

"Ride," she ordered. Alarice swung her mare

about and trotted to the south, following the faint woodland trail. Two doughty fighters accompanied her, but she did not know for how long.

Long enough, she hoped, for long enough!

"It's past midday and I'm starving," protested Vered.

"You're always hungry," said Birtle Santon. "Either that or complaining about the sanitary inconvenience of living away from the big cities."

"A bath doesn't hurt anyone," said Vered. "In your case, it might reveal a lighter shade of skin, should you clean off the caked outer layers."

Before his friend answered, they saw Alarice galloping back from scouting the dusty trail ahead. She reined in and said, "We've trouble. The wizard drawn by your use of the crown has laid his men in ambush not a mile down the road."

"Hard to retreat now," said Santon. "We could cut through the forest, though the trees are growing more sparse now. The rolling hills might hide us, even if the sounds of this creaking wagon carry from here all the way north to the Yorral Mountains."

"The wizard knows we approach," said Alarice. "His scrying spells are similiar to those that I use. If we do not appear soon, he will know that we try to evade him."

"So he comes after us later, rather than sooner," said Vered. "Does this give us a chance to prepare a trap for him? I feel more comfortable attacking than being attacked, especially if I can choose the battlefield."

"What you say has merit," Alarice said. "But I see nothing in the terrain that we can turn to our advantage. The wizard has positioned his men on either side of a narrow draw. We are too few to duplicate such a plan."

"What good does it do for us to run?" asked Vered. "This wizard watches us with his infernal spells and knows everything we do." He turned to face Alarice. "He does watch, doesn't he?"

"The use of magic is tiring," she said. "He might know we are here, but watch us constantly?" She shook her head. "That I doubt."

"So he uses the spell and drains himself until he is bedridden," scoffed Vered. "What matters this to him? He has a score of armed ruffians at his service."

"Magic is not the answer," said Alarice. Her cold gray eyes scanned the rolling hills. No opportunity for ambush suggested itself. Nor did it seem likely that they could tumble boulders off tall cliffs and crush the rebel band.

"Cast a spell and mask our path," said Vered. "But no, you said this is tiring. We will need to fight soon."

"Premonition?" asked Santon.

"Good eyes."

Clouds of dust rose. The wizard's fighters had tired of waiting and rode along the narrow, rutted road to seek them out.

"There are not a score," said Alarice, her face vacant and her eyes glazed with concentration. "Only ten."

"Three against ten," said Vered. "Why, these ruffians have no chance against us! You, Santon, you take the first three and a third. I'll take the next third, and Alarice can finish them off. Unless that does not include the wizard."

"It does. There are only ten. But the wizard is

more likely to use sword and shield than spells for this attack. Spells work too slowly, unless you are a master wizard."

"He isn't? You aren't?" Santon sounded disappointed.

Alarice smiled sadly and shook her head. "Never have I controlled more than a few simple spells. This is my weapon."

She drew forth her long glass sword. In the bright sunlight it shone like a solidified rainbow. She wheeled her mare about and said, "They come. Soon."

Vered heaved a sigh and climbed to the roof of the wagon. He drew his sword and a wicked basket-hilt dagger, spread his legs for a better stance, and began settling himself for the fight. Birtle Santon dropped to the ground and pulled his battle-ax from the wagon box. His left arm bulged as he swung the heavy ax about, getting the feel of it.

"Three and a third apiece," called Vered when the first rider came into view. "No slackers!"

The first wave of horsemen surged forward, lance tips shining in the sun and multicolored ribbon banners flapping from the shafts. Santon roared and took two steps forward to build momentum for his swing. The heavy ax passed through the leading horse's front leg and sent the rider sailing through the air to land hard near the wagon.

Vered shouted a warning to Alarice, but it was not needed. The Glass Warrior swung about, her fragile-appearing sword deflecting a lance. She put spurs to her mare and edged forward to lunge and impale the rider, her lethal glass tip penetrating leather armor and chest with equal ease.

Then Vered no longer saw what happened. Two riders had circled the wagon and he found himself engaged from two directions simultaneously. The young thief vaulted one sweeping blow with a lance shaft. He ignored that rider. His attention turned fully on the lancer charging from the far side. Vered used his dagger to parry; the lance tip drove into the top of the wagon. The shock brought the lancer up in his stirrups.

Vered's sword ended the man's life.

Vered twisted about and again parried a lance thrust. He took the opportunity presented when the other horseman foolishly turned away from the wagon. Vered leaped and landed behind the lancer. A quick slash with the dagger sent a fountain of crimson spewing forth. The horse reared and threw Vered off.

He hit, rolled, and came to his feet beside Birtle Santon.

"Some fight, eh?" he shouted. "How many?"

"Just the one," said Santon.

"I need only one and a third to go!" Vered rushed forward, a lance tip almost opening his skull. He thrust his dagger into the horse's flank even as his sword reached upward to gut the rider. If either attack had failed, the other would have proven effective. As it was, Vered scored easily with both. Horse and rider died in a pool of blood.

Santon had unseated another lancer. A powerful overhead swing with the ax shattered an upraised shaft. A return swing ended the life of the lancer.

"I still need a third of a rider. You need one and a third," called Vered. "But where are they? Have the cravens run? What manner of ruffian is this, to attack in overwhelming numbers, then flee?"

Vered turned in a full circle. He hardly believed his eyes. The fight had gone well, he thought, but how could it be over? It had barely begun, yet the corpses he counted totaled ten. He had accounted for three and Santon two.

His brown eyes rose to stare in surprise at the Glass Warrior. Her long blade dripped gore. "You have vanquished fully half the force," he said. Then, angrily, "How dare you! You took more than your fair share!"

"Calm yourself, Vered. She did us both a favor."

"The wizard?" Vered walked to a fallen man whose throat had been neatly slit. Only a thin line of red appeared beneath his chin, but he had died from the wound.

"A minor one," said Alarice. "I have seen him before in the southlands. Never have I heard a name."

"Too bad. I wouldn't mind it if you cursed him and sent him and the entire pack of ruffians to the hottest depths of demon-infested hell." Vered knelt down and used his dagger tip to lift the sorcerer's pouch. He opened it cautiously, spreading the contents on the ground.

"I see nothing of interest," said Alarice. "Take what you will, Vered. There's no magic potion hidden there."

"To hell and gone with magic potions," he cried. "I want gold! The wizard is as poverty-stricken as we are. What kind of brigand was he? Imagine, dying without a full purse. The impudence of it all!"

Santon and Vered searched the bodies and found fewer than a dozen coins, mostly silver and copper. No gold. Even the equipment carried by the rebel band proved worthless to them.

"We should only allow better-quality rebels to attack us. This is ridiculous. No booty. Pah!" Vered dropped down beside the wagon, his back against a wheel.

"We've gained a few horses. The ones you didn't gut in your clumsy attempts to kill the riders," said Santon.

"Horses. We can't hitch them to the wagon. These are saddle mounts, not work horses. They'd be more trouble than they're worth. What a wasted fight." His eyes turned back to Alarice. In a lower voice, he said, "But it was an honor seeing her fight. By the saints, what a warrior!"

"She's that and more," agreed Santon, emotions Vered had seldom seen in him rippling across the man's weathered face.

The pair sat in silence for some time. Then both spoke at the same time. They quieted, and Santon said, "What do you think of her quest to find the twins? A worthy one?"

"It would eliminate scenes such as this. No rebel bands. The countryside would be quieter, more peaceful, less suspicious."

"Our trade would be the easier for that," said Santon.

"What else do we have to occupy our time?" asked Vered. "We're wanted by too many local constables to travel freely. I had demurred originally because I thought she was no true warrior. But she equaled our combined best."

"Better than that," said Santon. "She hardly seemed tired from the exertion."

"Neither of us worked up a sweat," Vered pointed out. "She is quite a woman. One fine warrior. And the season is good for exploring. Who's to say that we wouldn't find the twins—and a sizable reward?"

"There is that," Santon said.

They sat in silence for another few minutes, then stood and began stowing their weapons so that they would come easily to hand. Wherever the Glass Warrior led them, they knew those weapons would be needed.

CHAPTER EIGHT

"There's no need to keep looking for the wizard's fighters," said Vered. "We finished them off." He sneezed, wiped his nose, then said, "Or perhaps it is not the wizard you seek. Could it be that your heart reaches out to Alarice?"

Birtle Santon glared at his friend, then turned his eyes squarely ahead to the double ruts they followed across the countryside. Rains had washed away much of what had been a road, and with the minor battles raging constantly, no one had the will or time to repair it.

"What's wrong with me looking at her? She's a fine-looking woman."

"She is," Vered agreed.

"You go whoring about whenever we find a town large enough."

"Most are large enough," said Vered.

"Who are you to pass judgment on what I think or feel?"

"We all need a vice or two. Makes life more interesting." Vered leaned back and put his feet over the edge of the wagon box. "It seems that you have more than a few vices, though, Santon my friend. If you add Alarice to the list, why, you might spend all your time trying to remember what to indulge in next."

"You mock me."

"Of course I do! It's all in good fun. You take yourself much too seriously. Loosen up. There is nothing wrong with lusting after a wench so comely."

"She's no wench."

Vered quickly apologized. "She's even better with that strange sword of hers than I am with mine. And I have grown accustomed to the balance of mine. Best weapon I ever stole."

They rode along in silence until Alarice reined in and waited for them to catch up. "Pull over," she said. "We need to discuss our course. The land is turning against us."

"But the day is beautiful," protested Vered. "As far as the eye can see, it is lovely. No storms, although the muddy road suggests we might be in for more rain this evening."

"We go to the southlands," she said patiently. "The way is dangerous and we must discuss how we are to proceed."

Santon pulled on the reins and the horse gratefully slowed and stopped. The animal bent forward in its harness, straining to graze at a patch of verdant grass. Vered swung down and released the horse to graze freely. He doubted the horse would run off. Its running days were long past.

"Here is the castle," Alarice said, her finger marking a spot in the damp dirt. "The River Ty runs along this course, then empties into the delta swamps."

"I've never been there, but others who have report only insects and disease. Why do we go there?" Birtle Santon settled down on his haunches to await the answer.

"Tahir d'mar killed King Lamost."

"I'd heard of Lamost's death," said Vered. "Never has it even been hinted that foul play helped him along to his grave."

"Tahir is a powerful wizard and adept at traceless potions carrying a hundred deaths in every drop."

"What did he hope to gain from killing the king? He certainly hasn't been active over the past decades," said Santon. "If he sought power, he failed miserably."

"These are matters I hope to explore with Tahir. I am sure that he killed Lamost *and* kidnapped the twins."

"He might have exploited that and gained a small part of Porotane as his own. Yet we go into the filthy bowels of the swamps. This Tahir could not have chosen such a spot for his domain."

"This is something else to discover, Vered. Tahir lives. My best scrying shows that. Why does he hide in a swamp laced with death and disease? Even a sorcerer cannot avoid all enemies. If I sought to harm Tahir, I would choose an insect carrying a deadly poison as my weapon. Should the victim swat it, another could be a-wing in seconds. This is opinion and not magic, but I feel that Tahir did not choose this retreat willingly."

"The twins are with him?" asked Santon.

The Glass Warrior shook her head. "I detect no sign of them, but Tahir must know. It is possible that both Lokenna and Lorens died soon after the kidnapping. Tahir might have decided they, too, had to die in some scheme that failed later. These are things we must learn."

"Is it wise to carry the Demon Crown into a wizard's stronghold, even if the stronghold is hidden by swarms of gnats and sucking swampland?" Vered worked over lines of approach and liked none of them. Alarice had picked the worst section of Porotane for attack. Who can charge properly through scummy swamp water? At best, he would look ludicrous. At worst?

Vered turned his thoughts from this sorry picture. That which worried a soul the most always came to pass. Better to consider only successful ventures.

"My scrying shows only that Tahir lives within the confines of the swamp. I have no clear idea where he is."

"How do we track within such muck? Better to simply stand on the fringe of the swamp and yell for him to come out. A challenge always provokes response." Santon sank back into silence.

"Not this wizard. Tahir scorns society. He thinks little of violating sanctions simply because it causes discord. Of all the wizards I have known, Tahir was the one most likely to have assassinated a king and stolen away the heirs to the throne."

"Might he have done it out of spite? He might not have sought power," suggested Vered.

"His motives are obscure, but Tahir wanted something more tangible than discord," said Santon. "This sorcerer isn't driven by insane urges. He seeks gain. All men do."

"But Alarice says he is irrational." Vered tried again to formulate a plan and failed. The Glass Warrior's quest took on disturbing aspects that he could not cope with.

Alarice made a motion that quieted the men. "This swamp lies many days' travel to the south and west," she said. "The land between here and the edges of the swamp is dangerous. Rebel bands roam freely."

"We've been across it a few months ago," said Santon. "You speak the truth about the land. The people are left homeless and many have taken to wandering. Some are even joining rebel bands, although they have no sympathy for the leader's cause."

"They join only to have food and protection," said Vered, cutting in. "It is a sorry state for any country's citizenry to be in. Possibly the worst in all Porotane."

"We can reach the swamp in a week, if we travel swiftly," she said. "Are you up to it?"

"Are the horses up to it," corrected Vered. "Mayhap the wagon has outlived its usefulness. What do you say, Santon? Leave it and ride our captured horses?"

"The roads get worse with every passing mile. If we want to reach this Tahir before he dies of old age, we'd be well advised to do just that. Let's ride."

The men chose horses from those taken from the soldiers and used two extra ones as pack animals. Their swayback horse that had served them so well they let roam free.

"Dinner," said Vered. "That scrawny animal will end up as dinner for someone. Mark my words."

"Why not?" Santon said. "You mark your cards."

But he, too, hated to set free their trusty

swayback horse. The Glass Warrior called, and he wheeled his horse about and trotted off, willing himself not to look back.

"This is our destination?" asked Vered, horror in his voice. "We have endured all manner of deprivation these past ten days. Starvation, no sleep, the saints take them—cannibals! And for what? So we can arrive at a place like *this*?"

The swamp extended in a noisome fan before them. Heavy-limbed mangroves appeared to sway and move, as if alive. The clouds of insects around these trees were more than Vered wanted to consider. The green slime-covered waters circling the thick tree trunks rippled with unseen life. When an unblinking amber eye rose and fixed on Vered, his hand flashed to his sword.

"I know not what it is, but it sizes me up for dinner."

"A swamp swimmer," said Alarice. "Nothing to fear."

Vered tried to outstare the eye that began moving slowly along the scummy surface. He failed. When he looked back, the eye had vanished beneath the water.

"What should we fear? I like nothing about this place." Vered swatted at a hungry insect working its way past his collar. His hand came away sticky with blood.

"We cannot ride aimlessly," said Santon. "Alarice, how do we find your murderous wizard in this slop?" His horse bucked and protested. Standing at the edge of the slime-covered pond, the horse had begun sinking into the muck. Santon got the horse moving and pulled free of the sucking mud.

The Glass Warrior stood in her stirrups and slowly scanned the swampland. Vered and Santon exchanged glances. They had no idea what she sought. The banyan trees, with their long armlike branches, dangled mosses to form feathery green curtains preventing anyone from seeing into the swamp. Of dry land, there was none in sight.

"There is much power locked within this land," Alarice said. "It is stunted, though. A power once great but now on the wane. This has to be Tahir d'mar."

"So much for the notion that wizards live lavishly. Why does he hide in such a place, unless another pursues him? Could this have something to do with the twins?" asked Vered.

"That direction," Alarice said. "We ride to the center of the swamp. I see a small island. Dry land. Tahir is there."

"How far?" Santon had increasing difficulty controlling his horse. The animal did not enjoy the sucking yellow mud around its hooves.

"Distance means nothing. Time? Two days' travel. Longer. I cannot say. There is more than swamp swimmers and catamounts."

"Catamounts!" Vered turned to Alarice. "The last of that species died before I was born. From all accounts, they fought fiercely and loathed humans."

"Many hundreds survive in the swamp," she said. "Otherwise, you are correct. They will not like being disturbed by our passage through their breeding grounds."

"Santon," Vered said in disgust. "Seldom will you hear this escape my lips. I have made a mistake. We should not have accompanied her. Not only will we be eaten alive by bugs, we disturb fornicating cats able to tear our guts out with the single swipe of a paw. And for what? So we can find a king-killer wizard who, in all probability, will be only too happy to slay us, also."

"True," said Santon. "There is one thing you can say about this, however. It's not dull."

Alarice put spurs to her mare and splashed off through the shallow swamp. Santon convinced his steed to follow. Vered coughed, wiped his nose, swatted two more marauding bloodsucker insects, then urged his horse after Santon's. As he rode he stared down into the murky water for hint of swamp swimmers, whatever they were. He had never seen one and had no desire to see more than the eye that had watched him.

"Take a care," Santon called back. "The path is narrow. A step to either side will cast you into deeper water."

"To think, we could be enjoying ourselves in a brothel," Vered grumbled. "Or lounging at the seaside, watching the beautiful blue waves crash against the shore. Or we could even be socializing with cannibals." A sudden splashing caused Vered to jerk about. Except for the expanding rings of ripples, he saw nothing.

Even dinner with cannibals seemed less objectionable.

An hour's ride brought them to drier land surrounded by stagnant ponds. Alarice dismounted and tended her mare. Santon heaved himself to the ground, too, but Vered remained in his saddle.

"Aren't you going to rest? This is the first solid ground we've found all day," said Santon.

"Solid? Does this muck look solid to you. See? You sink to your ankles in it." He dropped to the ground and moved around, stomping in small puddles. "What are we doing? The Demon Crown must have addled my wits. This is no fit place for me."

Vered stopped. Neither Alarice nor Santon paid him any heed. He fumbled in his pack and found a brush to curry his horse. As he pulled the brush free from the pack, he stared over the horse's back. The movement in tangled, low shrubs drew his attention. He stiffened, thinking this to be another "harmless" creature like the swamp swimmer.

When he saw the powerful, hairy arms, the immense shoulders, the tiny furred head, and the savage yellow fangs, he knew otherwise.

"Trouble!" he called, dropping the brush and drawing his sword. Vered slipped and fell to one knee in the mud. In the span of one frenzied heartbeat, the yowling creature had crossed the intervening distance and attacked.

Vered looked up into tiny red eyes filled with hatred and a mouthful of teeth capable of ripping him apart. He had no time to properly thrust. Instead, he braced the hilt of his sword on the ground, aimed the point in the creature's direction, and fell backward.

The beast launched itself and came down on the sword point, impaling itself. Sizzling hot yellow blood erupted from the gash in its chest. A few drops spattered onto Vered's boots and breeches; the acid blood burned through the clothing and into his flesh.

He yelped in pain and began kicking against the yielding ground to get away. Only Birtle Santon's quick reflexes saved Vered. The heavy battle-ax swung parallel to the ground and struck the beast's collarbone. The sickening crunch of the collision echoed through the swamp.

For an instant, the hairy monster stood and stared at the ax buried in it. Then the scream of agony drowned out all other sounds. The creature reached up and plucked the heavy ax from its body and cast it aside as if it were made of splinters.

Vered avoided the shower of yellow blood and drew his dagger. Gripping the hilt firmly, he thrust upward, seeking the creature's foul heart. The blade sizzled and hissed as the acid chewed away metal along the razor-sharp edge. Vered drove the blade up but found no secure berth. He pulled away and rolled, coming to his feet beside Santon.

"You've lost your ax, old friend," observed Vered.

"You've lost your sword."

Alarice pushed past them, her glass sword extended *en garde*. "It does little good to attack with steel," she told them. "Let me see how I fare with this beast."

The creature bellowed and beat its chest with heavy fists. Alarice did not let the challenge go unanswered. She stepped forward with a movement more like a dance step than a battle move and lunged.

The glass sword tip drove directly into the hollow of the creature's throat. It gurgled and choked on its own blood. The burning flow of acid blood had no effect on the Glass Warrior's sword. She twisted it savagely, drew back, and lunged again.

The thrust went straight to the creature's heart. It groped at empty air with its paws, then fell forward, dead before it struck the ground. Alarice wiped off her blade on the beast's matted fur back.

The deadly blood burned a small band where her sword had touched, then quieted as it ate into the corpse.

"What *is* that thing?" demanded Vered. He held up his dagger. The dull pits along the once-sharp edge made it almost worthless as a weapon. The acidic blood had eaten huge chunks from the metal.

"Who can say?" answered Alarice. "The swamplands are filled with creatures real and magical. This is an example of the latter. Tahir might have set it to protect his little kingdom."

"Let him keep his saints-damned kingdom," exclaimed Vered. "Why risk our lives against *things* like that? And look! I am filthy from rolling about on the ground."

"A true disgrace to your clan and your country," Santon said sarcastically. He hefted his battle-ax and swung it. "Balance is off. The beast ruined the temper of the blade. Look!"

"Forget the blade," said Vered.

"Vered, Alarice, look!"

The burly man's tone brought both of the others around to face a scaly monster wobbling up onto dry land from the pond. Scum clung to its back, giving it a curious color in the fading sunlight. But Vered did not concentrate on colors or texture.

"The teeth! Damn me if they all don't have twice the number of teeth they should!"

Eyes on the knee-high beast, he picked up his sword and tested the blade. It had suffered the same fate that his dagger had. He might be better off using it as a club. For slashing or stabbing the sword had outlived its usefulness.

Vered and Santon worked together well as a

team. They split, one making distracting noises while the other advanced. When the long-jawed monster turned to attack, the other began the noise. Back and forth they worked the dim-witted monster.

But neither could make a clean kill. Vered's blade glanced off a thick, armored back. Santon's battle-ax fared little better as he swung it down as hard as he could atop the flat head. Even attacking simultaneously, they failed to stop the monster's advance.

"This one is stronger than the both of us," panted Santon. "Not for the first time do I wish I had the use of both arms."

"Let's hope that wish is not for the last time," muttered Vered.

"Can you stop it with a spell?" Santon asked of Alarice. The Glass Warrior stood, staring off into the distance, as if listening hard for sounds no human could hear. His question shook her from the reverie.

"No, it's natural. Unlike the ape-thing, no spell drives it."

"Let me guess," said Vered as he dodged a savage snap of powerful jaws. "This is a swamp swimmer. The harmless animal you said not to worry over."

"It is." Alarice avoided the closing jaws and moved behind the swamp creature. "Dealing with them is simple. They are protected too well for ordinary attack. No!" she called to Vered. "Don't thrust into its mouth. It can break your blade."

Vered glowered at her and moved back.

"You have to distract it," Alarice continued, "then attack from the rear." The beast moved sluggishly toward Santon. As it did so, Alarice grabbed its tail and grunted as she lifted. The swamp swimmer's legs proved too weak to support it; it flipped over onto its back, exposing bone-white belly.

"Do we gut it?" asked Vered, not daring to advance on it, even in this helpless condition.

"No. It is formidable even now. As a hunter might try such a shot on a deer, so we must work on the swimmer."

Alarice's glass sword drove down toward the beast's anus. The swamp swimmer made a strangely soft noise as the glass blade vanished into its bowels. It kicked weakly, then slumped, head lolling to one side.

"Now?" asked Vered.

"It is dead," the Glass Warrior said. "But our problems are only beginning."

"What?" Vered and Santon said as one. They moved to stand back to back, ready for still more dangers.

"We are a long distance from Tahir. There is no way we can hope to fight through a legion of such creatures."

"You're not giving up," protested Santon.

"You can't! We've gotten dirty and bloody and gone hungry to get this far. We cannot surrender. We've yet to do battle with the murderer of our beloved King Lamost. And what of the twins?" Vered's face gained color as his indignation rose.

Alarice did not answer. She had not expected them to come this far, yet they had and she appreciated their loyalty. But the Glass Warrior knew that the most dangerous part of the journey lay ahead. Could she ask even more of these two adventurers?

CHAPTER NINE

Baron Theoll drew himself up to his full height and barely came to the guard lieutenant's shoulder. He glared at Oprezzi and, when this disapproval went unnoticed, pushed his way past to stand unsteadily beside the duke's bed.

Freow's eyelids fluttered and he stirred. Unfocused eyes opened and a parchment-like hand reached out. To whom Theoll couldn't tell. Nor did it matter. Circling the bed were the powers in Porotane's castle. The physician tending the failing duke mattered little to Theoll. The others, however, held his full attention.

The Lady Johanna he considered something of an interloper. Almost a year ago, she had arrived from a distant province a few minutes ahead of Gaemock's band of ruffians. The castle guard had fought off the rebels, and Dews Gaemock had retreated. Johanna had given proof of noble birth —she was the bastard child of Lamost's youngest nephew. The way she had declared this dubious lineage rankled. Theoll did not call her a liar openly, but the scheming she had engaged in warned him that her ambitions knew the same bounds as his own: none.

Johanna had begun bedding each of the

guardsmen until she found Lieutenant Oprezzi.
The man had the power Johanna sought and was
willing to trade it for a few minutes of fornication.
Theoll looked from Oprezzi to the cool, calm
Johanna. Those were damned few minutes the
guardsmen had had with her. He had watched
often enough to know.

He studied the woman closely. Her gown
proved demure for someone with such well-known
flamboyant tastes in clothing. Perhaps she thought
it improper to come to a death bed in party
clothing, yet the smile trying to force up the
corners of her mouth showed her true feelings.
Freow's death meant opportunity for her.

A castle coup? Theoll thought it possible.
Oprezzi had the loyalty of more guardsmen than
the captain of guards. The duke dies, Johanna
ascends the throne and takes Oprezzi as consort.
That seemed the most likely plot she would have
held out to the young and ambitious lieutenant.

Theoll pushed them from his mind. Others
gathered about the duke like vultures waiting for
their dinner to die. A few royal second cousins
who had no chance for the throne nonetheless
hoped for suitable recompense. A small estate. A
castle. A lifetime stipend.

A swift blade slid through the ribs and into
their black hearts would be their reward, if Theoll
triumphed.

That would remove those of distant claim to
the throne. Theoll followed this line of thinking
and frowned. What of Freow's family? His wife had
been killed on her way to the castle after Lamost's
death. No children? Not even a bastard? Theoll
wondered about Freow's manhood, yet he had

spied on the duke with numerous women, sometimes many at a time. Still, he thought it strange
that the duke had no family in the distant province.
He and his brother had not been close. Rumors of
discord—even a blood feud—between him and
Lamost had run the circle of Porotane society.

But no family? Strange.

"Excuse me, Baron." Theoll stepped to one
side and allowed Archbishop Nosto to stand beside
Freow. The cleric took the old man's hand in his
and held it gently. Theoll wished he could see the
archbishop's eyes. Despite his sincere-sounding
words and loving caresses, Nosto's eyes held nothing but polar ice. The cleric had begun his Inquisition, and it now ruled him totally.

Theoll could not decide if Archbishop Nosto
used it as a means to gain the throne for himself, or
only desired to choose the next ruler of Porotane.
Either way, Theoll had to cultivate the cleric's
friendship and loyalty. The meeting with the "demon" had done much to convince Nosto of the
existence of evil within the castle walls.

It would soon be time for the Question to be
put to Oprezzi. That would snap the backbone of
Lady Johanna's power, Theoll decided. She would
have no chance to forge new bonds with another
guard officer of sufficient standing in time to
oppose him.

Theoll winced at the pain in his legs as he
stood on tiptoe and peered past Nosto's shoulder
at the duke. The amount of poison had been
increased to accelerate the old man's decline. It
worked well. How he hung onto the thin strand of
life that kept him from the Eternal Abyss, Theoll
did not know. But soon, very soon Duke Freow

would die, and he would replace the old regent as king.

"Yeow!" Theoll cried. Someone had come up behind him and driven something hard and round into his posterior. He spun, hand on dagger. Harhar stood there, an idiotic grin on his face. The jester held up his rattle and shook it at Theoll. In other company, the fool would have died. Instead of driving his dagger into Harhar's gut, Theoll grabbed him by the collar and sent him tumbling across the room.

The jester hit and rolled and came to his feet, the rattle making odd sounds as he shook it vigorously.

"Why so sad?" Harhar called. "Duke Freow is stronger than ever. He will live, if you permit a jest or two to brighten his outlook."

"Get him out of here," Theoll ordered Oprezzi. To his surprise, the lieutenant glanced over at Johanna. He obeyed the tiny shake of her head and not Theoll's command.

"He harms nothing," said the physician. "The duke responds well to him. Let him stay. For a time, at least."

To Theoll's disgust, the jester's cavortings and salacious japes *did* help Freow rally. Color returned to the translucent cheeks and the eyes focused.

"I would rest," came a weak voice, but one lacking the edge of death that Theoll expected. The duke's gaze went around those at his bedside. He looked like a death's head when he smiled. "I am not dead yet, my dear friends. When I go, rejoice, for there will be a new ruler, a true ruler. I have sent for the royal twins."

"You know their location?" cried Johanna, obviously startled.

"I do, I do." Freow's eyes closed and he drifted into sleep, his chest rising and dropping slightly the only indication that life remained within his withered frame.

"All away, go, go," ordered the physician. He pushed the expectant onlookers away. Theoll allowed the physician to start him for the door. To his considerable irritation, the physician did not treat Harhar equally. The jester stayed behind.

In the corridor outside Duke Freow's chambers, Theoll tugged at Archbishop Nosto's sleeve with his good hand and pulled the man's ear down where he could whisper without being overheard.

"Oprezzi. See how he and Lady Johanna talk to one another?"

The archbishop said nothing, but his thin frame stiffened and his hands clenched. Even more revealing for Theoll was the way Nosto's jaw muscles tightened. The cleric had taken seriously the "demon's" condemnation of Oprezzi.

"He is a heretic, as you must know. He has strayed from the True Path."

"What?" Theoll cried, feigning astonishment. "I did not hear wrong then? I know that he and Johanna plot against Freow, but a heretic? That is a serious charge, Archbishop. I had hoped I was wrong. Your, uh, assignation proved fruitful?"

"I have the proof."

"He must be put to the Question. The full extent of his treachery must be learned." Theoll's voice dropped even lower. "Or do you already know facts I do not?"

"He has congress with demons."

"That is no way to speak of Johanna, although in bed she seems possessed." Theoll allowed himself a chuckle.

"Do not speak heresy, Theoll," snapped Archbishop Nosto. "These are matters of the utmost gravity."

"I beg your forgiveness, Nosto. I meant no disrespect."

"No, of course not. How could anyone following the True Path know of this swine's obscene behavior?"

"Tell me more," Theoll said. "I need to know more. I cannot accuse Johanna of poisoning Freow, but the thought refuses to leave my brain. She has come from a distant province with the flimsiest of claims to the blood royal, and yet she is now a pretender to the throne. She might assume the throne, should her royal line be verified."

"She is of no importance. It is Oprezzi who occupies my thoughts and prayers. I seek guidance in that matter," said Archbishop Nosto, "and the saints have failed to answer. I drift on a sea of heresy and know not how to proceed."

"Truly, a serious concern for everyone in Porotane. This lieutenant must not contaminate Johanna, should her claims to the throne prove valid."

"He must be put to the Question immediately. There is no other way to know his involvement with demonic forces."

"No!" Theoll said, too abruptly, too forcefully. He wanted Oprezzi in the hands of Nosto's Inquisition, but not yet, not until Freow died. Only in that way could he indict Johanna and remove her. A premature questioning of the young lieutenant would allow her time to respond and sway others to her favor.

"I have no choice, Theoll. None. By the saints, I shall find out about his involvement with demons!"

Archbishop Nosto pulled free of Theoll's grip and stalked off. Theoll controlled his anger. This precipitous questioning would remove Oprezzi, but not when the baron desired. Freow's death and Oprezzi's torture must come within hours if Johanna was to be discredited.

"Damn you, Nosto, damn you and all your fornicating saints!" Theoll bit his tongue and looked around to be sure that no one overheard his outburst. Still seething, he stormed off. New plans had to be made. He had to profit from Oprezzi's death. But how?

Baron Theoll slipped from the secret passages, his heart pounding furiously from his spying. This night proved exceptionally active in the castle's bedchambers. His eye hurt from being forced against too many spyholes and his legs throbbed mercilessly. Only his left arm gave him true difficulty, however; it hung useless and twisted at his side. He emerged into the corridor outside Nosto's quarters. For a moment, he considered slipping back into the secret panel before the red-clad Inquisitors in the corridor challenged him.

Too late. The one at the far end of the hall tugged his blood-red hood down so that the eyeholes were in place and pointed a ceremonial dagger at Theoll. "Halt!" the Inquisitor cried. "Halt and be identified to the Inquisition!"

"Baron Theoll of Brandon," the small noble said. "I come to speak with the archbishop on a personal matter."

"He is occupied with clerical matters."

"Does it have to do with a guardsman being put to the Question?"

Both Inquisitors adjusted their hoods and shuffled nervously from one foot to the other. A silent decision was made. The one closest to Theoll grabbed his good arm and swung him toward the door leading to Nosto's chambers. "Inside," ordered one. Theoll did not resist. Both Inquisitors had drawn their daggers and were ready to use them should he protest. He shrugged off this lack of respect and pushed through the heavy door and into Nosto's sitting room.

"Archbishop?" he called. "I'd speak with you."

Nosto emerged from an inner room wearing a hood similar to those of the guards outside, except his had the bone-white sigil of the True Path imprinted on the face. Theoll blinked in surprise, not at this but at Nosto's muscular development. The archbishop was naked to the waist, displaying power Theoll had not even guessed at. Tightly cinched around the cleric's waist was a hair belt.

Human hair, Theoll saw. He did not doubt that Nosto had taken it from previous victims— heretics—of the Inquisition who had confessed their heresy before dying.

Skintight breeches the same color as the hood disappeared into the tops of soft leather boots, also adorned with the white sigil of the True Path. In the top of the left boot was thrust a dagger like the ceremonial implements carried by those outside.

"You come at a bad time, Theoll. The work of

the Inquisition requires my full attention. Come back tomorrow. Tomorrow afternoon."

"Nosto, wait. Does the Inquisition go to put the Question to Oprezzi?"

"Yours is a secular realm, mine is religious. My duties as Inquisitor do not concern you, Baron."

Theoll's mind raced. He saw that nothing would dissuade Nosto from torturing the lieutenant. He had to turn this to his own benefit.

"Do you know the questions to ask?" he demanded of the archbishop. "Not the religious ones, but the secular. Who seduced Oprezzi? I have reason to believe that Lady Johanna is a demon in human form."

"Ridiculous, even I—" Archbishop Nosto cut off his words. Theoll stared at the tall, thin cleric. Had even Nosto succumbed to Johanna's influence? The vision he had of this whipsaw-muscled cleric and the lovely, lush-figured, frosty blonde Johanna together turned his gut to jelly. What a powerful alliance those two would make if he did not stop them!

"These are matters to investigate," said Theoll.

"What is the source of your accusation?"

"A dying messenger," Theoll lied. "He crossed a strife-torn Porotane from the lady's province to tell of demonic deeds before her departure. Many died, some horribly with boils disfiguring them. Each had been touched by Johanna." Theoll said no more. To do so would prejudice Archbishop Nosto against him. If Johanna and the archbishop shared a bed, it was better to let Nosto's imagination fill in any discrepancies. Because of his work as Inquisitor, he did a fine job of jumping to conclusions based on the flimsiest of evidence.

"Perhaps you speak the truth. You have always walked the True Path, and often revelation is given to the faithful."

Theoll bowed his head.

"Stay here. The Inquisition seeks Oprezzi. He will be put to the Question this night and truth will flow from the heretic's lips!"

"May I . . ." Theoll cut off his request and bowed his head again when he saw the determined set of Nosto's lean body. Religious matters brooked no interference by a mere baron. Theoll bowed even lower as Nosto left abruptly, the loose fabric of his hood snapping as if in a high wind.

Theoll released a pent-up breath, then counted slowly to one hundred. He peered into the corridor and saw that Nosto and the two Inquisitors had left on their mission of righteous interrogation. Even if Oprezzi sat surrounded by his fellows, none would dare defend him against the Inquisition.

Theoll almost laughed when he thought of the possibility that Oprezzi lay with Johanna. The notion of Nosto plucking the lieutenant from the blonde's bed amused the baron greatly. But he knew such was fantasy only. The guardsman patrolled the battlements, as was his duty. All day long Dews Gaemock's rebels had been sighted riding across the burned-out farmland surrounding the castle. What this scouting on the rebels' part portended, no one knew. Another siege? Doubtful. Trouble? All agreed on this point and vigilance rather than dalliance ruled the guardsmen this night.

He considered going to the battlements and waiting for Nosto and his Inquisitors to take Oprezzi into custody. He reconsidered. It would appear that he maneuvered the archbishop into the action. Theoll wanted no hint that he *had* been responsible. He turned to his secret ways in the castle walls and found a spiraling staircase leading four levels lower into the dungeons.

He went quietly along a passage so narrow that his shoulders brushed the walls. Occasionally he dallied to peer through a spyhole. Nothing caught his fancy. Theoll finally stopped behind a large wooden panel with a dozen different cutouts. He slid back several and peered through, finding the few that gave him the best view of the dungeons used by the Inquisition.

Theoll waited only a few minutes before loud shouts and the scrape of metal against stone alerted him to Nosto's entrance. He bent forward, eager eyes pressed against the wood panel. With a vantage point better than if he'd been in the room, Theoll saw Oprezzi being dragged between the two hooded Inquisitors, Archbishop Nosto following closely behind.

"There," ordered Nosto. "Place him there."

"I am a guardsman," protested Oprezzi. "You cannot take me from my post without imperiling the entire castle! What if the rebels attack? Who would command?"

"What if a lieutenant of the guard strays from the True Path and has congress with demons?" Nosto parried.

"I am no heretic!" cried Oprezzi. "I know nothing of demons. Praise be to the saints!"

"Blasphemer!" Archbishop Nosto struck the

helpless soldier with the back of his hand. Oprezzi's head jerked back and a tiny trickle of blood ran down his chin.

The Inquisitors heaved the guardsman onto a wooden platform and fastened him spread-eagled on it to stare in fright at the cold stone ceiling. While Nosto watched, his eyes gleaming through the eyeholes of his hood, the other two stripped Oprezzi of his uniform. The naked man struggled futilely.

"What do you want of me?" he asked, fear tingeing his words. "I am no heretic."

"The Question will be put to you later. Now we need know of your involvement with demons."

"There isn't any. I know nothing of . . . aiee!"

One of the hooded clerics used the tip of his blade on the man's bare chest, inscribing the sigil of the True Path.

"What of Lady Johanna?" came Nosto's query.

"What of her? She's a lady of the realm. She's of royal blood. What do you want from me?" Again Oprezzi shrieked in pain as the Inquisitors drew their knife-points over his flesh and duplicated the sigil on his trembling arms and legs.

"She is a demon. Admit it."

"I know nothing of that. She does not seem to be."

"Beneath you," said Archbishop Nosto, "are cages of famished weasels. The blood from your wounds drives them wild. Small panels in the wooden platform on which you lie slide back." Nosto gestured. An Inquisitor pulled a thin wooden sheet away, leaving no protection between helpless flesh and savage fangs.

Oprezzi shrieked in true agony now as the

weasels ripped his flesh. He surged and strained, trying to break the bonds holding him to the table. He stood a better chance of pulling his arms from their sockets. Nosto nodded. The panel was slammed back into the platform, denying the weasels their meal of human flesh.

"The doors open the entire length of your body. We can open them singly or in concert with others. No portion of your body will be denied them if you refuse to speak truthfully." To emphasize his determination, Archbishop Nosto drove his dagger between Oprezzi's legs. The lieutenant tried to move; his bonds prevented it. "The dagger sticks in the last door we shall open—unless you speak now."

Baron Theoll moved to other spyholes to get a better view of the torture. He hoped that the lieutenant did not die of fear before he confessed. So many of those facing the Question expired from sheer fright. Theoll needed Oprezzi to curse the Lady Johanna, to condemn her, to declare her a demon.

After that, Theoll was willing to let the archbishop have his heretic.

"Anything," Oprezzi said. "I'll confess to anything you want."

Theoll was disappointed in the young lieutenant. He had hoped the man would show more courage. He could have at least tried to protect his lover's honor. But no, the presence of voracious rodents beneath him produced a torrent of words.

Before Oprezzi stopped to catch a breath, he had condemned Johanna as both a demon and a poor lover. Theoll smiled wickedly when he saw Nosto begin to twitch in anger. The archbishop *had* shared Johanna's bed! Oprezzi's denunciation on that score did nothing to gain him mercy from the cleric.

"You have spoken enough of these matters," Nosto said to his victim. "What of your congress with demons?"

"I know nothing of it. I swear!"

Theoll's heart raced as one door after another opened. Bloody strings of flesh remained before Archbishop Nosto ordered the doors closed.

"Are you a heretic? This is the Question. Are you a heretic? Answer truthfully and beg forgiveness."

"No!"

Theoll knew the guardsman had had no demonic contact. But Archbishop Nosto had seen with his own eyes the demon in the wall of the pantry, heard the naming of Oprezzi, seen heretical activity.

Oprezzi denied it, blaming all on the Lady Johanna.

"Roll him over on the table," ordered the cleric. The hooded Inquisitors did as they were ordered, falling to their task with a will. Face down, Oprezzi was dangerously exposed to the weasels and their ripping teeth.

One by one the doors were opened, Nosto saving the one at Oprezzi's groin for last, as he had promised. Oprezzi confessed everything, but he never provided the details Nosto knew to be true.

Lieutenant Oprezzi died a heretic.

CHAPTER TEN

Vered cursed to himself as he tried to put the fine edge back on his sword. The whetstone seemed less the tool to use than a coarse rasp. The acid blood from the apelike creature had permanently ruined the cutting edge and the temper of the blade. Vered did not even look at his dagger. Most of the hilt had vanished because of the sizzling yellow blood.

"What do you mean you won't turn back?" Alarice demanded. The Glass Warrior stood and stared in disbelief at Birtle Santon. The man rubbed his withered arm with his left hand. A slight smile danced on his lips.

"Life's never been easy for me and Vered," he said. "That hasn't meant it's been interesting. Fact is, of late life has been dull."

"That's not what you told me before," she said, exasperated. "You said the constables track you mercilessly—"

"They do," cut in Vered.

"And that more nobles want to break you on the wheel than there are fiefdoms in all Porotane!"

"A sorry state when you have so many pretenders to minor posts," said Vered. He thrust his sword into the muddy ground and drew it back, as if this would produce a new edge. It only left the blade more nicked and dirty than before.

"You owe me nothing," cried Alarice. "You shouldn't have come this far. This is my duty, not yours."

"We go where we choose," said Santon. "That's the kind of life we *want* to lead. We've been fleeing. That's no fit existence for anyone. Even us."

"I don't understand this. Not at all," the woman said. "You have only savage death to look forward to in this saints-abandoned swamp. How does this allow you to lead a 'fit existence'?"

"Because we'd be doing what we want, not what some scurvy ruffian of a rebel leader or a petty baron or count wants us to do. They chase, we run. What life is that? We'd rather stay in one place and . . . ply our trade in that fashion."

"You want to steal without being punished?" Alarice shook her head. This made no sense to her.

"A notion worthy of consideration," said Vered.

"But . . ."

"We go where you go, Alarice," said Santon. His eyes locked with her steel-gray ones.

"There is nothing binding you to me," she said, not sure she truly meant this. Birtle Santon pretended to be old and tired, he had an arm withered by war, he stank of animals and dirt and sweat, his manners were crude—and she found herself liking him. And more.

The Glass Warrior dared not believe the feelings she felt for him were returned. Yet this seemed to be what the man implied.

"You mistake our wandering thoughts for real

logic," said Vered. "Consider: We return one twin to the throne. A reward? Possibly. Certainly, we would gain a royal pardon for past crimes. Even better, Porotane would be united, freeing us from the warlords and annoying rebels."

"You seek only to rob and plunder without interference from other thieves?" Alarice asked, amused now. She heard the steel under Vered's bantering tone. He desired a peace for Porotane as much as she. Commitment to a cause lay within this one's breast, no matter how he tried to hide it with ignoble reasons.

"Of course," Vered said. "Looting, robbing, a bit of purse-cutting. That keeps Santon and me alive. Why shouldn't we want free rein to continue?"

"No reason, save that the course through the swamp will be infinitely more dangerous than Dews Gaemock and his band of rebels or your petty barons threatening to put you on the rack."

"This Tahir d'mar," said Santon. "Are these his magical creatures?"

"The ape is not of this world. I can only surmise that Tahir conjured and sent it. The swamp swimmer is a harmless resident in these ponds."

"Harmless," snorted Vered, staring at the ass-stabbed monster. "Crowds of whacking big oafs would part in front of me when e'er I passed if I were half that harmless."

"The spells," said Santon, drowning out his friend's complaints. "Can you counter them or must we suffer their full impact?"

"I can use my own limited sorcery," Alarice answered. "It might not work as well as a quick blade, though. It takes time and preparation to cast most spells powerful enough to benefit us. I have neither the ability nor the strength to cast those able to win us free of the swamplands and their magical protectors."

"This blade is better used to pry open doors," said Vered. His work had availed him little. The sword was useless as a precision fighting tool.

"You begin to understand my fondness for glass weapons," she said. "Here, Vered. Take this short sword." She handed him a weapon drawn from a sheath on her saddle. "Use it as you would a regular blade, except in hammering nails with the flat."

Vered made a face as he swung the short sword. To be of use, he would have to crawl within the arms of the ape creature before lunging. Vered did not think this was a proper use—or a decent way to die.

"And you, Santon," she said. "Your battle-ax is still useful. Its edge hasn't corroded as badly as Vered's sword and the heavy spiked ball is still formidable, but your infirmity works against you. We must change that."

"You can fashion a glass arm?" Santon lifted his right arm. "Truly, you would be a sorceress second to none if you do that for me."

"That lies beyond the power of any wizard," she said. "However, I have something which might serve you well." She pulled a small round woven glass-fiber shield from her saddle and motioned to the man. Alarice worked to fasten the straps around his upper right arm so that he could twist and turn the shimmering glass shield.

"This is comfortable," Santon said in amazement. "I had seen yours and thought it would be difficult to use."

"It might not withstand the blow of a battle-ax such as yours, but it will turn aside a sword thrust—and resist the burning blood from the swamp creatures."

"I hardly feel whole again," Santon said, waving the shield about, "but I feel more secure. Let's not allow Tahir to rally his noisome beasts. Let's attack!"

"A noble sentiment," said Vered. "But where do we go? What do we attack? We must *find* the wizard before we fight him."

Vered fell silent when Alarice drew the glass rod on the gut string from her pouch. She closed her eyes. Lips moving in silent spell, she held the clear crystal far from her body. The swings became less random, and soon aligned with what Vered saw as due south.

"That path leads directly into the bowels of this foul-smelling swamp. Why are we cursed with the smell and texture of viscera all about us?" Even as he grumbled, Vered stood and brandished the glass short sword. He shrugged and smiled at Santon, then made a mocking bow and indicated that his friend should mount.

"How much distance can we make in this muck before sunset?" Santon asked of Alarice. The sorceress opened her eyes and stared up at the two mounted men.

"Enough," she said. Alarice held out her hand, first to Vered and then to Santon, in silent thanks for their courage and faith in her.

The Glass Warrior swung into her saddle and pointed out the path through the swamp.

Hardly had they ridden a hundred yards when Vered protested loudly. He swatted at the insects buzzing over his head and caught one between thumb and forefinger. "See!" he called. "See the menace we fight? I can battle beasts that don't belong in the miserable quagmire, but bugs? Never!" Vered's fingers closed. The insect let out a screech that sounded almost human. It died amid a flow of sticky red blood. With some distaste, Vered wiped his fingers on his tunic. The new stain mingled with the old and vanished instantly, much to the fussy man's disgust.

Riding alongside the Glass Warrior, Santon said, "Is it safe to camp when it gets dark? Should we ride directly for Tahir's palace?"

Alarice shook her head, fine white hair flying in a halo around her. "We must rest soon. There is no way to tell how far off Tahir is. And I do not think he lives in any palace."

"But he is a wizard," protested Santon. "All wizards live like royalty."

"I don't," she said. "I never have, but then I have little power when compared to the likes of Tahir." She sighed deeply. "I remember him as a decent fellow. Odd, but all wizards are strange in some respect, or we would not be able to cast spells. I rather liked him before . . ." Her voice trailed off.

"There is no doubt he murdered King Lamost?"

"None. I have received this information from Freow."

"Why didn't the duke do something about it before now? He's been searching for the heirs for over nineteen years."

Alarice told Santon the story of Duke Freow's perfidy—or that of the man posing for all these years as the duke.

"So," said Santon, sucking on his teeth as he

thought. "We have put up with two decades of civil war because of a man's quest for power. It always seems this way."

"Do you still want to find Lokenna and Lorens?"

"All the more!" he exclaimed. "The fake duke must be replaced quickly with true members of the royal family."

"Santon, Alarice," called Vered from the rear. "Something follows. I hear its heavy breathing. I swear by all the saints, I hear its belly rumbling in anticipation of a fine meal—of three fine meals!"

Alarice turned in the saddle. She wobbled as dizziness hit her like a solid blow. Only Santon's good hand reaching out saved her from a tumble into the filthy swamp.

"What is it?"

"Magic," the Glass Warrior said. "It swirls about us. Something is wrong. I feel so . . . disoriented."

"You can feel dizzy later," called Vered. "The thing comes up quickly!"

Santon scanned the area in front and to the sides. Too often an enemy launched a diversionary attack to mask the true thrust. And so it proved this time. From ahead came a huge man, one tall enough to stare Santon squarely in the eye when the adventurer sat upright in his saddle.

"Ahead! A warrior of immense size!" he cried. Beside him, he felt Alarice straighten. The way she wobbled told of continuing problems with balance. Santon hefted his ax and prodded his horse forward, being careful to remain on the solid portion of ground.

Vered whipped out the glass sword and wheeled about to face the challenge from behind.

But even as he prepared for the fight, all sounds stopped. He no longer heard the sucking of feet pulling free of the swamp muck. The snuffling and snorts faded away. And all wildlife ceased to howl and buzz and sing. It was as if he had been struck deaf.

Panicked, Vered fought his horse to turn around and join Santon. But his friend sat astride his steed, the man's confusion obvious.

"Where's this giant foe?" called Vered. He got his horse under control and joined Birtle Santon.

"I . . . he's gone. As surely as I sit here, though, Vered, I saw a gargantuan man. His arms were thicker than my thighs. He—"

"Wait, a moment, please," gasped out Alarice. Vered and Santon turned to her. She wobbled but maintained her seat. "Something has happened. A spell was cast—or we entered a spell."

"What do you mean 'we entered a spell'?"

"Powerful magic held a bubble around this portion of the swamp. We somehow penetrated it."

"Tahir!"

"I fear this is so," she said. "We blundered into a ward spell."

"But the giant. Whatever it was Vered heard. What of them? Where did they go?" Santon's head swiveled back and forth so fast, Vered feared it might come unscrewed.

"We are not in the swamp. Not the one we entered," said Alarice. "Stop, wait. Extend your senses and tell me what lies around us now."

"No insects," said Vered. "No sound. No bugs buzzing or biting. The wind still blows, though. I hear its soft sighing through the banyan limbs."

"The time of day has not changed," said Santon. "The sun remains just over the treetops.

But the odor of the swamp is . . . different. The decay is subtly changed from what it was."

"How can you tell?" demanded Vered. "Rot and decay are all the same."

"This is not the same. Alarice is right. Superficially, it looks the same but other things have changed."

"The ground!" Vered urged his horse forward. "Look! Solid." The horse pranced on dry dirt. "The pathway is clear."

He considered the implications of this discovery. He looked from Alarice to Santon.

"It leads to Tahir's 'palace'," the Glass Warrior said. "We have entered another realm—and this is the road to the one we seek."

"What of the giant?" Santon continued to crane his head about looking for the monster.

"A magical manifestation. A warning, perhaps, or a sentry placed to keep out unwanted visitors," she said. "We will find out for certain at the end of this path." Alarice put the spurs to her horse. It reluctantly obeyed, tossing its head and shying away repeatedly.

They rode in the eerie silence until Vered said, "I liked the bugs better. They gave something more than Santon's curses to listen to."

Then Vered cursed. The swamp opened into a lake. In the center of the lake rose a pitiful mound of black dirt that beggared the glorious title of "island." Built in the center of the lump rising from the lake sat a rude hut with thatched roof and no windows.

"Who lives in that?" Santon wondered.

"You spoke of immense castles and palatial estates where we wizards live," said Alarice. "That is Tahir's domain."

"That?" Santon and Vered spoke simultaneously, amazed and bemused.

"Tahir is a powerful wizard, but I begin to think that the spell we penetrated is not of his casting. Another, more powerful sorcerer might have bound Tahir to this swamp."

"But why? For killing Lamost?"

"Ah," said Vered. "Consider a more devious plot to ruin Porotane. What if Tahir only carried out the orders of another wizard? What if he were a mercenary and failed in his mission?"

"But he didn't," said Santon. "Until meeting Alarice, we both thought King Lamost died of natural causes. The kidnapping of the heirs, of course, might have been a failure. No claims for ransom were made—or none I heard about."

"None was made," confirmed Alarice. "That always seemed suspect to me. It made me believe the two had been killed, either by design or accident."

"If our thinking turns even more devious," said Vered, "it is not stretching possibility to say that Tahir might have succeeded in snatching away the twins and that he killed them. Accidentally or otherwise would not matter to a more powerful wizard."

"Another wizard who imprisoned Tahir in this wretched swamp for his misdeed," finished Alarice. "Aye, that is possible. Tahir loved his comforts. He would never stay here without good reason."

"I do not like the idea that our quest has ended, that Lokenna and Lorens perished nineteen years ago." Santon coughed and spat. The gobbet went into the water. Ripples appeared, then raced in concentric circles to infinity.

"Creatures too dangerous for description reside in the water. There'll be no wading across for us," said Vered, relieved. He had not liked the idea of getting wet. The lake water on his grimy clothing would produce a stench that would gag the very saints.

"A boat." Santon rode to the small craft. Oars rested within the frail shell. "Looks sturdy enough for the three of us."

"Mayhap we should consider leaving someone behind to guard the horses," suggested Vered. He eyed the boat with growing skepticism. "It doesn't appear strong enough for three, but for two . . ."

"All or none," said Alarice. "The horses will not be harmed. The land seems scoured clean of life."

"But not the water." Vered dismounted and tossed a stone into the lake. Again came the racing ripples indicating beasts just below the surface.

They tethered the horses and entered the boat. Santon pushed off, then jumped aboard before his feet entered the water. Grunting and straining, Vered rowed while Alarice sat in the prow studying the island and Santon crouched in the stern, his withered arm restlessly moving the glass shield as if readying it for combat.

Vered hazarded a glance over the side of the rowboat. He felt faint at the sight of human faces peering back at him—but attached to those all-too-human faces were piscine bodies. He jerked back and bent to the task of rowing. The sudden surge in speed almost tumbled Alarice from the boat's bow.

She laid a gentling hand on his shoulder and said, "They are those who have entered the water and were magically transformed. We do not want to join their ranks. Magic beyond my imagining plays around this island."

"And it is not of Tahir's doing?" asked Santon.

"Another. There are only a few wizards living able to cast such spells and Tahir is not one." She shook her head, white hair going in all directions. "Tahir was always too careless. Did I not learn his name many years ago?" She peered over the side at the swimming creatures and shuddered. "I do not relish the thought of meeting any of them, should they have control of the heirs."

"But you will," said Vered.

"I must. My word has been given to restore one of the royal blood to the throne." Both men heard the pain in Alarice's words. She wished to recant her promise but couldn't. Once given, honor demanded that her promise be fulfilled.

For the first time, Vered found himself wishing that the twins both lay dead. He cast a glance over the side of the boat again and caught sight of a leering face. He gulped. "If only they have not become fish," he prayed.

He stroked powerfully, putting his back into the effort. A sudden crunch and pressure told him that the rowboat had beached on the island. Vered reluctantly climbed out. As frightening as the journey had been, the boat provided a safety that wasn't likely to be found on the island. Even the crumbling black dirt beneath his boots felt odd.

Vered walked a few paces behind the others, trying to decide how this soil differed from that in the rest of the swamp. It occurred to him that he felt lighter, more nimble. Every step was into a spring that gently pushed back at him.

"It's as if the souls of the dead and buried try to rise up," said Santon. Vered almost bolted at this thought. But fear seized him and held the man firmly in place. His knuckles closed around the hilt of his glass sword until they turned white with strain.

"I shouldn't have doubted you, Santon," he choked out. "He *is* a giant!"

An immense man, easily twice as tall as Santon, came from the pitiful hut. The giant peered at them, as if not believing its eyes. Then it bellowed and charged.

All three readied for a fight that could end only in their deaths.

CHAPTER ELEVEN

Vered bellowed and whined and protested—
except during battle. He fell into a deadly silence.
His nerves calmed. His heart rate picked up and
blood rushed through his body, heightening his
senses, putting an edge to his reflexes. His keen
eyes studied the charging giant for weaknesses.
Through his mind flashed the chances of using the
glass short sword, of pounding at the giant with his
acid-blunted dagger, of a dozen different attacks.

When he moved, Vered didn't even realize he
had reached a decision. Three steps forward, a
quick drop, and his legs entangled those of the
lumbering Gargantua.

The monster man shrieked and threw out his
arms to catch himself. Even as Vered had executed
the perfect attack, so did Birtle Santon launch one
of his own. He stepped to one side and let the giant
topple past. He turned, batted away a huge hand
with the glass shield, then used the same motion to
power the up-and-down arc of his battle-ax. Santon
aimed well. The ax drove directly into the base of
the giant's skull.

Such a horrendous blow should have severed
any beast's head from its torso. Santon staggered
away as the shock of the blow vibrated all the way

up his left arm and into his body. He stared stupidly at the cutting edge of his ax. It had skittered off the giant's neck as if flesh had turned to steel.

"The edge," Santon muttered. "The acid blood dulled my ax!"

Vered untangled his legs and scrambled to his feet. The giant kicked about and almost sent Vered flying. The man twisted and drew the tip of his glass sword across the giant's hamstrings, trying to disable him. A screeching of metal on metal sounded.

Both glass sword and giant's flesh remained untouched.

"I should have cut his leg in half with that slash," protested Vered. He danced back and fell into *en garde*. As the giant rose to a sitting position, Vered lunged. The tip snaked in past a clumsy hand and struck the giant's left cheek. Vered jerked upward and guided his blade directly for the creature's eye.

Again he failed. The blade refused to thrust home into the giant's brain.

"What manner of creature is this?" Vered cried. "I refuse to be thwarted. How dare you deny me your death!" Vered launched a flurry of thrusts, none intended to do harm. He distracted the slow-witted giant while Santon sneaked into position behind the sitting monster.

Santon put all his strength behind the blow. The muscles along his left arm rippled with the power of the stroke aimed at the giant's spine. Again Santon staggered back, his killing blow turned away harmlessly.

The giant moaned and bent forward to rise to his feet. Vered kicked a supporting hand out from under the giant and sent him tumbling back to the ground, but again this diversion did not help Santon get in a killing stroke with his ax. When the monster stood, he towered over either man. Santon and Vered parted to keep the giant distracted, then attacked. Santon came in with his glass shield raised high to protect his head; his ax swung at waist level, aimed at the giant's thigh. Simultaneously, Vered attacked the tendons behind the giant's vulnerable right ankle.

The giant roared and grabbed. Both men were lifted into the air and hung, feet kicking. They might have been rats caught by a terrier for all the good their strength did them.

The giant cast them away, as if he considered them nothing more than debris. Vered hit the ground and rolled easily to his feet. Birtle Santon had the wind knocked from his lungs and lay gasping for breath.

Before Vered could renew his attack, Alarice held up a hand. Her gray eyes never left the giant. "Hold, Vered. Your efforts will only fail."

"If he's of flesh and blood, he is vulnerable. No spell can protect him indefinitely."

"He might not be human," Alarice said. She circled to place her body between that of the giant and the fallen Santon. "Tend to Santon. I would have words with Tahir d'mar."

Vered frowned. A huge tear formed at the corner of the giant's eye. It rolled like an ocean's wave down a grimy cheek and dripped to the ground. Where it landed a small plant sprouted and grew with astonishing speed. The giant knelt and gently plucked the plant from the ground, roots and all.

"It will die soon," the giant said, his voice

rumbling deep in his barrel chest. The action and words struck Vered and Santon as incongruous, but Alarice accepted them easily. The Glass Warrior waved back both men.

"So will all things, Tahir," she said. Vered and Santon exchanged glances. It hardly seemed likely that this mountain of impervious gristle and bulk was the wizard they sought. But Alarice had addressed him as such.

"You recognize me, woman of glass. After all these years, you still remember poor Tahir d'mar." The giant dropped the withered plant. It fell to dust within seconds.

"So, Tahir, you remember me, too."

"Of those remaining, I always thought you would be the one sent to find me." The giant collapsed to a cross-legged sitting position, hands resting on his knees. Even so, he almost looked them squarely in the eye.

"It has taken me all these years to learn you were the one who killed Lamost."

Tahir vented a sigh that sounded like gas escaping from a volcanic fumarole. "That spell was pernicious, devious, a glory to cast! He wasted away, with none in Porotane the wiser."

"You also kidnapped his children."

"I did," the wizard agreed.

Vered and Santon moved closer to each other, Vered letting Santon keep the glass shield between them and Tahir. Vered whispered, "He acknowledges the crime too readily. I fear a trap."

"No trap, short one," boomed Tahir. "It is no sorcery I use to overhear. Since my exile to this pathetic island, I have come to know loneliness. I spend my nights awake, straining to hear another's voice. Seldom do I hear even wind. This island is at the vortex of a spell so powerful I cannot escape it."

"The royal twins," urged Alarice. "What of them? They are not with you?"

Tahir laughed, the echoes dying in the distance. The wizard shook his head. "I am alone. I have been alone for nineteen years. See?" He indicated the hut. "Go, look, tell the Glass Warrior what you find there."

Santon looked to Alarice. She made no effort to stop him. Santon trotted up the slope and peered into the hut. The simple thatched hut was bare inside, save for a straw sleeping pallet. On a long wood pole Tahir had carved a line of notches, one for each day of his imprisonment. Santon reported this to the Glass Warrior.

"So, Tahir," she said. "You cannot leave. I take that at face value. There is no reason to deceive me with mere physical evidence. You always used spells to do your bidding. What happened after you took the heirs?"

"I do not remember you as being this anxious. Spend time with me. You still have a few minutes."

"What do you mean by that?" demanded Vered.

"Who cast the spell binding you to this island?" asked Alarice.

"What did he mean that we have only a few minutes?" shouted Vered. "Demons take the wizard forcing him to stay here. We're in danger!"

"Aye, that is so, noisy one," said Tahir. "Exactly at sunset, I must kill everyone on this island. That is part of my curse."

"Who?" Alarice asked gently. "The sorcerer must be of exceptional power."

"The strongest. I angered the Wizard of

Storms. It was he who cast me here, he whose spell binds me more firmly than life itself."

"The Wizard of Storms never leaves the Yorral Mountains," said Alarice. "What is his interest in Lokenna and Lorens?"

The giant shrugged. "Who can say? I dickered with him for the children. I slew Lamost and then . . ."

"You could not give over the twins," supplied Santon. "Why not?"

The laugh issuing from Tahir's lips carried pure evil. "False pride. I thought myself invincible —with the spells promised me by the Wizard of Storms, I *would* be invincible. I fell into another's trap."

"Another wizard has the children?"

Tahir's lips pulled back in a sneer. "He stole the children and forced me into this odious body. Then the Wizard of Storms exacted his toll for my failure. He sentenced me to this island forever."

"Then it was his spell we crossed in arriving in the swamps."

"Space is contorted. Long distances are short, short are long. I saw you and tried to approach, but the movement produced by his spell pulled you away. But you found me anyway." The giant stood, flexing powerful muscles. "Now that it is sundown, I am compelled to slay you. No hard feelings, Warrior. It is required by the curse."

"Why? What is the nature of the spell? Perhaps I can lift it—in exchange for information."

"You would do that for me?" Tahir shook all over. "No, I see that you would not. It is for the royal heirs that you would risk it." The giant laughed at her naiveté. "I cannot leave this island, I cannot entertain visitors during the hours of darkness—and I am immortal. Forever must I endure my solitude."

"The creatures surrounding this island," noted Vered. "The ones with human faces. What of them?"

Tahir shrugged. "The waters are cursed, also. Should you become totally immersed, that is what you become." With a bull-throated roar, Tahir charged. He picked up Vered in his powerful hands and lifted him off the ground. "That is what you *will* become, you chattering magpie!"

Tahir's muscles bunched as he rocked back to heave Vered into the lake. Santon attacked. He ran forward at full speed, the glass shield smashing into Tahir's kneecaps. He bowled over the giant. Although Vered rolled out of the wizard's grasp, Santon had not injured Tahir.

"Back," ordered Alarice. "There is nothing you can do to him. This is my fight." She drew her glass sword and moved forward.

"We can take him if we work together," said Santon.

"Stay back. Do not interfere." Even as she spoke, Alarice lifted her glass sword and held its tip pointed at the twilight sky. Green fire danced along its length.

"He uses sorcery against her," whispered Vered. "How can we fight that?"

"We can't." Santon swallowed hard and pushed his friend back. "We must let her fight this battle. It is not for us to triumph in this. We could not. Ever."

"You cannot be immortal, Tahir," Alarice said. "Your energies are too weak. You expend more than you absorb. You *must* die." Again the glass sword glowed with the vivid green glow as she sucked strength from the giant with her spell.

Tahir stumbled but did not fall. "You are clever, Warrior. But the same spell can be turned against you. I know your name! You are Alarice!"

Vered and Santon did not understand the sorcery dancing about them, but they saw its effect on the Glass Warrior. She stood her ground, but she seemed diminished. Her lips moved to cast counters, to renew her own assault on Tahir, but she weakened visibly as she worked.

"She turns to glass before our eyes!" cried Vered.

Santon moved forward, the glass shield riding high on his withered arm. He placed himself between the battling wizards. He shrieked and fell backward, but the ploy worked. Alarice regained her substance. The transparency developing in her body misted over and solidity replaced it.

She lowered the tip of her sword and ran forward. The lunge started from a distance and snaked toward Tahir with deceptive slowness. The tip of the blade nicked the giant's upper arm. Blood spurted.

"You are *not* immortal," Alarice called as Tahir jerked back and ran to his hut. She moved to follow, but got no farther than halfway before Tahir reappeared. In his brawny hands he held a great sword so massive that even the giant wizard had difficulty balancing it.

When he began swinging it, the men saw that no human could stand before the deadly arc. Tahir advanced, forcing Alarice to retreat. She made no attempt to parry with her glass weapon. Against this battering ram of edged steel it would shatter.

"Beneath your feet, Tahir. Look at your feet."

The giant yelped and danced away from some menace only he saw. Vered and Santon saw nothing; this spell Alarice cast only for Tahir. As the wizard backed in fright, Alarice again attacked. Her glass sword shone in the dusk. Another pink to Tahir's leg; more blood. Nothing serious, but Tahir had received two wounds and given none in return.

"You anger me, Alarice."

"Fight, don't talk," she chided. She slashed viciously for the giant's midriff and opened a long gash that bled profusely. Any ordinary man would have been disabled by this gutting cut. Not the wizard. Tahir fought on, his massive sword singing through the air. Alarice dodged easily, but dared not get too close. A single cut from that mighty weapon would behead her.

"Who did you give the children to, Tahir?" she asked. "Surely, you can tell me this small thing."

"Defeat me and I will tell you."

"How can I defeat you if you are immortal?"

Tahir roared with laughter. "That's the curse! I cannot be killed—and slaying me is the only way to learn the name that dances on the tip of my tongue." Tahir thrust out his tongue. The tip glowed a bright pink, shimmered, and vanished.

"Always the jape," Alarice said. She circled warily, studying the wizard for weakness. The instant before she lunged, a yawning pit opened at her feet. The Glass Warrior leaped over it in time to avoid falling face first into a pit seething with poisonous snakes. The vile stench from the poison dripping from their fangs rose and caused Vered to wrinkle his nose. He backed from the pit.

"She cannot defeat him alone. We must help." Santon started forward, but Vered held him back.

"We can do nothing in a battle fought with *that*." He used the tip of his glass sword to show the sinuously moving black mass at the bottom of the pit. Illusion it might be, but Vered would not chance it. Better to believe the snakes and death-giving poison fangs were real.

Swords he understood. Sorcery lay beyond his expertise.

"We must do something!" protested Santon.

"Think of it and I'll do it. Until that time, we stand and watch. If we interfere, we risk distracting Alarice."

Santon saw that his friend spoke truly. The Glass Warrior had begun to turn glass-transparent once more. Her hair vanished and bits of her flesh winked in and out of existence. But the glass sword she clutched so firmly remained solid and she used it well.

Tahir's body dripped blood from a half-dozen wounds.

"Alarice," called the giant wizard. "A trade. Do you agree to this?"

"What are your terms?" She continued to circle, not trusting her opponent.

"I sense that you carry the Demon Crown."

"How do you know this?"

"I may be imprisoned but I retain all my magical skills. The crown blazes within my brain, just as it must for you. Give it to me and I'll tell you the name of the sorcerer who stole away the royal twins."

They continued to fight as they negotiated. Even though every stroke threatened to divide Alarice in half, the great sword always missed by inches. Her ripostes lacked Tahir's power, but she had opened wounds all over his body.

"Ridiculous, Tahir, and you know it," she answered, beginning to strain. Her breath came in short gasps and her movements slowed. Tahir, for all the bloody cuts, seemed no weaker than when he had begun the fight. "What good would it do me to find even one twin but lose the Demon Crown? The crown is necessary to reunite Porotane. It must rest on a royal brow."

She weakened further. Vered had to restrain Birtle Santon. The man wanted to rush forward, but Vered saw the clever use Tahir made of the great sword. The wizard wove a curtain of steel around him that no ordinary mortal might pierce.

Just as it appeared that Alarice would fall victim to the wizard's sword, she moved with blinding speed. She lunged, the glass sword blazing so brightly that it might have been forged from a dazzling emerald. The tip found Tahir's navel. Alarice performed a quick skip and got her back leg repositioned for an even more powerful lunge. The scintillant glass weapon sank into the giant's gut.

Both Santon and Vered threw up their hands to protect their faces from the heat and light emanating from Alarice's sword.

Vered peered through his fingers. His heart turned to a lump of polar ice. Although Alarice's sword had pierced Tahir, it had not killed the giant.

"He must be immortal," moaned the man. "Not even a magical thrust stops him!"

The wizard bellowed in pain and grabbed the blade of Alarice's sword. Tahir jerked about and ripped the sword from the Glass Warrior's grip. Sobbing in agony, he pulled the sword from his body.

But Alarice had not stopped her attack. She leaped, acid-filled glass dagger lifted high above her head. She brought it down, its fragile tip penetrating Tahir's breast. Once in the wizard's body, she twisted the knife. Vered heard the *snap!* as the hollow blade broke.

Tahir's flesh sizzled as the acid raced through his heart.

"Look!" Santon bumped Vered with his shield to make certain the other man saw and confirmed the strange sight. The giant began shrinking, turning in on himself until a man slightly smaller than Vered struggled on the ground.

"The curse!" cried out Tahir. "You have broken the spell binding me to this pitiful island!"

"You are not immortal," said Alarice. She had retrieved her sword and stood over the body of her fallen opponent.

"No longer. Your spells and fine sword work defeated me. Oh, I tried to defeat you, I did. I could do nothing else because of the curse. But now I can die. Glorious day, I can die!"

"The children," urged Alarice. "What of Lorens and Lokenna? Which wizard took them from you?"

The laugh coming from Tahir mixed with a burbling sound. Blood dribbled down his chin; he turned his head to one side and spat. "It burns," Tahir said, almost in awe. "Your acid fills my veins already. I taste it on my tongue. It . . . it is strangely sweet, like a honey-filled pastry."

"The name of the wizard, damn you!" Alarice placed the tip of her glass sword at Tahir's throat, then leaned on it.

"You can no longer threaten me, dear Alarice.

Not as you did before. I am dying. Sweet oblivion is rushing up on me."

She pulled the sword away. "I can bind you, Tahir. I can bind your phantom to this island and be sure that you never see a proper burial. Would you allow your phantom to roam endlessly? Or will you trade the name for a consecrated grave?"

Tahir spat at her. "You evil bitch! I always hated you!" The wizard rolled into a fetal ball, arms clutching at his knees. "The pain grows. The acid no longer tastes so sweet."

He peered up at her, his eyes fogging over with death. "I . . . the name you seek is Patrin." Tahir jerked once, then relaxed. His face looked strangely serene.

"Alarice, is it true? Did he tell the truth?"

The Glass Warrior nodded. "Tahir spoke the truth. For that small favor I will not bind his phantom to this land. He will receive a formal burial."

"What's wrong?" asked Vered. "Your words convey a strange sorrow."

"He spoke the truth, damn him!" cried Alarice. She thrust her blade into the dirt beside Tahir's diminished corpse. "Of all the wizards, Patrin of the City of Stolen Dreams is the worst. Better I had never learned his name. Better I faced the Wizard of Storms himself!"

Vered and Birtle Santon exchanged worried looks. Of Patrin they had never heard, but dread began to build within them.

No one looked upon the City of Stolen Dreams and lived to tell of it. No one.

CHAPTER TWELVE

Birtle Santon rubbed his hand against dirty breeches and stepped back. Vered and Alarice rolled Tahir d'mar into the shallow grave. The wizard lay at the bottom of the grave, a serene expression on his handsome face.

"He knows nothing can happen to him now," grumbled Vered. He ran grimy fingers through his brown hair and looked up at Alarice. "What did you mean when you promised him you would not doom him to wander as a phantom?"

"Just that. Once the grave is consecrated, his soul is at rest." The Glass Warrior stared at the corpse, as if trying to come to a difficult decision. "No," she said at last, "I cannot do such a thing to him, although it lies within my power. He gave me the name I sought."

"How can you turn him into a ghost?" asked Santon. "Such power is reserved for saints—or demons."

Alarice smiled sadly. "Alas, it is a simple spell. Most wizards are able to conjure it."

"Why aren't we overrun with phantoms then?" Vered began scooping the loose dirt up in his hands and tossing it onto Tahir.

"In some parts of the country, the phantoms outnumber the living," she said. "The places where battles have raged are the worst. Who properly buries the dead after a major defeat?"

Vered looked over his shoulder, as if a ghost crept up on him. "Never seen one. Not sure I want to."

"Tahir did give you the name of this Patrin," said Santon. He saw the way Alarice reacted. "Is Patrin so evil?"

She shivered. "He is. Never have I encountered a man more evil. If any had conspired to steal away the twins and create a reign of confusion, it would be Patrin."

"What of this Wizard of Storms? The one who locked Tahir to this island. He must control vast power. He seems the true villain."

"Patrin I have met and know all too well. The Wizard of Storms is a recluse, content to weave his spells and avoid human contact. Unless Tahir lied, and I see no reason for him to have done so, there is more afoot than we understand. Porotane's rulers must play an important part. How, I can't say."

Vered finished moving the dirt back to the grave. He stood and brushed off his hands while Santon stamped down the rich black dirt with his boots.

"Why we do this is a mystery," he said. "There are no animals on this island. Save the one we've just buried."

"The spell is gone," said Alarice. "With Tahir's death, nature reasserts control."

As if to emphasize the truth of her statement, Vered yelped and swatted at an insect boring hungrily into his neck. His hand came away bloody.

"See?" she said. Taking a deep breath, the Glass Warrior started reciting the burial ceremony that would keep Tahir's phantom from rising to walk the world endlessly. Finished, she made a gesture over the grave as if dismissing a servant. "That takes care of Tahir."

"You sound skeptical," said Vered.

"Not skeptical. Tahir is gone for all time. Sad perhaps. The information I sought is mine—and the easy part of the quest is finished."

"The *easy* part is done?" exclaimed Vered. "How can you say that? We've fought magical ape creatures, a wizard turned into a grotesque giant, the damned insects, the sucking swamp, the . . . things in the lake. How can you *possibly* say the easy part is behind us?"

"Because it is. You and Santon are free to leave, should this please you." Alarice spun and stalked off. Santon and Vered followed quickly, going to the boat. The Glass Warrior sat in the boat, arms crossed over her chest, deep in thought.

"Let's both row," said Santon. "You take that side, I'll take this. And match my rhythm. I can't handle the oar with one hand as well as you can with two."

"Anything," Vered said, "if I don't have to look down into the lake." The thought of vanishing beneath the magical waves, then having his body transformed into a fish's, upset him more than words could tell.

They rowed across the lake. As they went, they both commented on the changes being wrought around them. Birds flew overhead, their dark forms visible in the dim light of the rising moon. Fish swam in the lake, occasionally breaking the surface in pursuit of a succulent bug. And from the shore toward which they rowed came the normal sounds of swamp creatures snuffling and screeching and hunting and dying.

"Do we ride on?" asked Vered, once they beached the boat. He started when he felt Santon's strong hand gripping his arm. Silently, they watched the boat dissolve like salt poured into water.

"What happened to it?" whispered Vered after several seconds, hardly daring to speak.

"Sorcery," said Santon. "The boat was part of the spell."

"Whose spell, Patrin's or the Wizard of Storms'?"

Santon didn't answer. He turned to Alarice, who worked to pull her bedroll from the saddle and spread it on the ground. She prepared for the night. The way she chose her sleeping site told Santon that she intended to sleep alone this night. She had been worrying deeply over something since leaving the island.

"Could this Patrin upset her so?" he asked Vered. "She has vanquished a giant, a wizard, the man responsible for the death of a king and the kidnapping of the twins. She can conquer anyone, warrior or wizard."

"She doesn't think so. See how she sits?" Vered prepared a small cooking fire and fixed a meal, though neither of them had much appetite. Alarice refused to even look in their direction.

The men spoke quietly after eating, then stretched out in their blankets. Vered lay flat on his back, staring at the stars and trying to work out the constellations. As always, he failed to find the patterns officially sanctioned by the royal astronomers, but he found constellations of his own making. Each was more lewd than the last.

He amused himself with the Negligent Whore and the Obedient Dog, invented a few more combinations, and finally sat up, tired of the pastime. Santon snored heavily, long since fast asleep. Vered turned to Alarice. The Glass Warrior sat tailor fashion, her gray eyes glinting with reflected starlight.

Before her on the ground rested the Demon Crown. It glowed a pale green, as if it had rested on the brow of royalty. She reached out; the glow intensified. As if succumbing to a fever, Alarice shivered and worked the crown into its crystalline box without touching it. She put the Demon Crown back into the velvet bag and leaned back, her arms circling the knapsack.

Vered wondered what thoughts coursed through her head. Did she desire the power the Demon Crown offered to the right person? Or did she desire only surcease, an end to this search for the heirs?

Vered turned over and lay down, momentarily worrying about snakes and insects crawling beneath the blankets with him. Better a willing woman. But such was not to be had. He drifted off to a sleep troubled by giant wizards and fish with men's faces.

Vered awoke with a start, not sure what disturbed him. He lay back, unmoving and straining to hear. It took several seconds for him to realize that he heard nothing—and this was what awoke him. He reached out and gently shook Santon. The man rumbled deep in his throat, stirred and tried to pull away.

"Santon, trouble. The animals have fallen silent."

"Spell," Birtle Santon mumbled, more asleep than awake. "The spell keeps them away."

"The spell died with Tahir."

Santon came to a sitting position in a movement so abrupt that Vered drew back, hand going to his worthless dagger. The man's eyes took on an inner light as he stared at Vered, then cocked his head to one side, listening intently.

Santon began buckling his shield onto his limp right arm. Vered reached for his glass short sword and opened his mouth to alert Alarice. The blow to the back of his head doubled him over. Vered rolled to the side, pain blasting through his entire body. The glass sword fell from his numbed fingers. An infinity away he heard Santon bellowing incoherently.

"Alarice, to the attack!" yelled Santon.

Vered struggled to hang onto the frayed thread of consciousness. The Glass Warrior did not respond. He tried to rise to aid his friend. His legs weighed like lead; his arms twitched feebly; the pain centered in his head blotted out the world and left only a red curtain.

Through the battle in his head came sounds of the battle without. Vered rolled onto his back. His blurry eyes caught glimpses of moving figures. The flash of light off a round shield might have been Santon. Vered blinked and cleared his vision. He could not let his friend down. To lie helpless on the ground spelled both their deaths.

But who dealt that fate? Vered did not know

or care. The attack might come from ruffians roving the countryside, Dews Gaemock's band of rebels, even remnants of the wizard's soldiers they had left unslain on their way to this miserable swamp.

Vered sucked in a lungful of air and gave voice to his battle cry. When he realized it came out as a kitten's mewling, anger forced away the last of the pain he felt. Vered came to his hands and knees, only to be knocked down again by a glancing blow. He rolled and used the momentum to get to his feet.

Somehow, he still clutched the glass short sword in his hand. His motion more falling forward than lunging, Vered thrust at the nearest moving shadow. A mortal man's cry of pain told of a direct hit. Vered fell to one knee but felt stronger from his minor triumph. He parried a thrust, disengaged, and rammed the tip of his blade into his opponent's armpit. From the spastic jerk he felt, he knew that their foes numbered one less.

Vered swung his sword and took the legs out from under another. Strength flowed into him like rainwater into a cistern. He drew his dagger and used it to parry. For stabbing it proved worthless. Repeatedly, he met solid armor. These were no starving farmers banded together to rob careless travelers. They fought with military precision and skill and their accoutrements were of the finest quality.

"Santon," he gasped out. "What happened to Alarice?"

"Don't know," came the reply. "Don't see her. But we need her. I count three in front of me."

"Another three here," said Vered. He rolled

his blade around his opponent's and carried it out and away, to splash in the lake. "Go fish," he called after his retreating foe. Vered hoped the man immersed himself totally in the lake. Perhaps the spell lingered.

The remaining two forced Vered back until he fought with his spine pressing into a cypress. They separated and engaged him from each side, one attacking until he responded, then the other trying to hamstring him.

"Santon, can't hold off these two much longer." Vered riposted, missed, and nearly lost his head when the enemy behind swung his sword two-handed in a powerful cut. "Santon? Santon!"

No response. Vered's heart missed a beat when he saw that he no longer faced a pair of swordsmen. Three more joined the battle. Santon had fought his last.

"Aieee!" he shrieked, hoping to shock his foes into temporary immobility. Vered tried to fight his way through the ring of steel. A powerful blow sent him tumbling face forward into the ground. Dirt entered his mouth and nose, choking him. A second knobbed hilt smashed into the base of his skull.

Blackness settled over him like an old, familiar blanket.

Vered awoke to pain. Not since he had been lost and starving after his village had been burned had he felt this lost and miserable. His eyes fluttered open. A slow smile crossed his lips.

"Truly, I have died and am in the arms of the saints."

"He's all right," said Alarice. She dropped his

head from her lap. He winced at the sudden pain. "I had feared the blow might have addled his wits permanently, but his skull is too thick for that."

"Being partially of royal blood helps," Vered said. He touched the back of his head. Alarice had bandaged him expertly once again.

"A sorry trio we are," the Glass Warrior said. "Not even posting a guard, being taken unawares, the theft." The bitterness in her voice hurt Vered worse than the wounds to his head.

"What theft?" he asked. He looked past the Glass Warrior to Birtle Santon. The man stood behind her, his expression baleful.

"The Demon Crown," said Santon. "The ruffians took it from her."

"That's all they wanted? Just the crown? How did they know we had it?"

"I fear that these are assassins sent by Baron Theoll. A squad followed me from the castle after Duke Freow entrusted this mission to me. I thought I had eluded them, sending them along a false trail to the Uvain Plateau."

"Assassins?" Vered tried to think. The effort hurt too much. "Why did they not kill us instead of taking only the crown?"

Alarice snorted derisively. "You are not the only one able to fight. When you woke Santon, I had already drawn my sword. You two did well, but I did better. At least, I drove them off."

"I accounted for two," said Santon. "And you, Vered, you killed one and wounded two others."

"I remember being backed into a tree. Santon, your attackers finished you and came for me!"

"Nothing of the sort. Where those extra ruffians came from, I'll never know. I fought well, but it was Alarice who drove them away."

"With the Demon Crown," she said in a tone lacking any emotion. "More important than finding the twins is recovering the crown. With it Theoll can rule Porotane."

"He is of royal blood, isn't he?" Vered tried to stand. Alarice had to help him remain on his feet.

"Just shows that some bastards can be legitimate."

Vered saw the bodies at the edge of their camp. Either Alarice or Santon had stacked them neatly. The cloud of insects on them caused Vered's nose to wrinkle in distaste. Death could be so messy.

"Which direction?" he asked. "They cannot have ridden far, not in this sucking swamp."

"It's that very swamp that makes it difficult to find them," observed Santon. "I've circled about, trying to find spoor. I can only guess that they head in that direction." He pointed north.

"They take the Demon Crown to Theoll." Vered stretched and tried to get some feeling that wasn't entirely pain back into his body. "We should start out immediately. No time to lose."

Vered looked from Alarice to Santon and back, hoping one of them would argue. When neither did, he vented a huge sigh and went to saddle his horse. The white agony in his skull had died down to a dull throb. He had felt better; he had also felt worse. To regain the crown—to keep it out of Theoll's grasping fingers—he could endure anything.

Ten minutes later, the three rode slowly north. Alarice had tried scrying with her gut string and crystal and found the results inconclusive. The residual magic from Patrin's binding spell muddled her responses.

"Is there another spell to home in on the crown?" asked Santon. "Such a powerful magical ornament must radiate energy."

"There might be," said Alarice. "I know nothing of it, though. I am a sorceress with little power. What spells I cast are elementary. Anyone with a modicum of ability can duplicate all I do."

"I doubt that," said Santon. His green eyes locked with her gray ones. A shadow of a smile crossed his lips. Then he spurred his horse and rode ahead to find Vered.

"What from the rear echelons?" asked Vered when his friend pulled up next to him.

"No hope of tracing the crown magically," Santon reported. "Have you found their trail yet? You're the best tracker in Porotane."

"Go on, make it difficult for me. Make me feel guilty if I can't locate it."

"Sorry."

"We ride less than an hour after them."

"What? You did find their spoor!" cried Santon.

"Of course. Hasn't it been said, even recently, that I am the best tracker in the kingdom?" Vered grinned broadly. It hadn't been easy finding the assassins' trail in the quagmire, but he had. A thread caught on a shrub. A bit of bark missing from a tree trunk. A stone with a fresh nick on it. Those were the clues that only a master hunter could observe.

Santon thrust out his shield and motioned Vered to silence. Ahead in a small, swampy clearing stood a horse. The animal tried to crop at a patch of grass but its tether proved too short.

"What do you make of that?" asked Santon.

"One thing only," said Vered. He turned in the saddle and motioned to Alarice.

"I fear you are right." Santon paused, then in concert with Vered, rode into the clearing, alert for danger.

They dismounted and went to the horse. Bloodstains on the saddle showed where the rider had been injured.

Neither man paid attention to the moans coming from behind a fallen tree trunk. They turned, backs together, and readied glass blade and battle ax.

"The trap is sprung," said Vered.

From three sides came armed soldiers. They advanced, anger shrouding their faces like dark storm clouds. They had expected Vered and Santon to fall completely into their trap.

"What would we have found by the trunk?" called out Santon.

The answer came from the man Santon had already guessed to be the leader. "Poisoned needles in the fallen man's clothing. But you insist on making our task difficult."

"Seems as if a few of you are shirking your duty," observed Vered. "Shouldn't there be a *solid* ring about us? Why let us have an escape path?"

The leader turned and looked over his line. His eyes widened. "By all the saints and demons, where are—" He never finished. Alarice had ridden around the perimeter, seeking out the ambushers. She had slain three and rode down hard on another. Her glass blade flashed. An assassin's throat exploded in a bloody welter as the tip drew along a line below his chin.

The leader feinted, then waited, hoping to draw out Vered or Santon. Both men stood their ground. As long as a friend remained at his back, the other knew a modicum of security.

"Get them!" cried the enemy leader. Those were his last words before Alarice's clever sword found a berth in the man's mouth. His sword fell from lifeless fingers. He tried to bat away the sword thrust down his gullet and failed, already being dead. The officer sagged away from Alarice, the sword pulling free.

The remaining five men tried to flee. Vered and Santon took quick steps forward. Santon's blade killed one man; Vered's short sword ended another's flight. Alarice engaged a third, making short work of him.

"The last two run," shouted Vered. He sprinted after one, diving and tackling the man before he could vanish into the tangled under-growth around the clearing.

Vered struck the man twice, both blows land-ing squarely in the center of the man's face. He threw up his hands to prevent Vered from making further attacks.

"The Demon Crown," came Alarice's cold voice. "Where is it?" She shoved the point of her sword into the hollow at the captive's throat.

The soldier looked from Vered to Alarice and saw no mercy in either's face.

"Speak or die!"

"He . . . Vork . . . our leader. He has it. Had it!"

From across the clearing, Birtle Santon called, "I have it. It's untouched. Still in the velvet bag."

"Vered, check it," she said. Her steely gray eyes never left the man trembling under the point of her glass sword.

Vered rose and went to verify the crown. He place his hand on the crystalline box. The answering green glow showed that it responded to the royal blood sluggishly flowing through his veins. "It's no decoy," he told Alarice.

A strangled cry answered him. Both men were halfway across the clearing when Alarice emerged. She thrust her blade into the soft dirt to cleanse it.

"They were assassins. They deserved worse than a quick death, but that's all I could give them. It will do." She took the Demon Crown from Santon and stared at it. Her face became an unreadable mask. Vered wondered what thoughts fluttered through her mind. Did she see paradise or perdition in that crown fashioned by a demon's hand?

Vered shrugged it off. They had recovered the crown. He turned and surveyed the clearing, counting the dead bodies. He stopped, frowned, and counted again.

"There's one missing," he told Santon.

Santon counted. The two men cursed. To Alarice, Santon said, "One of the killers is missing. Vered caught one of two remaining after your attack. We must track down the last one or he will return to Theoll for reinforcements."

"Let him," she said, her bloodlust momentarily sated. "It is more important to find Lokenna and Lorens. We must seek out Patrin and the City of Stolen Dreams."

Vered shivered at the Glass Warrior's words. She made their goal sound like a death sentence.

CHAPTER THIRTEEN

Birtle Santon hitched the shield higher on his withered right arm. All day the arm had been hurting. The hot sun and the dry wind did nothing to soothe the pain building in his body. Nor did Alarice seem willing to slow their breakneck pace. They had left the swamps where Tahir had died and found firmer footing on rolling lands that pleased Santon. He had grown up in farmland much like this, and seeing it once again caused cherished memories to bubble to the surface of his mind. But the grassy lands had given way to more barren stretches within a week.

And still Alarice plunged on, driven by her quest. Santon tried not to stare at the woman as they rode. To do so would be intolerably rude, but she attracted him strangely. Pretty in a wild way, yes, but the Glass Warrior offered more than simple physical beauty. He smiled. The way the hot, dry wind whipped her white hair back into a never-resting banner highlighted the firm jaw and softened the sharp, hard lines of her cheekbones. But nothing softened her determination or the steel-gray hardness of those eyes.

Santon had seen action in the past twenty years that had toughened him, but he felt like a kitten mewling for milk in comparison to Alarice. They had shared the comforts and joys of one another's bodies. For Santon it had been more than physical. For Alarice, he could not say. He doubted that she felt any emotional attachment. But he could hope. The road had been long and lonely for him. Having someone as fine as Alarice to share it made the journey worthwhile.

Santon turned his eyes to the terrain ahead. He should not allow himself to feel more than simple gratification with her. The Glass Warrior's quest consumed her totally. He should keep matters between them on an impersonal plane. He closed his eyes and tried to settle the churning of his mind and emotions. He should. But he didn't. So much about Alarice attracted him—the quick mind, the devotion to duty, the loyalty, the independence tempered with need for another.

He opened his eyes and caught full in the face a blast of dust that caused watering in his eyes. He blinked the dirt free. What others had there been in the woman's life? He did not know, and Alarice never spoke of her past. For that, he felt some small thankfulness. His own past had been blighted, then lit with love and blighted anew too many times for the subject to be a comfortable one. To reveal that part of his life to Alarice would be giving away all he had.

"Santon, what do you see yonder?" Vered's insistent tug on his left sleeve caused him to jerk about, startled.

"What? Where? Can't see for all this dust."

"You need to show more care," said Vered. "Your eyes pour tears." Vered looked at him strangely, then lifted his arm and indicated a collection of low hills off to their right. "I caught the glint of sunlight on metal a few minutes ago, but have seen nothing since."

"It might be nothing more than debris long discarded. The weather seems dry enough to prevent rust for many a year."

"This time of season is deceptive," said Vered. "Dry winds now, wet and cold autumns. Still, you may be right in this. It might be nothing more than my fertile imagination since I see no dust rising from horses' hooves."

"We should investigate, though," he said. "It pays nothing but death to allow an enemy to come up on us from behind once we enter the mountains."

Santon peered into the distance and saw the ragged, torn black peaks of the Iron Range. Crossing them would be difficult. Getting into the narrow, torturously winding passes and finding armed men behind would be fatal. His eyes slipped from the mountains back to the prairie lands to the right of their travel.

"Let me scout. You stay with Alarice."

"Not good, Santon. Dividing our forces only weakens us, if you happen to find trouble."

Santon laughed. "You think I am so inexperienced that I'd take on an entire band of brigands without letting you in on the fun? I go only to spy, not to fight."

Alarice overheard their conversation and dropped back. Her mare tossed its head and looked sideways at the men, as if thanking them for this brief respite from the demanding pace her mistress set.

"Why stop?" she demanded. "We must reach

the foothills soon. The heat of spring melts the snows quickly. I have no desire to be caught in the Iron Range with floods cutting off the passes."

"Vered saw riders. I'll check them out. They might be nothing more than traders beginning to move from winter quarters to the south." Santon knew better than this. The nomadic traders who roved Porotane seldom appeared until midsummer, when the festivals began, with the plays and gatherings of musicians. The springtime carried too much work for farmers intent on getting seeds in tilled ground. Only after the saints blessed the ground and the first green shoots rose did many in Porotane think of frolicking.

Santon turned melancholy at the thought of the many festivals lost to the civil war. Even with crops growing, not many people had time for proper festivities.

"Or I might have seen nothing. A trick played on me by these accursed winds." Vered brushed dust from his cheeks.

Alarice stared at him. Vered shrugged. "All right. I *saw* something, and do not think it was a reflection from a harmless castoff."

"We dare not linger here. We must reach the mountains soon if we are to get through before summer."

Santon knew the true reason behind Alarice's concern. Although mountain flooding posed a problem, it mattered less than entering the Desert of Sazan on the far side of the Iron Range in summer. The desert heat melted metal, or so he had heard. Santon had no reason to doubt the tales told by others, fantastic though they seemed. He had witnessed stranger occurrences with his own eyes.

"How long will it take to find Patrin and the City of Stolen Dreams?" he asked.

Alarice shrugged. "I have no idea if my scrying spell works on the city. It is a place where intense magic dwells—and Patrin is its ruler. If he thinks to affect the politics of Porotane, he plays a game deeper than any he has chosen before."

"No wizard seeks out visitors," said Vered.

"Me least of all," added Alarice. "Patrin and I have never been on friendly terms. If he truly kidnapped Lokenna and Lorens, that dislike has become total enmity."

"Then there will be no surprises when we find this City of Stolen Dreams," said Santon, his mood darkening even more. "That does not resolve the dilemma of our distant watchers." From the corner of his eye, he, too, caught a glimpse of movement. A rider? An animal hunting late in the afternoon? With the sun at their backs and their shadows long on the ground, they would be ideal targets for ambush. An attacker might have the sun in his eyes, but they would be silhouetted as they rode.

And the wind! It switched direction constantly. What had been in their face a few minutes earlier now came from the rear. Somehow, this boon from the saints did not keep the grit from Santon's green eyes or pasty mouth.

"We should camp soon," said Alarice. "We can wait for them to come to us—if they mean us harm."

"Another night of watches," sighed Vered. "Before we find the twins, I shall be a hundred years short on sleep. When one ascends the throne, my first request of the monarch will be for a month of never being awakened!"

"Sounds like death to me," said Santon.

"Birtle, you are much too gloomy," said Alarice. "The reason we ride is serious, but you need not carry the full weight on your shoulders. We do this together." She reached over and laid a hand on his. The smile warmed him. He tried not to think of the eyes and the cold depths within them.

They rode for another hour, then camped. It took the men another hour to tend to the horses and prepare a simple meal. While they worked Alarice used her scrying spell to discover the identity of any who followed them into the Iron Range.

"I'd be tempted to say that we do the hard part," said Vered, staring at the Glass Warrior while she concentrated. "We tend the horses, we make the meal, we stand the watches, but this time I stand mute."

Alarice's face was drawn and white. Her eyes were closed and sweat beaded on her forehead in spite of the hot breezes still blowing. Finally, she sagged forward, her hands falling limp to her sides.

"Are you . . ." began Santon. He knelt. Alarice opened her eyes and smiled weakly.

"I am unharmed. This scrying proved more taxing than before. Someone counters me. I cannot tell who the wizard is, but it must be Patrin. Somehow, Tahir's death alerted him. Perhaps when the imprisoning spell vanished it triggered a magical alarm. I don't know."

"I've been to the top of yon tree," said Vered. "From the topmost branches I've watched for the past half hour and seen nothing. If we are being tracked, they have no desire to approach before complete darkness." He cocked his head to one side. "The moon rises in another two hours from behind the mountains. An attack would come from that direction. We would shine in moonlight and they would be invisible to us."

"So," mused Santon. "If they rode parallel to us all day, they would continue on, then circle back and come at us. When? We have a two hour period of grace before moonrise. Call it another three hours before the moon rose too high to afford them any benefit from the attack. One should keep watch, then, for two hours, all three of us until the moon is overhead, and the usual watch afterward?"

"Sounds good," said Vered. "Since I crawled up that damnable tree and got sap all over me, you can take the first watch while I clean off." Vered made a face as he pressed his hands together and started to pull them apart, only to find the sticky sap gluing them together. The expression on his face when he saw the sap on his clothing told of extreme contempt for any pursuit in which he would sully himself.

Santon prowled to the perimeter of their camp and began carefully studying the terrain. If attack came, he wanted to know the land better than the enemy. Less than a hundred paces along the route of his careful scouting, he got the eerie feeling of being watched. He did not turn; he moved onward slowly, adjusting his shield as he went. The feeling of being stalked increased.

Only when he had a large boulder to put at his back did he turn, his battle-ax singing as it whipped free of his leather sling. Santon held back his chagrin. He had been *sure* that someone stalked him. Try as he might, Birtle Santon saw no one.

But the feeling persisted—and grew.

He retraced his path, every sense straining. The wind had died down shortly after twilight. He scented nothing but cloying blossoms in the air. His ears picked up only faint sounds from Alarice and the muffled curses Vered uttered as he peeled the sticky juices from his hands. A horse neighed, then fell silent—one of their own. Santon's sharp eyes studied the dirt for signs of passage other than his. He had moved so carefully he had left only faint smudges marking his trail. Nothing else had passed this way.

Santon still *felt* eyes on him.

Heavy ax swinging restlessly, he walked on. A sudden gust of wind brought him spinning around, the blunted edge of his battle-ax slashing through a vicious arc. The ax went through empty air and his glass shield protected him from nothingness. But Santon jumped back in surprise when his attack produced an anguished cry.

"Who's there?" he demanded, seeing no one. His hand tightened on the handle of his weapon. "Come out and fight like a warrior. Your death will not be any less easy if you hide."

"My death was not easy the first time," came a moan that might have been wind in tall trees had it not formed true words.

"Where are you?" Santon lowered himself into a defensive crouch, his ax moving slowly from side to side, ready for instant use.

"Here." A tiny spiral of dust rose. Within the column of dancing brown motes appeared a faint glow. The glow intensified until it took on the vague form of a man. Santon felt as if he peered into another world—and, in a way, he did.

"A phantom!" he exclaimed.

"I roam these plains seeking my body. It is a lonely quest. Would you aid me?"

"I cannot," Santon said, relaxing his extreme posture. He lowered his battle-ax and moved the shield to one side for a better look at the ghostly figure. The phantom hovered two paces distant. The face glowed with an eerie pinkness and the body tapered off into the bottom of the swirl of dust; Santon could not tell where dust began and ghost-body ended. The features proved too indistinct for him to identify the phantom.

"I was lost in a battle on these plains over fourteen years ago. Since then I have sought aid from all who pass. You must help me. I've become so tired of roaming, neither alive nor truly dead. I have none of the bodily woes of the living but all the sorrows are mine to suffer. Forever! I cannot bear this burden much longer."

"What will happen if you can't?"

The phantom rippled like water in a pond filled with myriad fish beginning to feed. "I will surely go insane. Instead of knowing I should seek out my corpse, I will wander and embarrass myself completely, performing irrational acts. This behavior I have seen in others."

"Who were you? In life?"

"Dare I tell you?" the phantom wailed. "If I fought on the wrong side in the battle, you might think it a boon to let me suffer. I was only a petty soldier, a pikeman. Nothing more. I had nothing to do with the officer corps."

"Your allegiance does not interest me. I'll help, if I can."

"You will?" The phantom's excitement caused it to come apart. Bits of glowing substance flew in all directions, slowly coalescing as the ghost regained control. "How I have longed for one such as you."

"Where do you remember last?" asked Santon.

"Nearer the Iron Range. In a pass. Just going into a pass. We had ventured too far from the main body of our force. My squad started into the mountains when the enemy came from behind. We were trapped, unable to move forward quickly enough."

Santon nodded. These were the fears Vered had voiced about entering the Iron Range without being sure if any tracked them. He raised his eyes and studied the sky. The moon poked above the hills. The time for attack, if it came from their mysterious followers, if they even existed, would come soon.

"We enter the Iron Range on the morrow," Santon said, "and we have reason to believe we will be similarly attacked."

"By those camped a league toward the mountains?" asked the phantom.

"You've seen them? How many? Do they plan to attack us tonight?" He let his battle-ax drop and hang from its leather wrist strap and reached for the phantom, thinking to shake the information from the ghost. His hand passed through the ghostly substance. Santon experienced a momentarily tingling sensation in his fingers and nothing more.

"Sorry," apologized the phantom. "It is difficult for me. The ruffians yonder refused me aid. I became so enthused that I neglected to offer a trade of information when you so kindly agreed to help me find my corpse."

The phantom reformed after Santon's hand had sundered it.

"Come along. You must talk with Alarice."

"The Glass Warrior?" asked the phantom. "Many have spoken of her but so few have seen her. This is a signal honor for me."

"How do you know her name?" demanded Santon, instantly suspicious. He did not see how the phantom could be a spy for those following them. There was no need for the ghostly being to appear to him. Simply drifting disembodied around their camp would provide adequate intelligence for an attack.

"I . . . I know so many things and do not understand why. You are Santon. It is as if all living are known to me. In exchange for this worthless boon, I know naught of my body." The glowing column shook, as if the phantom cried ectoplasmic tears.

"Who follows us?"

"Do you want their names? Those I can give. But who orders them after you?" The phantom made a gesture Santon guessed to be a shrug of nonexistent shoulders. The man silently motioned for the phantom to follow. They returned to the camp. Alarice's cold eyes instantly locked onto the phantom.

"You found us a spy," she said with no enthusiasm.

"For us, against us, who can say?" Santon warmed his hand on the small cooking fire. Across from him Vered lay sleeping lightly. "I'll make a quick circuit of the perimeter and return. If they are to attack tonight, it will come soon."

"They will," said the phantom. It spun about, its substance agitated and glowing more brightly. "I don't want you hurt. Santon promised to help me find my body."

"I can help," said Alarice. "I might be able to scry your body."

"You are a wizard! But of course. The stories of the Glass Warrior say you are. It becomes so hard for me to think like this. Oh, thank you, thank you!"

Santon snorted and returned to his patrol. He had little liking for dealings with phantoms, yet this might prove to their benefit. If he had his way, entire battalions would be dispatched to scour Porotane to find the unburied bodies and properly consecrate graves for them. Leaving their shades to wander like this one did was needlessly cruel. Santon smiled without any humor. To die in battle was a risk all took. To drift aimlessly in search of your body after dying—that was a burden no one should bear.

Tiny sounds alerted him. He fell to his knees and hid behind a low tangle of shrubs. The moon had risen too high in the sky to cast good shadows on attackers from the east. Santon knew that the moon would illuminate him well for the enemy, though, if he ventured out into the open. He lay in wait, not daring to move. He wanted to shout, to alert Vered and Alarice. To do so would precipitate the attack and gain him nothing.

Three men skulked past him, not even noticing him. Santon kept his shield and battle-ax low to prevent vagrant moonbeams from reflecting and warning them.

Only when they had passed by and he had

assured himself a second wave did not follow did he turn and silently stalk the stalkers.

The one in the rear sensed him. Santon rushed forward, battle-ax raised. The man emitted a squeak more like a mouse than a human before the heavy spiked ball behind the ax blade crushed his skull. Santon's strong wrist flipped the ax around. The blade cut into the second brigand's leg. He fell to the ground, screaming in pain.

"Die, fool!" cried the man who had been in the lead. His sword flashed toward Santon's breast. A quick movement brought the glass shield into play. The blade deflected and Santon used the shield edge as a weapon, driving it into the man's arm. This caused the brigand to stumble off balance. Santon's ax assured that the assassin need never worry about his clumsiness again. Brains spattered over the moonlit ground to glow phosphorescently.

Panting with the exertion, Santon recovered. He stood and stared at the bodies. Death had come so quickly. It always did. Only now did he realize how it might have been his corpse cooling on the ground. His hand shook and sweat made the handle of the battle-ax slippery. No matter how many times he faced danger like this, he reacted strongly afterward, his stomach churning and threatening to regurgitate. Santon held down his gorge and concentrated on scouting. If three had come, there might be more.

He found no sign of other assassins creeping through the night. He returned to camp.

"You took your time returning. You got them?" asked Vered, casually lounging on his bedroll. For all the man's flippancy, Santon saw the tension in his body. Santon reacted physically to danger; Vered tried to laugh it off.

"Of course. Were there others?" The small movement of Vered's hand toward his sword showed that there had been. Vered had already cleaned the gore off his blade.

"Five," said Alarice. "Eight, all told."

"I got three. Does that end the madness for the night? I need sleep."

The phantom spoke up. "Five remain in camp."

Santon squatted down and stared into the embers of their fire. "Do we leave them be or take them out?"

"You promised the phantom that we'd find his body?" asked Alarice.

"I said that your magic might help us. I made no definite promise. But he can aid us. He died in an assault similar to the one we feared in the mountain passes."

"His body lies a hundred yards from their camp."

Santon sighed. Always it came to killing. For too many years he had been the best. He tired of it. "Let's go," he said, rising to his feet. "If I am to sleep this night there are five more who must die."

"Don't you even want to know whose men they are? Whether they are simple brigands or Theoll's soldiers?" asked Vered.

"What difference does it make? They want us dead. We must kill them first."

Vered rose like a feather on a summer breeze. "That's what I like about Santon. He's such a philosopher."

The five in the brigand camp died under ax and sword before the moon rose to zenith.

CHAPTER FOURTEEN

Baron Theoll pulled himself up to the greatest height possible and still the assassin towered over him. Trying not to be obvious about it, Theoll moved around the table between them and perched on one edge, a short leg swinging slowly, to prove to himself that the pain had fled. He glared at the man. He might be taller than the baron but the assassin knew who was the more powerful. His paleness had turned to a pasty white before he had finished his sorry report.

"You let these two ruffians and a woman defeat you?" Theoll asked in a voice both low and menacing. "How is this possible? You were the best in all Porotane. None came close to your skill or stealth."

"They . . . it was magic, Baron. It had to be. We could not fight them. They . . . they summoned demons!"

Theoll snorted derisively. He knew better. The Glass Warrior had proven more dangerous than he'd thought possible. He had underestimated the woman's abilities. Even though the assassins had found her true path into the swamps after being misled north, they had failed against her. And the Demon Crown had slipped from his grasp!

"There is more," Theoll said. "Tell me."

"The two with her. They fight like a dozen warriors."

Theoll shook his head. Everything fell apart around him. His carefully built plans turned to ash. His assassins, the pick of all in the kingdom, proved ineffectual against a wizard and her two pets. His fists clenched so tightly that the fingernails cut into the flesh. Tiny crescents of blood formed. Theoll jumped to the floor, staggering slightly as his weakened legs yielded under his weight, and spun to prevent this worthless creation of his from seeing his infirmity.

Never let weakness show. Never. Especially to underlings.

Before Theoll formed the proper reprimand, a page burst through the door and stood breathless.

"What is it?" Theoll had little time for such intrusions. The boy would be punished.

"Baron, Dews Gaemock attacks the castle!"

"Impossible. Gaemock's forces withdrew. He can't reform his siege until fall." Theoll cocked his head to one side and listened hard. The pounding footsteps of hundreds of soldiers came to his ears. "Damn," he said, knowing that the page spoke truthfully. To the assassin, he said, "Wait here. Don't stir until I return."

It pleased him to see the man frozen to the spot by the command. Theoll motioned. The young page fled. Theoll followed closely, checking his dagger and making certain that the light leather armor he always wore covered the vital spots on his body. He burst into brilliant sunlight and squinted. By the time his vision cleared sufficiently, the battle raging below had progressed—too far.

"Who are they?" he demanded of the guard captain.

"Not Gaemock's troops as we first thought," the captain answered. "It might be a band of ruffians we found a few weeks ago. They headed to the sea and we ignored them."

"What do they hope to gain?" Theoll watched the flow of battle with a critical eye. Porotane's troops—he thought of them as his own—had been caught unawares. Their position proved poor for defense; the field commander showed a spark of intelligence. Unable to defend, he had attacked and split the rebel band in half.

"Lieutenant Squann's forces have been reduced by almost a hundred, with losses to the rebels of only a score," said the guardsman. "If Squann had not attacked when he did, they would have been wiped out."

"He should concentrate on the northern flank. Give him covering archery fire against their southern half."

The captain motioned and sent runners off to the far reaches of the castle's battlements. Flight after flight of feathered death arched into the air and fell in rebel ranks. The rebels had depended too heavily on surprise and too little on planning. Either an arrow had felled their leader or the leader failed to keep discipline in his ranks. The southern formation disintegrated, letting Lieutenant Squann commit his full force against the other half.

Theoll watched with little pleasure as the field commander killed every rebel that fell within sword range. No quarter was offered, although the rebels tried to surrender. Theoll wondered if this Squann knew he was being observed. Possibly. But the chance existed that Squann was vicious and offered no quarter under any circumstances. The baron made a small notation in a book he always carried with him to check out this commander. The assassins had done poorly. He needed new recruits for his personal guard.

"Why do they continue to attack?" he asked aloud.

"The rebels expect Duke Freow's death to weaken our resolve and crack our solidarity. They hope to assume the throne by a clever thrust at the proper instant. Yes, Baron, that's definitely the way I see their battle plans forming."

Theoll glared at the guard captain. This man was stupid. Oprezzi had been cunning, if not careful in his sexual liaisons with the Lady Johanna. But Oprezzi's replacement? Theoll suppressed the desire to throw the verbose fool over the battlements and to his death.

The baron spun and stalked off. Squann had turned the attack. The neighboring countryside would have to be scourged of all future threat. The spring and summer crops must not be allowed to suffer under the thousands of hooves of rebel cavalry. The food had to be used to supply the castle throughout the autumn and winter months. Theoll knew that Gaemock would never stop.

Kill him and perhaps end the single-minded drive for the throne. Maybe. Theoll had nightmares of Dews Gaemock's phantom ascending the throne, placing the Demon Crown on a vaporous skull, and ordering everyone put to death. The small baron shoved such nonsense away. Let it inhabit his dreams, not his waking moments. He hobbled back to his quarters, then paused.

An idea formed. The guards had abandoned

their posts in the castle corridors to protect the walls. Freow would be unattended. Theoll's fingers tapped along the hilt of his dagger. Making his decision, he hurried to the duke's quarters and burst inside.

One muscle strained against another as Theoll fought to keep from drawing his blade and plunging it into Freow's thin chest. The duke was not alone. Harhar capered and japed between baron and duke.

The jester turned and stared at the baron. "What is it, my lord? Do you come to help me entertain our duke?"

Theoll weighed the chance of killing the jester and the duke. Such would be for the best. Harhar carried in his dim-witted brain the knowledge of how Archbishop Nosto had been duped into putting Oprezzi to the Question. That little play had crushed Johanna's chance to ascend the throne. Her power gone, she had pulled back to defensive positions, trying vainly to reform her power base. With Nosto so firmly on Theoll's side, few would even talk to Johanna.

Harhar should die to protect the guilty knowledge of Nosto's deception. Theoll dared not have the archbishop turn the Inquisition against him.

But the jester was strong and young and the element of surprise had passed. In the corridor he heard the shuffling of guards returning. Theoll cursed his bad luck.

"I came to see how the duke is," he said lamely.

"Stronger. Stronger because he enjoys my jokes." Harhar did a handstand and began relating a preposterous story about two ducks and the king's handmaiden.

Theoll went to the duke's side and stared at him. Freow's eyelids quivered and then popped open. Theoll almost cried out in shock. For months the slow poison he administered had taken its toll on the duke. As if some horrid magic erased all that, Freow looked and acted stronger than ever.

"Theoll?" came a weak voice. "How nice of you to visit me."

"My . . . duke." Theoll bowed. "I am pleased to see you recovering from your grave illness." Theoll almost choked when Freow sat up in bed unassisted. The poison should have robbed the old man of every ounce of strength. He should have died by now!

"I recover too slowly," said Freow. "It is as if I have come through a veil of fog and the bright light of day has yet to burn all traces of the mist away from my tired old brain."

"You fare well, my duke." Theoll again cursed his missed chance. The poison had failed. He should have driven the dagger deep into Freow's putrid heart and seized the throne!

"My jests cheer him," declared Harhar. The lank-haired jester turned a set of powerful handsprings that brought him to the foot of the bed. He jumped straight up into the air and caught a bedpost. Harhar hung like a gigantic fly on the wall. Theoll wilted under the jester's hot, dark scrutiny.

Behind him he heard guards enter and resume their posts. Theoll bowed deeply and backed away, all thought of assassination passed. He would have to devise another scheme.

All the way back to his chambers, Theoll

stewed. When he finally entered his secure rooms, he boiled over. The lone assassin returning from the attempt to steal the Demon Crown from the Glass Warrior cowered.

"You," snapped Theoll, pointing at the assassin. "You failed once. Will you fail me again?"

"Never, my baron, never!"

"No, you wouldn't dare." Theoll slumped in his chair and stared at the frightened man. He had selected for courage as well as ability, yet this man almost burst into tears at the mere sight of his lord. Theoll rejoiced in this. It showed someone feared him. He had considered removing this abysmal failure permanently, executing him painfully as an example for others.

Theoll thought better of such a dire course now. The assassin would risk anything to serve him in return for his miserable life. If anything, that fear might make him all the more effective a tool to use against Duke Freow.

For a fleeting moment, Theoll worried over the failure of the poison. It had sapped the duke's strength for months. Why did it suddenly reverse itself when death should have been imminent? Could it be interference by the Lady Johanna? Theoll discarded that notion. Johanna's power had been broken with Oprezzi.

"Archbishop Nosto," he murmured.

"Baron?"

"Silence," he ordered. He had forgotten the assassin's presence in the room. His thoughts returned to the archbishop. Nosto might scheme against him. The Inquisition provided a convenient vehicle for obtaining information and exerting considerable power. Too many in Porotane feared heretics for the cleric's pogrom to be stopped. Had Nosto decided to save Freow and use him as a puppet?

Theoll shook his head. The notion was too preposterous. During the peak of Freow's rule, Nosto had been virtually exiled. Freow and Nosto had clashed constantly. Only when the duke took to his death bed had the archbishop again dared to return to the castle. The Inquisition had followed soon after.

An even more ridiculous idea was Nosto's assuming the throne. Never had a cleric become king of Porotane. The Demon Crown would destroy one so closely aligned with the saints. The tension between demon artifact and belief provided much of the power generated by the Demon Crown, or so Theoll believed. Archbishop Nosto could never surrender himself adequately to the immense demonic power of the crown to use it.

And without the Demon Crown on a true king's head, the civil wars in Porotane would continue. Should Archbishop Nosto assume the throne, the entire land would be split asunder in a matter of weeks.

Theoll pushed such nonsense from his mind. Nosto might lust after power but he found it by posing the Question, through the Inquisition, by acting the Inquisitor for the saints.

Some other power opposed him. But who might it be? Theoll had eliminated all the other players. He snorted. He had eliminated the strongest, but the factions against him still presented a difficult obstacle to overcome. If he killed Freow outright they would unite against him. Perhaps even Archbishop Nosto would turn on him. The cleric had lain with Johanna, of that he was sure. What other vices did Nosto have that he knew nothing about? The poison had been his best chance and its effect seemed blunted now.

Another sought the throne. If he could not decide who it was, he had only one clear choice. Freow must die quickly so that Theoll could immediately ascend the throne. Such a move would throw the opposition into disarray long enough for him to consolidate his power. Then none would dare oppose him!

"You will obey my commands?" he asked the assassin. The man's head bobbed up and down as if on springs. "Good. You will prepare for this mission carefully. You will make no mistakes. Is this understood?"

The man bowed his head.

Theoll tented his fingers and rested his chin on the peak. "Very good. You will assassinate Duke Freow in such a manner that it appears to have been done by, say, the Lady Johanna. Yes, she is a good choice."

"I am to kill the duke?"

"By the saints, you haven't turned deaf as well as stupid, have you? Yes, yes, *yes*! You will slay the old bastard. You will do it so that none can suspect me of the crime."

"When, my lord? It might take time so that none links us. I have been under your command for over a year."

"I understand that, fool. I'm not asking you to perform a suicide mission. I want you to kill Freow and leave subtle clues pointing to Johanna as the instigator. You are not to be caught or even suspected of the crime."

Theoll hesitated. He had the feeling that he

chose a weak tool for this task. The man had failed
once. The Glass Warrior still had the Demon
Crown—she still lived!

Theoll had no other choice. "You will do as
ordered. I desire Freow's death within a fortnight."

"Yes, Baron." The assassin left quickly—and
Theoll was left with a feeling of frustration.

Loud rapping came on the barred door of
Theoll's sleeping chamber. The small man came
awake instantly, hand on dagger, heart pounding
and ready to face danger. He sat up and peered
over at his bed—he never slept in the bed for fear
of assassination. For weeks he had moved about
the room, sleeping in chairs, under tables, even on
the narrow, cold window ledge.

"Baron, come quickly. There is trouble. Duke
Freow!"

Theoll wanted to laugh aloud. In only four
days his assassin had done his job!

He pulled on clothing and went to the door.
Outside stood a small squad of castle guards.

"What is it?" he asked, trying to keep the tone
of his voice somber. "Am I needed?"

"At once, Baron. Hurry please."

Theoll almost ran to keep up with the escort's
quick pace. He burst into Freow's chambers, ready
to spout inane condolences. Instead, he choked.

Freow sat up in the bed, looking healthier
than he had in over a year. Surrounding the bed
were Archbishop Nosto, the physician, Johanna, a
few minor nobles, and Harhar.

"We are glad you came so quickly, Baron,"
said Nosto. "There has been an attempt on the
duke's life."

Theoll's eyes darted around the room. He saw feet sticking out from under a blanket on the floor. The lump under that blanket had to be the body of his killer.

"Yes, an assassin. He was slain before he could work his perfidy on the duke."

"But who . . ."

Nosto shook his head. "We do not know." The cleric stared straight at Theoll. Nosto knew but could not prove it.

"What happened?"

"I slept," Freow said. His voice cracked occasionally but came out strong otherwise. Too strong for Theoll's liking. "I heard noises, a struggle. The room was dark but I saw two dark figures. The killer was killed."

"How? By whom?" demanded Theoll.

Freow shrugged. "I did not see. The guards claim it was none of their rank." The old man smiled feebly. One parchment-skinned hand lay outside the coverlet as a tribute to the physician's skill in caring for the decrepit duke. "It would seem that I have an unknown protector in the castle."

"The saints smile on you, Duke," intoned Archbishop Nosto.

"Yes, I'm sure that is it." Theoll's mouth had turned drier than the Desert of Sazan. His poisons had failed. His assassin had failed. Who guarded Freow so well?

Who?

CHAPTER FIFTEEN

Vered put his hands over his ears to keep down the din from their horses' hooves echoing along the dark iron canyons. It muffled the sound a trifle but did nothing to diminish the pounding inside his skull.

"Not even rags stuffed in my ears help," Birtle Santon said in a too-loud voice.

"Is this the only pass?" complained Vered. "Surely other, quieter routes to the Desert of Sazan exist."

Alarice rode alongside. Her lips moved but Vered heard no words. She repeated; he caught the gist of her comment.

"Sorry," he said. "Santon and I never got used to silent communication. That's one reason we did so poorly in battle." Vered smiled as he remembered. "No commander dared send us on the dangerous missions. We chattered like birds quarreling over a tasty morsel. The others used sign language or semaphore. Not Santon and me."

The echoes from his voice rang from the iron walls of the canyon and returned to haunt him. He gazed up from the floor of the narrow canyon they followed. The walls had an ugly blackness to them, the only color being spots turning to rust from constant exposure to the elements. Truly, he knew why they called this sorry collection of rock the Iron Range. Such purity of ore he had never seen. Vered would have exchanged a fraction of the hematite for a grassy slope or a gently flowing stream.

They had encountered neither since entering the pass after slaying the brigands.

Alarice held up her hand. Vered reined in while Santon continued on to scout their path. In a voice low enough to be heard but not so loud that it triggered new echoes, Alarice said, "This is the spot where our phantom friend died."

Startled, Vered looked around. "So far away?" he said. "The remains were found not a league from where we slew the brigands. Your scrying proved remarkably accurate."

"Especially so since Patrin blocks my attempts to see into the City of Stolen Dreams."

Vered jerked nervously when the phantom appeared at his elbow. The sudden swirl of air caught up tiny bits of debris and dust laying on the floor and spun them in blinding circles.

"Is this truly the spot where I was slain?" asked the phantom. The intense longing in his voice communicated to Vered and touched the man's heart.

"Here you died. Your body was taken out of the pass, possibly for burial, possibly to prevent your enemy from learning the true numbers of your casualties." Alarice shook her head, sending a wild frizz of snowy white hair away from her eyes. She pointed. "There. You died there at the base of that hillock."

The phantom drifted toward the indicated spot and hovered. Vered knew it might have been his imagination but he thought the ghostly pillar took on added substance and became less transparent.

"Yes, I feel it. Here. I died here!"

Alarice whispered in Vered's stoppered ear. "The remains should be laid to rest on this spot. The digging will be difficult. The ground is extremely hard."

Vered kicked at the scattered rocks with his boot and found the layer of soil beneath. It looked as if they would have to blast through solid iron ore. Frowning at something he uncovered, he dropped to one knee and pawed through the rocks. A rusted corps insignia came to light. He lifted it for closer examination and saw that the medallion was brass, that the red splotch was dried blood. He sagged. Fourteen years, the phantom had said. For that long this bit of military uniform had lain exposed to the winds of winter and the searing heat of summer and still the blood remained.

"That was mine," said the phantom. "An insignia from the left shoulder of my uniform."

Vered nodded. He recognized it as such. "This is where you died," he said. He took out his dagger and scraped at the ground. It resisted. He worked until sweat poured down his face. The Glass Warrior added her blade to the chore. After Santon returned to report that the way ahead was clear for another day's travel, he added his nicked ax blade to the task. Hours later they had carved a shallow crypt in the stone.

Vered wiped the sweat from his face and sank back, the hard canyon wall supporting him.

"That's enough, is it not?" He had become increasingly disheartened as they dug, in spite of the phantom's enthusiastic encouragement for their task. Vered had found that the blood shed in this forgotten battle had seeped into the ground and turned the very soil rusty. The amount of life's blood needed to perform this transformation measured in gallons—and what distressed him the most was his ability to imagine such carnage. He and Santon had seen worse during their days together.

"Give me a hand," said Santon, struggling with the sack containing the remains.

"Then I'd be the one lacking a pair," said Vered. Santon glared at this tasteless joke at his expense and said nothing. Vered grunted as Santon pulled the sack containing the remains from the back of a packhorse and dropped it fully on Vered's shoulder. The smaller man staggered under the load, then turned and made his way to the grave. He tried to lower the sack as easily as he could. It landed with a *thunk*! loud enough to give birth to new echoes.

"I feel strange," the phantom said. "It . . . I cannot tell you what is happening."

"Rest easy," Alarice said. They piled rocks over the sack, then built a small arch above to mark the grave. She began the death litany.

"Peace," the phantom said. "I feel tranquility settling over me like a warm, comforting blanket. Thank you, my dear friends. For so many years I prayed for this. Thank you . . ."

The words vanished into echoes, drowned by the Glass Warrior's recitation. When she finished, all trace of the phantom had gone. For several minutes, the trio simply stared at the grave.

Vered broke the silence. "May we be as lucky to find peace in death."

Alarice looked at him sharply. "You don't have the second sight, do you?" she demanded.

"No. I have trouble predicting what I'm going to say and do next. The future is closed."

The Glass Warrior relaxed. "This quest has been difficult for me. It will become even more taxing before we . . . succeed."

Vered and Santon exchanged glances. Not for the first time, Vered wondered at the Glass Warrior's age. Alarice walked with a spring in her step and fought with reaction and strength that would be the envy of a new lieutenant of guards, but a miasma of age about her descended now and again. Vered thought she had come by the white hair honestly, by living through ages undreamed of by ordinary men. She might match Santon's thirty summers or she might be three hundred. He could not tell.

"When do we leave these demon-damned passes?" asked Santon. "The echoes are driving me insane."

"Such torture is used by the Inquisitors," said Vered. "They place a bell over their victim's head, then ring it occasionally, when it is least expected. The sound is terrible, but the uncertainty is worse."

"There is no uncertainty to *these* echoes," said Santon. "We talk. Echoes. We ride. Echoes. Even the echoes spawn echoes."

"We must ride for another few days. How many, I cannot say."

"Our water runs low," Vered said. "We use more for the horses than I anticipated. The heat radiating off these accursed iron walls are cooking the water from our bodies, too." He tried to spit and couldn't form enough to clear the grit in his mouth.

"There is water," she said. Alarice closed her eyes and turned slowly. When she completed a full circle, she pointed to their left. "In that direction. A small spring. The lip of the basin is rusted but the water within is pure."

"Thank the saints for such a small favor," Santon said glumly. "It'd be my luck to find water poisoned by the heavy metals."

They mounted and rode until they found a crossing canyon. Vered swayed in the saddle, the heat putting him to sleep. The exertion from digging the shallow grave had also drained him, but putting to rest the shade of the fallen soldier had buoyed him. To become trapped between death and life, to wander endlessly seeking succor, was a fate he wished to avoid. To help another escape this limbo must give him a better chance. The Death Rota carried all acts good and ill performed while mortal and living. This day Vered had negated several of the reprehensible entries against his name.

"There," came Santon's booming voice. Vered struggled to open his eyes. The tiny puddle of water surrounded by the rust-brown iron shore looked more appealing to him than the coldest beer, the frothiest ale, the headiest brandy. He spurred his steed forward and dismounted.

"Should we sample the water first to be sure it won't harm the horses?" he asked. Better that one of them turn sick from unsuspected poison than to kill their mounts. No one could escape the Iron Range on foot. Not amid this sweltering heat and interminable twists and turns of rocky canyon.

"The water is pure," Alarice said. "I detect no spell placed on it. And my scrying shows nothing harmful within." She dangled a cord with a catamount's fang tied onto the end. The hot wind whipping along the canyon failed to stir the tooth. "If the water had been tainted, the tooth would point downward. It reacts only to my magic."

Vered knelt and cupped his hands. The water almost burned his lips. He spat it out. "It's almost boiling hot."

"Not that hot," said Santon. Although he sampled gingerly, the bigger man did drink. "The taste is peculiar."

"That comes from the iron. It is not harmful," Alarice said. She dipped her empty water skin into the pool and filled it. The wind caressed the exterior of the damp bag and evaporation cooled the contents. Only then did she drink. A satisfied smile crossed her lips.

"What can we do for the horses?" asked Vered.

Santon laughed. "They seem not to mind the temperature. Just be sure not to let them drink too much and begin to bloat."

Their three horses, plus the two captured animals they used as pack animals, shouldered one another to the side to stick their noses deep into the pool. They lapped noisily. The echoes annoyed Vered. He considered totally clogging his ears with mud to shut out the sounds.

Vered settled down and began to drift off to sleep. The heat soothed him, swaddled him, and took all burden of thought from his mind. His head swayed, then his chin dipped.

He awoke suddenly when he heard cackling laughter. Vered looked around, his brown eyes bloodshot from the heat. Shimmering curtains of heat waves danced from the walls and along the canyon they had traversed to reach this spot. But of others he saw naught. Again lethargy crept up on him and sleep controlled his mind.

—mine!

"No," Vered mumbled. "Can't have me." He stirred, wrapped his arms around himself, and noticed the sweat flowing copiously from his body. Too hot. He drifted into deeper sleep.

—you are my slave!

Vered experienced a moment of drowning, the fluids claiming his life being those that had given him life. Blood and sweat mingled and rose around him. He panicked. He fought, trying to escape. Ever higher rose the waters of death. Vered threw back his head, trying to keep his nose and mouth above the flood. The harder he tried, the more he sweat. The more he sweat, the higher the waters rose.

—surrender to me, my little one. you are mine!

"No," mumbled Vered. He thrashed from side to side. The lapping waves crested over his head. He felt himself sinking, a sailor on the seas of his own juices.

Sudden searing pain caused him to scream. His eyes popped open and he stared up into Alarice's concerned face. She held her glass dagger in one hand. A tiny drop of blood—his blood!—dripped from the tip.

"Do not go to sleep. You must not," she said. The concern in her voice frightened him.

"What's happening to me?"

"I had not expected to find any still alive. But one roams these mountains."

"What? A wizard?"

"A wizard's creation. A mind leech. It hunts only when its prey sleeps."

"I was drowning." Vered dragged his hand across his face. It came away drenched with sweat. He reached out and touched his shoulder; the hand found a bloody streak where Alarice had cut him to force him from his trance.

"I'm sorry. Pain is the only way to combat the lure of the mind leech."

"It made me think I was drowning," Vered said, his voice cracking from strain. He looked directly into the woman's cold gray eyes. "What would it have done to me?"

The shudder passing through the Glass Warrior's body made Vered not want to hear the answer —yet he had to. Alarice said, "It saps your will. Slowly, you become its slave, doing its bidding. The more you resist, the more ways it finds to break your resolve."

"When we're awake, can it get us then?"

"No, not as easily. I felt it tugging at the edges of my mind, but it sensed my control of magic. The mind leech is a cowardly beast, never risking physical contact. It hunts with its mind—and this is how it triumphs."

"It uses slaves to kill for it? The slaves tend it?"

Alarice nodded. "They hunt, they protect, they obey. Submit once, and its insidious mind probe slips into your will. Submit further and you are doomed."

"So it's a physical being," said Vered. "One that can die?"

"Vered, no. I know what you are thinking," said Alarice. She took a step away. "We dare not seek out the mind leech. There is no time. Patrin. The City of Stolen Dreams. We must not tarry."

"This creature might be sent by Patrin," said Santon. "To kill it is to weaken Patrin."

"To attempt to slay a mind leech is easy. To accomplish such a feat is almost impossible. Any fear you might have would be turned against you."

"We dare not let it rove the Iron Range," said Vered. He yawned. "Besides, we can never win free of this wretched, hot place before falling asleep."

"You are especially vulnerable to it now, Vered," she said. "It has almost taken you."

"Then we *must* find it. No other way exists for us to safely escape the mountain passes," said Santon.

"Is there *any* fear in your heart, armless one?" she asked.

"Fear?" Santon shook his head. "Bitterness? Yes."

"I think there is fear," Alarice said. She circled, her dagger point raised. "Is there not a small shred of fear that your left arm will wither like your right? To lose that arm in combat? To fall and break it and starve to death?"

"Don't be ridiculous." Santon's voice lacked confidence. Both Alarice and Vered heard the worry hidden by years of denial.

"How dangerous is it facing a mind leech— with real fear lurking inside you?" asked Vered. He hastily added, "I'm seething with fear myself. It wouldn't do for me to approach this matter without knowing the full extent of my danger."

Santon's heavy breathing slowed. Vered had lessened the tension the one-armed man felt. But what might happen if Birtle Santon confronted the mind leech and this gnawing, buried fear was turned against him?

"The creature is able to attack several at a time. Simply presenting a united front will not permit us to triumph," said Alarice.

"Are there spells you can cast to destroy it?"

"No, Vered, none. I am not a wizard of Patrin's class." She laughed without humor. "I am unable to magically defeat even a creation like the leech."

"We must try," said Vered. "The three of us. Can you predict success with this monster lying in wait for us? An unsuspecting moment, a drifting into sleep, an unrecognized fear, and we are victims, not rescuers."

Alarice's face contorted in anger. "By the saints, you are right. Damn you for that!"

"Where do we find the leech?" Santon asked. "Near, I trust. Watching Vered yawn and stretch is making me sleepy, too."

Alarice looked around, up the towering walls of iron. "High. It will have its lair high so that it can look down on its prey. And near. It is a living creature as we are and needs water."

"Since this is all the water we're likely to find in this miserable stretch of the Iron Range, let's go upslope," said Vered.

"It might lair near the snow line." The tallest peaks retained heavy white caps and only reluctantly allowed thin trickles of moisture to creep downward. In another few weeks or even days, the spring sun would send down torrents from the melting snow.

"Dangerous," said Alarice. "The mind leech is sensitive to temperature. Physically it is weak. Only through strength of mind and the mental weakness of its prey can it survive."

"Let's look for traces of its slaves obeying its

will. I've never known slaves to be particularly neat nor slave masters to care," said Santon.

They tethered their horses and went into the searing heat of the iron canyons in search of spoor. Only a few paces farther into the canyon Vered discovered a well-chewed carcass. He called, waited for the echoes to die, and then motioned to the others. He pointed silently.

Alarice closed her eyes. She turned slowly, trying to locate the mind leech. When she stopped and her face turned as white as her hair, both men acted. As one they started up the slope, the loose rock coming back downhill in dusty torrents. Vered reached the top first. His short sword swung as he yelled in attack.

"Boars! Three demon-damned boars!"

The rush of one tusker sent Vered back-pedaling too fast. He lost his balance and slid down the slope, enduring minor cuts and abrasions until he regained his feet at the bottom.

"Careful, Santon!" he called. Vered remembered what Alarice had said about the mind leech finding the festering sore of fear in a man's mind and using it against him.

"Careful be damned. Get your ass back here and help me!" The heavy battle-ax rose and fell. An anguished squeal told of porcine death. Vered and Alarice hurried back to the top of the slope. Santon held at bay the other two tuskers.

The yellowed fangs snapped and flashed at Vered, taking away part of his breeches. He avoided the filthy fang and the possible infection it offered by a hairsbreadth. Off balance again, stumbling forward, he lunged with his short sword. The glass tip penetrated the boar's flank. The ponderously heavy pig died without a sound; Vered's blade had found its heart.

Vered laughed joyously. The adrenaline flowed through his arteries. The fight brought him to full awareness of his world, gave him confidence —and allowed him to know his true enemy.

Birtle Santon stood over the last boar, his heavy ax lodged in the animal's thick skull. Santon was Vered's enemy. Santon would split his skull asunder as he had done to Vered's ally, the tusker.

Vered pulled his blade free and advanced. In the distance he heard the Glass Warrior calling to him. He ignored her. Santon must die. Kill or be killed!

The expression on Vered's face when he lunged and missed by a fraction of an inch told of his expertise. None bested Vered in battle! Not even a demon in human form like Santon.

"Vered, stop, don't!" Santon used his shield to deflect a lunge.

"Both of you, stop," came Alarice's harsh command.

Vered saw fear on Santon's face. He knew he could not fail. He redoubled the speed and power of his attack, working around, trying to pink Santon's good arm. Only by playing on his fear of losing his left arm might he slay this foe.

"I don't want to do this, Vered. Please, don't force me." Santon parried the blows with his heavy ax, but his protective glass shield accomplished more.

"The mind leech," pleaded Alarice. "It creates fear to gain control over you."

"It has Vered," Santon cried in anguish. "I don't want to harm him."

The Glass Warrior did not reply. Vered circled even faster. His heart almost exploded in fear when he saw the woman enter a shallow cave.

"No, stop, don't go in there!" he shouted. Vered broke off the attack he launched against Santon. He had to stop the Glass Warrior!

Santon used the edge of his shield to smash into the side of Vered's head. The smaller man went spinning, blood matting his brown hair. The impact jolted Vered and pain burned through his brain—and cleared it!

"The mind leech," he gasped. "It used me. Alarice is going after it. We must help her!"

Santon looked at him skeptically, then indicated that Vered should precede him into the cave. Vered wasted no time. He had not detected the leech's insidious presence in his mind. He had been too wrapped up in the heat of battle. But now he knew the sensations. The instant he entered the cool mouth of the cave, he felt the leech again trying to subvert him.

"Santon," he said. "It works on me. Help me!" Vered turned to his friend. Santon stood in silence, as immobile as a marble statue. The expression on his face told Vered that the leech had taken over the man's mind.

Without thinking, Vered dropped to the cave floor and kicked out, his legs scissoring. One foot went behind Santon's ankle. The other foot snapped into his kneecap. Like a giant tree felled in a forest, Santon crashed to the rocky ground. When he sat up, the dazed look had passed and one of chagrin replaced it.

"The demon-damned thing had me!" he exclaimed.

"Alarice. We must help her." Together the

men hurried into the depths of the cave. Less than ten paces into the low-ceilinged cave they found the Glass Warrior. She stood with sword drawn. Her entire body trembled, as if she fought against unseen bonds.

"There," she said between clenched teeth. "There it is. The mind leech!"

Vered almost laughed. The pitiful creature cowering against a cave wall could hardly be the magical beast capable of subverting his mind. It was smaller than a princess' lap dog, a sickly pink in color, and had eyes as round and wide as yellow spring flowers. A long, slender tongue probed constantly from between its lips. No teeth showed as its lips drew back in a grimace.

"We must kill it!" Alarice shrieked. The echoes down the iron cave assaulted Vered's ears and sent new waves of pain into his head. The surge of agony pulled him free once more of the mind leech's power.

A heavy hand tried to restrain him. Vered twisted, grabbed Santon's left wrist, and broke free. The fear on Santon's face came not from within but from the leech's fear for its own death. It had again taken over Birtle Santon.

Vered dodged to one side, tripped Santon, then used his dagger on the mind leech. The first prick produced a tiny spurt of thin, orange blood. Vered felt the lifting of mental pressure as the leech panicked, sensing its own death.

Vered had no chance for a second strike. Alarice's glass sword slashed past, barely gutting the mind leech before Santon's ax decapitated it.

The magical creature's death released them totally from its mental influence. The trio sank to the cave floor and shook in reaction. Alarice reached out and put her arms around both men's shoulders. For a long time, no one spoke.

Then Santon said, "See? I told you. I'm not afraid of losing my arm. I'm afraid of nothing!"

"At least one of us has kept his sense of humor," said Vered. It was all he could do to keep from staring at the dead mind leech and reliving the horror of its bondage.

CHAPTER SIXTEEN

Vered almost tumbled from the saddle. Exhaustion had taken its toll on him over the past three days. They had defeated the mind leech, but the heat, the constant pounding echoes, the hardship of traveling through the barren Iron Range had worn him down.

"There," came Alarice's quiet voice. For a moment, he thought he had gone deaf. No echo returned to torment him. He rubbed his bleary eyes and sat straighter in the saddle. Hot winds blew at his back. For a moment, this confused him. Then he realized that they had finally escaped the black mountains and had emerged on the side most distant from fair, green Porotane.

Shock rolled through him. He had never recovered fully from the encounter with the mind leech. Afraid to fall asleep because of the nagging fear of having his mind taken over, Vered had become increasingly tired. The heat radiating from the high walls of the iron canyons had also sapped his strength, but now he stared out across land presenting a true challenge.

Vered was not sure he had the strength for it.

"Never have I seen such desert," he said. The barren waste appeared stripped of all vegetation.

Huge dunes of ochre sand rose like waves in the ocean. The tireless winds had cut creases into the sides of the dunes in their quest to move the ponderous mounds from one location to another. Here and there Vered saw the grit whipping along the ridges. The winds caught it and sent it upward, sometimes over five hundred feet high in a miniature tornado. More often, the winds played sleight of hand and hid the airborne sand behind the dunes.

"The Desert of Sazan," said Santon. "Only once before have I seen it. Luckily, I skirted the edge on my way south to Rievane."

"We must cross it. Straight across. In that direction." Alarice stared into the heart of this sprawling, overheated monster.

"Water," said Vered. "Do we have enough? Just looking at it turns my mouth into a furnace."

"How far do we need to go before finding the City of Stolen Dreams?" Birtle Santon hooked one leg across the saddle pommel and bent forward. "Vered has a point. We could never find water if we begin wandering aimlessly."

Alarice silently held out her scrying cord and crystal. The sunlight caught the facets of the glass splinter and turned them into glittering rainbows. Santon raised his hand to hold back the blinding glare. Vered found himself drawn into the ever-changing pattern as Alarice spun her spells.

The crystal spun in circles, never stopping until the Glass Warrior's spell came to completion. Like a true compass needle, the crystal pointed in the direction Alarice had indicated.

"Perhaps it means we should follow the hind end and go back into the Iron Range," said Vered.

"The City of Stolen Dreams," she said. "I . . . I cannot see it. Patrin still prevents direct viewing through a scrying spell, but I can do this much. My power seems to grow."

"Enough to confront Patrin directly and challenge him for the twins?" asked Santon.

"We don't even know if this Patrin has them. All we truly know is what Tahir told us—and I brand him a liar. He might have been imprisoned, but what evidence do we have that it was Patrin's doing?"

"Ah, Vered, you doubt even the rising of the sun every morning." Alarice put away her scrying crystal.

"There's no way to know if the sun will rise until it does," he pointed out. "Simply saying it will because it always has before is to deny change."

"I'll wager that it does," said Santon. "How much on the rising of the morrow's sun?"

"Fifty gold pieces," said Vered.

"Do you want odds?"

"Fifty to one."

"You seek twenty-five hundred if it does not?" Santon laughed. "What a crazy bet! If the sun does not rise, what matters gold?"

"At least I'll die with money owed me. The saints might appreciate that and enter it in the Death Rota."

"We will not die. We will prevail." The Glass Warrior spurred her mare forward. The horse hesitated when the hard hematite of the Iron Range turned to shifting sands beneath her hooves, but Alarice's insistence kept the animal moving. Vered and Santon followed, silently agreeing with the mare that they should not venture forth.

Vered let the Glass Warrior ride ahead. In a low voice, he said, "We can stop this now. There's no need for us to continue with her. What use can we be against Patrin?"

"We've not been promised riches," agreed Santon. "Nor are we likely to find anything but death."

"The Demon Crown is a dangerous relic. The wearer might become perverted by its power. The war might worsen."

"Even with a strong ruler, the civil war might have raged overlong," said Santon. "There is nothing to suggest that a new ruler will put an end to the warring."

"You mentioned Rievane to the south. What sort of city is it?"

"A fine one," said Santon, remembering with relish. "Women come into the street and beg you to join them in their soft bed and share their soft flesh."

"What of their men?"

"Few. Most go into the desert to hunt artifacts. They are gone much of the time, leaving the women—and how fair and beautiful they are!—to pine away."

"My kind of place."

"Ah, yes, Vered. And mine. And the women. They are alone so much of the time, they seek out companionship in foolish ways. Gamble? They are worse than even you! Anyone who could not come away from Rievane with a pouch brimming with gold is a fool."

"And the women."

"Yes, and the lovely, lovely women."

The men fell silent, each lost in his own thoughts. But neither looked to the south toward Rievane. Both stared at Alarice's back, the proud set of her head, the straight back, the determination in her mount. Vered's mind turned over and over as he wrestled with the problems of following the Glass Warrior. She offered hope to Porotane.

For Vered and Santon, she offered hardship and pain and probable death. Vered forced his body to forget some of the tiredness. He saw how Santon responded to the woman. Alarice had a quality about her that he found appealing—for Santon it had been irresistible. He could not deny his friend Alarice's companionship and love.

He forced such a notion from his mind. He had no designs on Alarice, and Santon's attachment to her had no bearing on his own decisions. He and Birtle Santon had gone their separate ways often enough in the past, only to rejoin and rediscover their friendship. If he let Alarice and Santon continue and headed for Rievane or some other spot to while away the time, neither would object. Vered had to admit that he stayed with Alarice because of the adventure it afforded. Life had not been dull, but it had become routine.

Brigands and rebel bands and renegade wizards and constables. Dodging them and trying to live the best he could took on a deadly sameness. Danger followed by flight and a seeking of new territory. Alarice offered something different and, as much as it wore him down physically, Vered had never been more excited about the future.

"Baron Vered," he said to himself, letting the title roll from his tongue like a honey lozenge.

"Rogue Vered," Santon said gruffly, interrupting his fine daydream. "We'll be lucky to escape this alive, much less with fine and fancy titles."

"One can hope," Vered said. "Restoring a monarch to the throne ought to be worth something."

"A title is little enough. What would you be like as a ruler of a small barony?" asked Santon. He answered his own query. "Miserable, that's how you'd be. So would I. What do we know of rule?"

"More than Freow, if Alarice's tale is even half true."

"He has done well enough, for a common ruffian," said Santon. "But would you want to live as he does?"

Vered's face tightened as a breath of hot desert wind brushed by. Pillars of dust rose on either side as cyclonic winds pulled aloft huge amounts of sand. He laughed aloud. Even if he had to live in a miserable place like the Desert of Sazan, Vered would not trade places with Duke Freow.

"My feelings, too," said Santon. "We have a freedom to roam."

"A freedom to do!"

Alarice had reined in. They came even with her. She said in a voice carrying a steel edge, "We also have the freedom to die. There. The City of Stolen Dreams."

"So soon?" Vered peered into a haze of dust blowing across the dunes. He saw nothing.

"Patrin's magical city is in the center of the Desert of Sazan."

"But," protested Santon, "we've ridden less than an hour!"

"We could ride for eternity and never find the city—if Patrin desired it."

The woman's words caused Vered to shiver, in spite of the furnace winds gusting around him.

"You say that Patrin *wants* us to enter this phantom city of his?" Vered did not like the implications. He felt like a bug being drawn into a spider's killing web.

"That is true," Alarice said.

Vered started to ask where this mysterious city was when he heard a deep rumbling. It built to a roar. He fought to keep his horse from bolting. The sound mounted, higher, deeper, until Vered felt his internal organs grinding against one another. And appearing through the brown haze came a city shimmering not with heat but with magic.

"The City of Stolen Dreams," Alarice said in a low voice. "The place where all your dreams can be snatched away and you are left hollow and haunted."

"Patrin steals dreams? Truly?" asked Santon.

"He tends the poisoned gardens of your mind, finding those weeds most likely to destroy you. The fine plants Patrin plucks and kills. What remains is vile."

"He drives his victims insane?"

"Worse, Vered," said Alarice. "He leaves them bitter and knowing that their lives were once better. Your fondest ambition, your greatest dream, *that* is Patrin's target."

"What are we to do? How do we fight him?" Birtle Santon looked uneasily at his withered arm. Vered read the concern in his friend's face. Recovering the use of that nerve-injured arm was Santon's dream. To lose that meant to lose much of the will to live.

"No sword can defeat Patrin. His weapons are magical. He is not the greatest of all wizards—the Wizard of Storms is that—but Patrin is powerful."

"More powerful than even the Glass Warrior?" came a rumbling voice. "Such humility. I never thought to hear it from you, dear lady."

Vered looked about but saw no one. He had almost called out to Alarice, named her name. He did not know if Patrin held this power over her, but he would not be the one giving it inadvertently to Patrin.

"Come. We ride to the City of Stolen Dreams," she said. Slowly, the trio rode forward. Outwardly, they showed no fear, but Vered fought hard to keep his hands from shaking. His horse trembled, eyes wide and nostrils foaming. Alarice's mount reacted similarly. Of Santon and his horse he saw nothing. The man rode behind.

But the Glass Warrior gave him courage. She rode, back ramrod stiff, hand easy on the reins, and with a determination to her that outshone any possible fear. Courage lay not in having no fear but in overcoming it.

The hollow clicking of the horses' hooves against paved street startled him. Vered looked around, then spun in the saddle and peered behind. The Desert of Sazan had vanished totally. Everywhere he looked, he saw a fabulously rich city. Buildings constructed of jasper and jade and onyx. Fixtures of silver and precious stones. Windows of stained glass depicting valiant scenes of combat and courage, crystalline sheets with beveled edges opening into lavish suites and courtyards with delicately spraying fountains filled with subtle perfumes. Everywhere he looked he saw opulence and . . . emptiness.

"Where are the citizens of this fine city?" he asked.

"There are none. Who can live without dreams?" asked Alarice.

Again Vered shuddered. To Santon he said, "My aspirations are simple but they are *mine*. I have no wish to lose them."

"Speaking seems sacrilegious," said Santon. "Any sound in this dead city is wrong."

Vered looked along intersecting streets, some paved with gold and other precious metals, some homey and quiet and begging for the laughter of children and the soft sighs of lovers. No sound reached him. Only the muffled clicking of their horses' hooves interrupted the deathly silence.

"Where do we find Patrin?" he asked the Glass Warrior.

"We ride until we come to him. As before, it might be an hour or it might be eternity. This is Patrin's center of power. We do his bidding or die."

"Why doesn't he just kill us?" asked Vered. "We disturb him. Surely, a wizard who hides in a place such as this does not wish to waste time with our like."

"Patrin did not exile Tahir and steal away the twins for amusement. He has plans. Somehow, we must fit into the matrix of those schemes."

"She has a point," said Santon. The man looked around, his sharp eyes missing nothing. "Patrin's power is immense to maintain such a city. He wants more, and we can give it to him."

"Very observant, Birtle Santon," came the booming voice. The three halted. From a small, simple peasant's hut walked a man of medium height, age, and coloring. Of his clothing, Vered saw nothing out of the ordinary. In truth, the harder he tried to find something unique about this man, the more he failed.

"It is a trick of Patrin's," explained Alarice. "He manipulates his image. I am uncertain that any has looked upon his true visage."

"Always the skeptic, eh, Warrior?" The man held out his hand. A tiny sun appeared. Vered held up his own hands to shield his eyes from the intense glare. So bright did the miniature sun grow that Vered saw the bones within his hand as the light passed through his flesh. Then the burning orb winked out of existence, as if it had never been.

"Your dreams are common," said Patrin. "Hardly worth my time." The wizard sighed deeply. "So few have uncommon dreams these days. Do you have any idea why this is so, Glass Warrior?"

"You rob humanity of its best, Patrin."

"Hardly, my dear. I find *your* dreams of interest, but they are not out of the ordinary. In fact, they fall into a category that perplexes me. You do not seek personal gain or glory on this quest of yours."

"You were always able to discern truth in motive," said Alarice.

"I do more than detect it, I collect it," he said. Patrin turned to Santon. "Your dreams are painfully mundane. You seek her love." Before Santon could protest, the wizard pointed to Vered. "And yours. You have a different set of ambitions. You talk of baronies and titles. Those are not what you really seek. You dream of unending friendship. Fear of loneliness drives you more than attaining any other goal."

To this Vered said nothing.

"You begin to bore me, Patrin. You know why I have come."

"Ah, yes, the royal twins. I know that you've spoken with that fool Tahir."

"Your spell killed him."

"Hardly possible. I turned him into an immortal creature so hideous that he would cringe whenever he saw his own reflection. What other fate could I give to a wizard who thought so highly of his good looks? What held him in the swamp, that's another matter and one not of my doing."

"He died."

Patrin peered at Alarice, as if believing her a liar. Slowly, the expression turned neutral. "You speak the truth. Tahir is dead. You countered my spell? I had no idea you controlled such power, Warrior."

"Another wizard's spell chained him to the swamp?" asked Vered. "The Wizard of Storms?"

Vered saw a flash of fear cross Patrin's face. He hid it so quickly that Vered began to doubt he had seen any emotion.

For the first time since entering the City of Stolen Dreams, Vered felt that success might be possible. Alarice had made Patrin out to be incredibly powerful. That he might be, but there were others he feared. This Wizard of Storms produced definite anxiety. And what of Alarice? She had protested for so long that she possessed only tiny powers. What magical spells were hers to command? Vered had the feeling that she had told them very little about her true abilities.

"You must be tired after your travels," Patrin said, suavely moving from a topic that disturbed him. "Enjoy the hospitality of my city. The entire city. Sample the dreams I have placed about it. See what can be yours."

Patrin whirled and vanished through the doorway of the simple hut. Vered took two quick paces and followed. He peered into the hut; it was empty.

"He vanished," Vered reported.

"Patrin always had a flair for dramatic entrances and exits," said Alarice. She looked from one man to the other. "Thank you for not mentioning my name aloud. He may try to trick this knowledge from you. As you value your life, so should you value my name. None of us will leave the City of Stolen Dreams alive if Patrin learns it."

"But you know his name. Can't you use it against him?" asked Santon.

The expression on Alarice's face told them more than they desired to know. Vered felt the coldness in his belly spread until icy fingers clutched at his heart. Alarice had been using this against Patrin, in spells so subtle that they had not detected them. Without these magics, Patrin would have slain them instantly.

"Yes," she said softly. "I am your only defense against him."

"Can you overwhelm him?" asked Vered. "With either spell or sword?"

"It must be with magic. While he remains within the boundaries of this city, Patrin is invincible against physical force."

Vered frowned, a disturbing thought occurring to him. "If this is so, why did he leave to imprison Tahir?"

"Patrin's reasons must have been more important than life itself to him."

"Power," said Santon. "Only more power

would draw a wizard from such a fortress." He looked around the empty, haunted streets.

"And it has to do with the Demon Crown," concluded Vered. "Can Patrin wear it?"

"No more than I," said Alarice.

"There is more to this than a sage can unravel," declared Santon. "Certainly more than I can consider on an empty belly. Is Patrin's offer of hospitality to be taken as truth?"

Alarice's face had become pinched and drained of blood. She nodded slowly. "He can do nothing to us."

"Your spells?" Santon moved closer. His good hand rested on her shoulder.

"Yes." She leaned heavily on him. Vered led the way into the heart of the City of Stolen Dreams, letting Santon and Alarice follow at their own pace. He marveled at the richness of the place—and worried at the souls lost to afford Patrin this luxury.

"This seems a good spot to spend a few hours," he said. A magnificent structure rose in the architectural style of Lubraenian palaces. Filigreed arches rose over curtains beaded with precious gemstones. Buttresses lifted and met the soaring walls, supporting and adding an element of grace and delicate beauty. Vered went inside. There lay the true attraction for him.

"Nothing is lacking," he said. "Except a few servants."

The curtains rattled as a plainly dressed man pushed through. Vered smiled and motioned to the servant.

"We need food and drink. Some white wine. From the Uvain Plateau, of course." Vered hesitated when he saw the look of anger cross the servant's face. "You *are* a servant?" Vered demanded.

"I am ordered to serve you," the young man said with more than a hint of bitterness in his voice. "I am Lord Patrin's apprentice."

"A wizard's apprentice serving me. I like the idea."

Santon and Alarice had finally followed him inside. Alarice stopped and stared at the apprentice wizard. She said, "Well, Vered, you like the notion of a young sorcerer serving you, eh?"

"I do," Vered declared. But something in the woman's tone put him on guard.

"Then you must love the idea of a prince serving you." Alarice bowed deeply. "Prince Lorens, we have come to take you back to Porotane to assume the throne."

Vered's mouth opened and closed. No words came out. He stared at the apprentice wizard— and king of Porotane.

CHAPTER SEVENTEEN

Vered struggled to find words. Nothing came out.

"Prince Lorens," said Alarice. "We have come in search of you."

"I am not a prince. I am Lord Patrin's apprentice." He stiffened and took a step away from the Glass Warrior. "He warned me of your lies. I am a commoner, not of royal blood. He told me you would try to drive a wedge between us."

"No lies," said Alarice. She examined the young man carefully. Fully twenty-four summers, he resembled dead King Lamost enough to dispel any doubt about his paternity. "Your uncle, Duke Freow, has ruled as regent until you were found. The duke is dying. It is time for a true heir to regain the throne and put an end to the wars raging in Porotane."

"This is my home." The sullen expression on the young man's face angered Vered.

"Porotane is your home. You and your sister were kidnapped."

"Yes," cut in Santon. "What of Lokenna? Is she also in this dead city?"

"My sister?" Lorens almost spat out the name, as if it left an acid taste on his tongue. "She has gained what she sought. May the demons take her!"

Vered and Santon exchanged glances. There seemed little need in pursuing this line of questioning. Lorens had been found; Alarice was convinced of his blood. Why seek out the sister?

"You cannot turn your back on Porotane. Your people need you."

"My lord needs me. No one else." Lorens glared at her. "If you speak the truth, why has it taken so long for someone to locate me? I have not hidden. Why has the duke not summoned me previously? My lord does not prevent travelers from entering our city."

"You do not believe," said Alarice. "You must be convinced."

"That is not possible." Lorens crossed his arms and glowered.

Without another word, Alarice pulled out the black velvet bag cradling the Demon Crown. She tugged at the fabric and withdrew the crystalline box holding the crown. Inside, the demonic circlet glowed more brightly than when Vered had donned it.

"The Demon Crown," Lorens said. His arms dropped to his sides and he moved forward to stare at the crown. "I have read about the demon Kalob's gift in my lord's grimoires. I always doubted." Eager hands took the box and lifted it. Vered squinted to keep from being blinded by the green-glowing crown.

"Put it on," urged Alarice. "Wear the Demon Crown and know the truth. Patrin has lied to you. You, Lorens, are the true heir to the throne of Porotane."

Lorens opened the clear crystal lid and lightly

touched the crown. The blaze of glory did not strike the young man dead. Instead, the green deepened in hue, became less eye-searing. Lorens lifted the crown and placed it gingerly on his brow.

"I *see*!" he cried. "Beyond the city, I can *see*!"

"You are the rightful king of Porotane. This is your father's legacy. You must return with us and take your place in history."

Lorens spun around and around, his face contorted with·insane rapture.

"Santon, Vered," the Glass Warrior said urgently. "Take the crown from him. He is like one drunk."

"Drunk with power," said Vered. Knowing that only he could touch the Demon Crown, he motioned for Santon to attack low. When the one-armed man hit Lorens behind the knees and sent him toppling, Vered snared the crown before it struck the floor. He recoiled in shock as. the magic flowed through him, even in this brief contact. He *saw* again—and the lure of such power proved almost more than he could bear. If it had not been for Alarice lightly touching his arm and drawing him back, he would have followed the images blasting into his brain wherever they took him.

"Here, Vered," she said softly. Alarice held out the opened crystalline case. He dropped the Demon Crown into its receptacle. The instant it left his hand, he sagged to the floor, drained.

Vered blinked and saw that Lorens had experienced much the same enervation. But the royal heir recovered quicker.

"The Demon Crown," crowed Lorens. "Such a treasure! It surpasses any of the dreams my lord has hidden away in the city."

"It will be yours—when you ascend the throne." Alarice stashed the box back in the velvet bag.

"Mine. It's mine! I want it now!" Only Santon's powerful left arm circling Lorens' neck kept the young wizard from ripping it out of Alarice's grasp.

"He's king of Porotane," protested Vered. "Leave him be, Santon."

"He thinks he's a demon-damned commoner. I think he is—"

"Santon!" The Glass Warrior's sharp command silenced the man. He released Lorens, who returned to his sullen glaring and surly manner. The apprentice spun and stalked from the room.

"And he never did bring me food or the fine Uvain Plateau white wine," said Vered.

"He is Patrin's pawn. The wizard has molded Lorens to his will over the years." Alarice looked worried. "And what of his sister? What became of Lokenna?"

"What'll become of us?" demanded Santon. "He'll tell Patrin that we have the Demon Crown. Do you think the wizard will let us go free without leaving it behind?"

"A moment," said Vered. "If Patrin is so powerful, why did he not sense the presence of the crown? It is a potent artifact. Surely, a sorcerer of his acumen must be able to sense such power."

Alarice smiled faintly. "I am not without my own spells. But I am sure that Patrin knows that we carry the Demon Crown. I worry more about Lorens. He is heir to the throne, but he must *want* to rule. He has had no training, other than that given him by Patrin."

"We install Lorens as king and Patrin will

become the true power, no matter what the youngling king does with the Demon Crown." Santon settled into a chair and rested his chin on his hand. "Was that the wizard's plan?"

"Patrin is powerful within the City of Stolen Dreams," said Alarice. "Controlling Lorens and the crown would make him even more of a force to be reckoned with. But it cannot be the full scope of his plan."

"This Wizard of Storms," said Vered. "Patrin is terrified of him. Could he use Lorens and the Demon Crown against him?"

"Ah," said Alarice. "There is more than a hint of truth to what you say, Vered. The crown might give Patrin the power to upset a delicate magical balance between two foes."

"Then Porotane means nothing to Patrin?" asked Santon.

Vered shook himself and rubbed circulation back into arms and legs. The effects of his fleeting contact with the Demon Crown passed. He left Alarice and Santon to their weighty discussion of Patrin's motives and their future plans. His belly grumbled and he could not spit because of the dryness in his mouth. More than reason, he required food and wine.

The pair chattered away while Vered explored the room. He had picked well. The furnishings outshone anything he had seen in Porotane. A single gold-legged couch or a finely wrought chair would fetch a pile of coins big enough to keep him happy for months. Years!

He circled the room, half-listening to his friends. Vered stopped and looked at a small stoppered vase placed carefully in a wall niche. The vase had the look of a storage vessel. Thinking it might contain dried fruit or grain, Vered took it from its shelf. He turned it over in his hands, studying the patterns on its ceramic surface. Vered shrugged. The patterns meant nothing. He preferred his art to represent something.

With a flick of his thumb, he broke the wax seal.

Vered shrieked, dropped the vase, and grabbed his groin. He felt himself growing to monstrous proportions. Pain shot into his gonads and then turned to a pleasure even more intense. Women moved around him to stroke, to touch, to lewdly expose themselves.

He cried out again, whether in pain or joy he could not tell. Scores of women, beautiful creatures all, pawed him, begged him for his attention, pleaded for him to take them. He doubled over, sobbing.

A cool hand touched his forehead. He jerked away. A rougher, more forceful grip shook him.

"Please, no, I can't," he moaned. "I hurt! I cannot!"

"Vered." The hand on his collar lifted until his feet left the floor. Then waves of relief laved away the confusing sensations in his loins. He became aware of Santon straining to hold him aloft and of Alarice's soothing voice. Her words took form in his ears; he recognized a tranquilizing spell and gratefully succumbed to it.

Birtle Santon dropped him and stepped back, grumbling. "What foolish thing did you do this time?"

"Nothing. I was hungry. The jar. I opened it." Vered's recollections became jumbled after this. His eyes went wide when he remembered segments of all that had happened. "I grew. Oh, by the saints, how I grew!"

"You stayed the same size." Santon snorted derisively.

"No, not all of me. Just a part." Vered looked guiltily to his groin. "There. To proportions more than—"

"Enough," interrupted Alarice. "You have opened one of the dream traps."

Vered did not understand.

"Why do they call this the City of Stolen Dreams?" she asked. "Patrin strips away the dreams, the longings, the ambitions of those who venture into the city."

"Someone wanted to—" Vered blanched.

"You know now why Patrin considered your dreams to be paltry in comparison."

"But to—"

"Enough," Alarice insisted. "Do not open any more of the dream traps, unless you wish to experience the bizarre fantasies Patrin has stolen for his own amusement."

"I could have satisfied every whore in Porotane and still had enough energy left for all the ladies of the court," marveled Vered.

"Why do you need a jar for that kind of daydream?" asked Santon. "Haven't I listened enough times to such maunderings from you? How you'll—" Santon cut off his diatribe when Alarice pulled back from the pair of bickering men.

"What is it?" Vered asked of the woman.

"Patrin. Lorens must have reported to him. He comes for the Demon Crown."

"How?"

"He'll use Lorens as a pawn," she said. "We dare not harm the prince. Our quest would turn to dust, if we did. But we cannot allow him to seize the crown and use it for Patrin's gain either."

"A pity we didn't leave the crown hidden in the Iron Range, then lured Lorens out. That would keep the crown free of Patrin," said Vered.

"What keeps the wizard away from it is Alarice's spell," snapped Santon.

For an instant, it was as if time stopped. Birtle Santon knew instantly what he had said. The mocking laughter told that Patrin had been spying and had overheard.

"So?" came the wizard's voice. "The lovely white-haired lady's name is Alarice. My spells now carry your name, Alarice, and are magnified in their power tenfold. More!"

"I know your name, too, Patrin," she said, but the stricken look told that she had lost much of her leverage. Repeatedly, the Glass Warrior had said that Patrin was the superior sorcerer. She had held him at bay only through knowing his name—and his ignorance of hers. That advantage had vanished in an instant's carelessness.

"I am sorry," Santon said. "I did not think."

"No," mocked Patrin. "You did not. But I applaud you for the slip. In fact, should you give me the Demon Crown without further struggle, I will allow you and your friend to leave the City of Stolen Dreams unharmed."

"And the Glass Warrior?"

"You mean Alarice?" the wizard taunted. "She must remain behind. For her, I have special plans. She has dreams. No," he hurriedly corrected himself. "She has *dreams*. I want them for my own!"

"Santon, Vered, leave the city. At once," she said. "You can do nothing against him. This is my battle."

"No," they said as one. "We all leave or none does."

"Foolish bravery on your part," said Patrin. He entered the room. At his elbow stood Lorens. The apprentice wizard basked in his master's approval. "That was your only opportunity."

Patrin's lips began moving, but no audible sounds emerged. Vered felt himself being crushed to death. He saw Santon struggling in an unseen grip, too. The magical death coming at them from all sides could not be evaded. They stood struggling futilely, the weight of the world slowly pressing the life from them.

"Lord Patrin, the bitch!" warned Lorens.

Alarice drew her glass sword and walked forward, as if she had no care to occupy her. The glass tip rose and pointed at Patrin. Vered thought she would lunge. Instead, she paused. Red lightnings danced along the tip, growing in power.

"Patrin, die!" the Glass Warrior shrieked. The flaming crimson bolt leaped from the tip of her glass rod and smashed squarely into Patrin's chest. The wizard staggered. Vered gasped in relief when the pressure around his chest suddenly lifted. Alarice's attack had drawn Patrin's full attention.

Vered wiped sweat from his eyes and sucked in huge draughts of air to steady himself. But Vered saw nothing he could do to aid Alarice. She and Patrin stood less than a pace apart. The air between them turned silvery, then translucent, then flowed into a liquid carrying writhing, slippery beasts unseen on this or any other world. Their spells constituted an attack more powerful than any he could mount with his puny glass weapon.

"Santon, get him. The apprentice!" Even as he called to his friend, Vered dived forward, his body crossing in front of Lorens' legs. The apprentice went down in a heap.

"I curse you!" shrieked Lorens. "You are mine. You—" The young man's head snapped back when Santon's powerful fist struck him squarely on the jaw.

"You didn't have to break it," said Vered. He ran knowing fingers along the line of the fallen Lorens' jawbone.

"I broke my hand." Santon rubbed it against his chest.

"He'll be all right. He's just knocked out." Vered rolled out from the tangle of legs and came to his feet, ready once more to aid Alarice. Both he and Birtle Santon stood and stared.

The magics burned and froze, surged and waited. For any not dealing in the most esoteric of spells, this battle would mean instant death.

"She's losing," said Santon, anguish in his voice. "See how she looks? Her face, her lovely face!"

Alarice faded and lost opacity even as Patrin grew in stature.

"The Demon Crown will be mine!" cried Patrin. "You are yielding to me, Alarice. Yield and die miserably!"

"He uses her name as a weapon." The sound of Santon's pitying voice tore at Vered. He knew his friend blamed himself for this. If he had not carelessly uttered the woman's name, Patrin could not have used it against her in his spells.

"We must do something." Vered rocked from

side to side, indecision eating at him. He was no wizard. Neither was Santon. How could they fight magic when they controlled none?

"The City of Stolen Dreams," said Vered, almost in wonder. "That's it. It must be!"

He pushed Santon aside and ran to the wall. He quickly went along it until he found another niche containing a sealed dream trap. He seized the jar and ripped off the wax seal. In the same motion, Vered heaved it at Patrin.

"What are you doing?" cried Santon.

"The dreams. Let him deal with them *and* Alarice."

"See how he uses them?" raged Santon. "He grows more powerful!"

And so it seemed. The dream trap had broken at Patrin's feet. Whatever had been contained within fed the wizard's abilities. Alarice weakened even more, sinking to her knees, battling and losing.

"No!" cried Vered. "That is just one jar. Throw them all! Let him experience a hundred perverted dreams!" Vered began heaving the magical dream traps at Patrin. When Santon saw the effect on the wizard, he joined his friend. The pair tossed the fragile jars from two sides. Try as he might, Patrin could not dodge both. Vered had no idea what dreams—what nightmares—they released, but the effect on Patrin was dramatic.

The wizard's lips pulled back in a soundless shriek. He tore at his hair and jerked from side to side, as if they drove burning spikes into his belly.

"Alarice," whispered Santon. "She is destroying him with her magic!"

Vered dared to hope again. The Glass Warrior stood on shaky legs and turned her full attention to Patrin. The man clawed at his face now, gouging out bloody chunks. When he tore out his eyes, Vered knew the wizard posed no further threat. Patrin sank down and seemed to melt. Alarice's magics reduced him to a smoldering puddle of grease.

"Dead," she gasped out. She fell face forward onto the floor. Santon rushed to her and turned her over. He cradled her head in his lap. The eyes looking up had lost their gray coldness. Only love shone there now.

"Alarice, my darling," Santon said, holding her close.

"I love you, too," she said in a voice almost too faint to be heard.

"We've won."

"Yes, Santon, we've won. You've won."

Something in her tone caused Santon to stiffen. "You're going to be fine. You'll recover. You're just tired, drained. The battle . . ."

"The battle killed me. Patrin's spell burns on within my breast. No one can halt its slow progress."

"No!"

"Yes, my love." She swallowed. A frail hand reached up to touch Santon's cheek. "Promise me. Promise me you'll return Lorens to Porotane and see him crowned as king. The land must be united or my death is in vain."

"You won't die. You won't," Santon said.

Vered put his hand on his friend's shoulder and squeezed gently. Vered reached over and closed the Glass Warrior's eyelids. "She has succeeded, Santon," he said quietly. "She achieved her goal." In a lower voice, he added, "She loved you very much."

Birtle Santon held her while the building around them turned translucent, transparent, slowly vanished. Even when the streets and other buildings faded from sight, Birtle Santon held her.

Only when the harsh desert winds whipped around him did he lower her head to the sand.

CHAPTER EIGHTEEN

Birtle Santon stood and stared at Alarice, no expression on his face. But Vered saw the tear slowly rolling down one dusty cheek and leaving a muddy track. The hot winds whipping across the Desert of Sazan quickly sucked up the moisture and left only a dried trail to mark its passing.

"Patrin killed her," said Santon.

"She destroyed him," said Vered, hand on his friend's shoulder. "She destroyed his greatest work, too. The City of Stolen Dreams is no more." He gestured to take in the emptiness of the desert. "When the wizard died, his dreams died with him."

"Evil dreams. They were evil."

Vered felt the powerful muscles ripple under his grip. He tried to stop Birtle but the man was far too strong. Santon whirled and drew his battle-ax, intent clear. A few paces away lay Lorens. Patrin's young apprentice stirred, one hand exploring his jaw where Santon had hit him.

"You can't," pleaded Vered. "He's our king!"

"He's the demon-damned wizard's apprentice."

"Lorens is the heir to the throne. Alarice

wanted him on the throne. She risked her life—
she *gave* her life!—to put him there."

Santon had passed beyond reason. He
shrugged his powerful shoulder and sent Vered
reeling. The smaller man hit and rolled, somer-
saulting over and coming to his feet. Without
thinking, he charged like a rogue bull. Vered's
arms circled Santon's waist and the force of his
charge carried both men forward. Santon's ax fell
from his grip and dangled by the thick leather
thong. This prevented him from swinging it and
splitting Vered's skull.

"Stop, think, damn you. Think about why
we've come this far!" Vered fought a silent Santon,
but the life had gone from the man. He fought
without purpose. When Vered got behind him and
pinned him face down in the sand, Santon ceased
to fight.

"There," Vered said. "Will you behave?" He
rolled off and stayed on one knee, ready for
renewed wrestling. If Santon had the fire of old
Vered knew he would have been an easy victim.
Santon might lack an arm, but the left had overde-
veloped and was prodigiously strong. As a result of
this and his many hours of practice, few men with
normal strength and two arms could best him. The
exhaustion Vered felt welling inside him told that a
strong breeze might knock him over. A fight was
beyond his winning.

"He doesn't deserve to live. Patrin trained
him."

"Away from the wizard's influence, he might
be different."

"Normal?"

"What wizard is normal?" asked Vered. "Except Alarice," he added hastily.

"No," said Santon. "Even she was not of the common people. She was special—she was also a wizard."

Vered went to Lorens' side and helped the man sit up. A large bruise had formed on his chin, and a lump the size of a small egg made speaking difficult for him.

"Where's the city?" he asked, his bright blue eyes darting about. "And my lord? Where's Patrin?"

"Dead," Vered said with some enthusiasm. "The Glass Warrior perished in the battle, too. That was a magical fight about which legends are born and ballads sung."

"My master is dead?" Shock clouded Lorens' face.

"Does this bother you? He seemed a cruel and thoughtless master."

"But he was all the family I've ever known."

"What of your sister?" asked Santon. The man's intent seemed clear. If Lokenna lived, the apprentice could die for his master's sins.

"She is dead. Long dead. She betrayed me. Only Lord Patrin helped me."

Santon slumped. "Then you are the one and only true ruler of Porotane. We have come far to install you on the throne."

The shock began to fade as Lorens gathered his wits. "Is the City of Stolen Dreams truly gone?"

"Like that." Vered snapped his fingers.

"My master *and* my home have deserted me."

Vered refrained from pointing out that Patrin had not willingly left his apprentice. Had Alarice been less capable, Patrin would have killed them all and taken the Demon Crown.

"The crown," Vered said to Santon. "Where is it?"

"There." Santon picked it up. The black velvet bag seemed none the worse from dirt or wear. He peered inside. "It still glows its ghastly emerald color."

"The Demon Crown?" Lorens forced his way to his feet. He wobbled slightly, then reached for the bag. "Give it to me. It's mine!"

As if one brain powered three arms, both Santon and Vered shoved the bag holding the crown from the young man's grasp.

"Not until you ascend the throne," said Vered. "Those are the orders given us by Alarice."

"But the Demon Crown is rightfully mine! I am of the royal blood. You told me so."

"Patrin did lie to you on this point," Vered said cautiously.

"Whether my master did or not is meaningless. I can *use* the crown. Such power should not be wasted."

"Such power is for the good of the people of Porotane," Santon said gruffly. "As the Glass Warrior ordered, so shall it be. You will be crowned when you assume the throne and not one instant before."

"I can force you to relinquish it," Lorens said in a nasty tone.

"Of course you can," Vered said smoothly, before Santon could give a toss to his wrist strap that would put the handle of the battle-ax in his meaty grip. "But how are you going to survive? Simply wearing the Demon Crown does not provide you with the knowledge we possess."

"I am a wizard. Patrin taught me well."

"Then conjure me a drink. I am thirsty. You

promised a fine white wine from the Uvain Plateau. I never received it."

"I cannot do such magic."

"So reduce me to ash," snapped Vered. "And then let yourself die in this miserable desert. The Desert of Sazan is not known for its caring attitude, whether you wear a crown or not."

"How far is it to the edge of the desert?"

"A day's travel," said Santon. The smile crossing the wizard-king's face turned nasty. Santon added without pause, "To the Iron Range. Another week crossing it. I doubt if any this far north of Rievane know the waterholes as well as Vered and I."

"The Iron Range is hot and dry, drier than the desert."

"And on the other side of this mountain range?" asked Lorens.

"Brigands, warring rebel bands all too eager to slay any pretender to the throne and seize Porotane for themselves, others." Vered did not mention the legions of phantoms roaming the land. Let those come as a surprise to the would-be king. Vered slowly began to agree with Santon about removing this arrogant demon-spawn permanently.

If Alarice had lived, would she permit such as Lorens to rule Porotane?

Vered had no answer. He could only hope that Lorens became more civil and the lingering effects of Patrin's life-long education wore off.

"You have made your point," said Lorens. "Lead me to Porotane. Until then, we need one another."

"No," said Santon, dark rage barely masked. "You need us. We have no use for you."

Vered whispered to his friend. "We get off to a bad start with the next king of Porotane."

"Why change our ways now?" said Santon. He turned and lumbered off, finding their horses on the far side of a sand dune. Ten minutes later, they rode slowly for the edge of the Desert of Sazan.

"We needed Alarice and her scrying tools," said Santon. He turned in the saddle and peered at the towering black peaks of the Iron Range. It had taken three times as long for them to find their way back to Porotane as it had to traverse the passes originally.

"I miss her, too," said Vered. He sat astride his horse, feeling ready to die. He had not bathed in a month and smelled like a charnel pit. His skin itched constantly, his clothing hung in tatters, his belly grumbled from the pitiful food they were able to find, and for a taste of good wine he would have cheerfully wrestled Kalob and forty other demons.

"Is this all there is? I expected more." Lorens rode the strongest of the three horses. The other animals had died en route. "If I am to rule, I want Porotane to be exquisite, a gem, a work of art!"

"It's endured twenty years of civil war," said Vered. "Actually, this is a quieter section of the country."

"Quiet? With that howling?"

"What howling, Lorens?" demanded Santon. He cocked his head to one side and strained. Turning to Vered, he said, "It is a familiar sound. I think it is a phantom."

"We have too little time," said Vered. "We must ride for the castle. Duke Freow leaned against death's door when Alarice left. He might already be gone."

"That would mean Baron Theoll has assumed the throne," said Santon. He spat.

"Maybe not. The duke was a strong one," said Vered.

"It matters naught who is on the throne. The regent, this duke who is supposed to be my uncle, does not sound fit to rule. And the baron of whom you speak with such loathing, cannot stand against me. Not when I wear the Demon Crown."

"In that you are probably right," said Vered. He touched the saddlebag where he carried the crown in its crystalline case. "The mere sight of anyone wearing the crown will rally many to your banner."

"Will it bring you, Vered? Or you, Santon?" Those bright blue eyes fixed firmly on the men. "I know you hate me because my master killed the Glass Warrior. But they were enemies. She killed the only teacher I've known."

Vered saw a hint of the true and likable Lorens shine forth. "Hate you?" he said. "No. Distrust anyone who can use such power as is offered by the Demon Crown? Definitely."

"I can accept that. I must. But what of that horrid howling?"

"A phantom," said Santon. "No other cause presents itself."

"Let's ride. Due west, then to the north until we find a branch of the River Ty. We can follow it to the castle."

"What of this phantom? I have never encountered one."

"Ride and we can talk," said Vered.

Barely had they gone a hundred yards when a miniature whirlwind caught up leaves and debris from the trail in front of them and carried it high into the air. The familiar mistiness of the phantom's body took on substance.

"That is a phantom?" asked Lorens, fascinated. "All it needs is a proper burial to be put to rest?"

"Something like that," said Santon. "This one seems intent on blocking our way."

"You there, phantom," called out Vered. "Why do you stop us? We are simple travelers on our way to . . . the Uvain Plateau."

"Liars!" whined the phantom. "You are spies. You report back to those in the castle. You report to Theoll!"

"Not him," argued Vered. "We have no desire to see the baron grow more powerful."

"Spies! I will stop you from reporting."

"Reporting what?" asked Santon.

The phantom's torso darkened and the mistiness turned to opaque body. "You cannot pass me. You will die on this spot as I died."

"A trade," said Vered. "We'll find your body and—" His words were cut off by the phantom's attack. Vered had not appreciated the power locked up within the ghostly beings until this instant. The wispy arms reached out and then solidified around his throat. He choked. The phantom spun wildly about its central core and rose, taking Vered with it. The brown-haired man found himself being lifted high into the air.

Strangling, he fought to pry loose the phantom's fingers. Only the fingers choking him had substance. Cool, moist fog met his feet and hands as he strove to free himself.

The blood pounded like drums in his temples and his vision blurred. Vered's struggles diminished as his strength fled. He had been close to exhaustion before encountering the phantom. This battle gave promise of being his final one. He fought, but the struggles grew ever weaker.

The howling he heard he thought came from within his own mind. Did demons come to ferry him to hell? He knew that the saints could not make such a soul-rending noise. And what had he done to entice them when the final entry on the Death Rota had been made?

He gasped when he fell hard to the ground. It took several seconds for Vered to realize that the phantom shrieked in anguish, not demons. The ghost whirled around and around, stirring up a miniature cyclone with its body. With a tiny *pop*! it vanished.

"What happened?" he asked, rubbing his throat. He felt the weals circling the flesh. This had been all too real and wasn't the product of exhaustion delirium.

"I had never dealt with phantoms before. The spells are difficult to remember. It took several tries before I drove it off." Lorens sat on his horse, his expression one of awe. "The spell I used worked!"

"You're a wizard's apprentice. Why shouldn't your spells work?"

"But you don't understand. Patrin never allowed me to cast a spell. Oh, simple ones to start cooking fires, things like that. This was a powerful one."

"You destroyed the phantom?" asked Vered. He pulled himself back onto horseback.

"I can't. Only consecrating the phantom's

grave can do that. But I drove it off."

"Listen hard," said Santon.

"Not more phantoms," groaned Vered. "I've had enough of just one. If it's gone and found a dozen friends . . ."

"Hoofbeats. Many. The ground trembles under them."

"The phantom scouted for a band of ruffians," said Lorens, his eyes unfocused and his face slack. What he concentrated on, neither man knew or was willing to ask.

"Never heard of a phantom spying for rebels, but it might be possible. By the demons, why not?" Santon pointed. "Let's try to hide. In our condition, we'd never be able to outride or outfight them."

"A sage suggestion," Vered said.

They rode into a small copse and dismounted. It took long minutes to tether their steeds and build up a shielding wall of brush. Any rider chancing more than a casual glance in their direction would surely see them. But it was all they had time for. The riders pounded hard into view.

"Let's hope they keep riding," said Santon.

They did not. They reined in and milled about the spot where the phantom had originally appeared.

"Can you hear what they say?" asked Vered.

"Give me the Demon Crown," said Lorens. "With it I can learn much."

Vered felt himself torn by the request. Lorens' attitude had changed only slightly. Still self-centered, still obnoxious and demanding, he was the perfect apprentice for a demon-spawn like his unlamented master Patrin. But Vered could not deny that the wizard-king had saved his life. And occasionally sparks of humanity shone through the tough veneer of his arrogance.

Vered reached for the saddlebag containing the Demon Crown.

"Do you know what you are doing?" demanded Birtle Santon.

"We need information. With the crown, he can get it." Vered drew out the box containing the crown. To Lorens he said, "Remember what happened the first time you wore the Demon Crown."

"I did not know what to expect."

"It is like a powerful drug. It will become *your* master if you let it. Wear the crown for only a few seconds, then return it to the box."

"If I don't?"

Santon moved slightly, the heavy battle-ax in his hand. His intent was obvious. Lorens nodded and held out his hand to accept the crown.

The brilliant green glow faded to a more bearable emerald when the Demon Crown came into contact with Lorens' flesh. He quickly lifted the circlet to his head and placed it squarely on his own brow.

Vered watched in fascination. A shock went through Lorens' body. He stood rigidly, teeth grinding, eyes screwed shut. Sweat beaded his forehead and began to run down into his eyes. But it mattered little. Lorens did not see with eyes or hear with ears. The Demon Crown provided those senses for him.

And what else? Vered wished he knew, but such knowledge was barred from him.

"The leader," Lorens said in a low voice. "He rides for a rebel called Dews Gaemock. The phantom did spy for them. It was the brother of one in the band. Baron Theoll's troops killed him. No, not Theoll's. One close to him. The Archbishop Nosto might be the one doing it during the Inquisition."

"The Inquisition!" exclaimed Santon. "They put their own people to the Question!"

"Quiet," said Vered. "He does not dare wear the crown much longer. We must learn what we can."

"Farther. Oh, by the saints, I am traveling so far!" Lorens staggered. Vered supported him, then eased him to the ground where the wizard-king sat, eyes still closed. "I see Gaemock. I *see!*"

"What do you see?"

"He has many phantoms scouting for him. They cannot enter the castle. Spells bind them if they do. They suffer horribly, but Gaemock uses them well in the field."

"What of the company not a bowshot from us?" asked Santon. "Gaemock might be foremost among the rebels, but these are the ones most likely to gut us."

"Turmoil within the castle. Death. No, not death. But close. Theoll. I see him. Such a small man, so insignificant-looking." Lorens cackled evilly. "He is no worthy opponent. I can crush him beneath my boot heel as I would a desert scorpion."

"The rebels," insisted Santon.

Vered licked his lips nervously. He cast a glance over his shoulder in the direction of the rebel band still in the clearing where they had encountered the phantom. Had they summoned back the banished spirit? Or had they seen the hoofprints heading for this copse?

"Theoll engineers Freow's death. He places

poison in the duke's food. But another—who?—I cannot see who!—removes it. The duke has an unknown protector. Archbishop Nosto? Possibly."

"Damn the court intrigues!" raged Santon.

"You're right," said Vered. "He's too caught up in spying on Theoll." Vered sucked in his breath and held it. Quick hands grabbed the Demon Crown from Lorens' head. The explosions in his own body burned and froze, but Vered got the crown back to the crystalline box. He dropped the magical crown and shut the lid. For long seconds, visions fluttered before his eyes.

"Duke Freow will die within a few hours," said Lorens. "And Baron Theoll will ascend the throne of Porotane."

"For us, that means naught," said Santon.

"Why not?" asked Vered. "We might have to fight both rebels and the baron's soldiers to get Lorens into the castle if the duke dies before our return."

"Prepare to fight just the rebels. They've seen us!"

Vered peered through the screen of bushes and saw that his friend spoke truly. The rebels had found their hoofprints and were slowly following them directly to their hiding place.

CHAPTER NINETEEN

Vered pushed aside the branches and saw the rebels moving quicker now that they had a spoor. Some worked to free swords and battle-axes. Still others unlimbered bows.

"The archers won't be of any good in the forest," said Santon. "When they are mounted, we have a small advantage on the others."

"Damned small," muttered Vered. He drew the short sword of shining glass that Alarice had given him. Against so much steel it seemed a puny weapon. But something of the Glass Warrior's courage went with the blade. Vered felt himself forgetting his tiredness and surging with strength.

"Can you use a sword, Lorens?" asked Santon. "If so, take the one sheathed on my horse."

"Alarice's blade?" asked Vered, startled. "You'd let him use her weapon?"

"We need all the fighting prowess we can muster," said Santon. "They are upon us!"

With that, the burly man lunged through the thin wall of bushes and swung his battle-ax. He grunted as it cut into a rider's fleshy thigh. The rebel shrieked in agony and toppled from his mount. He landed heavily and tried to wiggle away. The blood fountaining from his thigh weakened him quickly. Vered saw him die before the next rider knew what was happening.

Santon's ax swung again, this time the heavy spiked ball on the back of the ax head crushing a horse's leg and sending its rider tumbling. Vered pushed through the gap in the bushes left by his bigger companion. The short sword lacked the reach needed, but the dense trees and tangle of underbrush aided Vered. The rebels could not get into position quickly enough to launch a concerted attack.

Vered batted aside a steel blade and leaped upward, the tip of the glass blade working under leather armor. He felt an instant's resistance, then the blade sank into the rebel's side. Vered doubted he punctured any vital organs, but the rider fell from his horse. Just eliminating one of the score against them counted heavily.

Santon fought like a madman, felling two more. Vered fought but had less success. His opponent proved more wary and retreated quickly.

"They fight like a legion!" cried one rebel. "But there are only two."

This bit of information filtered along the rebel ranks. They withdrew to the edge of the forest and formed a ragged battle line. Santon and Vered caught their breath as the ruffians prepared to attack.

"We're dead men," said Vered. "They know our number."

"And surprise is lost to us."

"Even worse," moaned Vered, "they stopped using their muscles and started using their heads.

They'll flow over us in one rush like the River Ty overflows its bank every spring."

Santon sucked in a deep breath, then exhaled slowly. "Our lives mean naught—"

"Speak for yourself!" cried Vered, incensed.

"—in comparison to Lorens. We must see that he gets to the castle. If Freow is dying, Lorens must ascend the throne."

"You've changed your tune greatly from wanting to slit the royal bastard's throat."

"Alarice died finding him. For her memory, I'll see Lorens on the throne."

"We're not likely to see anything but our own deaths," said Vered. "Look."

"The phantom that Lorens banished. It has returned." Santon sagged slightly. "So much for our apprentice wizard's spell-casting."

"It is another phantom," Lorens said from behind. "The rebels use a dozen or more of the ghosts to scout for them. This one is recently appeared. I can banish it, too, but other spells occupy me."

"Be sure to compose the last verse of your death song. You want the saints to look favorably on you when they come for your soul."

"I will not die this day. Nor will you."

Vered ducked as an arrow winged toward him. The broad head slipped with liquid ease into a tree trunk to his side. He tried to imagine what that arrow would have done to his body. He shuddered at the thought.

"They stand back and think to pick us off," said Santon. "Stay behind the trees and—Lorens! Stop, wait, don't!"

Santon dropped his ax and tried to grab the

wizard-king. A dozen arrows drove him back to cover.

"He goes to his own death so willingly," Vered said in wonder.

Arrows flew until the air whistled with their passage. Strangely, however, none touched Lorens. He floated in a bubble amid the feathered flights of death.

The rebel leader held up a sword, motioning for the archers to cease. Lorens stopped a dozen paces from the mounted man.

"I go to the castle," said Lorens. "It is not wise to hinder me. I go there to accept the monarchy of Porotane."

"Oh," scoffed the rebel. "So you're another pretender to the throne? The woods are filled with them. But in you I detect something of the wizard. Well, good Sir Wizard, the woods are full of sorcerers aspiring to the throne, too."

Lorens said nothing. The fifteen men in the rebel party spread out slightly, without being ordered to do so. Vered saw the tension mounting in their ranks. Their leader would order Lorens' death at any instant.

"I am of the royal blood," said Lorens.

"Aren't they all?"

A dozen archers loosed arrows. None arrived at their target. Lorens held out his hands, now glowing a pale red. From each finger flew a crackling red spark that intercepted an arrow. The arrows stopped in mid-flight, turned, and wobbled off in unexpected directions.

"A nice trick, wizard," said the rebel leader. "I have seen better, though." Without another word, the rebel whipped his sword around and urged his horse forward. He rode Lorens down.

Vered winced. The apprentice wizard's spell failed him at the last instant; the rebel's sword slashed through the upper portion of Lorens' arm producing a cut bloodier than it was dangerous. The rebel turned his horse and prepared to gallop back for the killing stroke.

Vered felt the sudden tension in the air. Even Santon, who professed no magical abilities at all, stiffened in expectation. In the distance a phantom howled, "The spell. He casts a powerful spell!"

The flames that engulfed the rebel band produced no heat, but the searing light dazzled Vered. He turned away. The light reflecting off the leaves and trunks of the trees proved almost as blinding. Then it vanished as suddenly as it had appeared. He turned back to see Lorens standing alone in the small clearing.

"What magic is that?" wondered Santon. "I've never heard of a wizard able to command such force."

Vered rushed out to Lorens' side. The man stood stock still, his blue eyes glazed over. Vered touched him. Lorens toppled forward, as rigid as any tree felled in the forest. Vered tried to break the wizard's fall and failed. Together, they went down in a heap.

"Whatever he did, it drained him completely," said Santon. He rolled Lorens over and examined him. "I've seen men look like this—after a week-long debauch."

Vered scrambled to his feet and looked at the tiny piles of gray ash that marked where the rebels and their horses had been. "And that is how I feel after a week-long binge." Vered ran his fingers through the gray ash. He brushed it off and moved away, trying not to shake too hard. "I'll get the horses. You get Lorens into shape for travel. We've a long journey ahead if we are to arrive at the castle before Duke Freow dies."

Vered stumbled off, avoiding walking on the ash as he returned to the grove where their horses pawed the ground nervously. He soothed the animals, then led them back to the clearing. Santon had Lorens sitting upright, but the wizard-king showed no signs of life.

"Is he all right?" asked Vered.

"He lives. The spell-casting took everything out of him. How long this shock will last is beyond my knowing."

They heaved Lorens over the saddle and tied him down. The ride would be uncomfortable, but in his present condition, he would not notice. Vered climbed into the saddle and found this almost more than he could do. His body rebelled at any strain he placed on it.

"No more fights," he told Santon. "I have no reserve strength to draw upon."

Santon's shaggy head nodded. He rode with shoulders sagging.

"What a fine trio we make. All hail the conquerors returning to install the rightful king! Why, I am so exhausted, even the promise of a coronation orgy does nothing to perk me up."

"You're not exhausted," Santon said. "You must be dead."

Vered saved his strength and did not answer. But he wondered at the truth in his friend's words. How would he know when he died? Vered glanced about and found a pair of shimmering columns marking the spots where phantoms stalked the land. Would he end up like them? Or was death something else? He was too tired to ponder such philosophical notions. Vered let his horse go where it wanted. His head rocked forward and he slept.

"More trouble," moaned Vered. "I'll never get to bathe or change into decent clothing." He leaned forward in the saddle, hands spasmodically clutching at the pommel. Arrayed around the castle were rebel troops.

"I thought Alarice said that Dews Gaemock had retreated for the year," said Santon. "She scryed constantly to learn of Freow's fate."

"It seems that Freow's impending death—perhaps actual death, by this late time—has brought out the vultures."

"Gaemock's not that bad," said Santon. "Truth to tell, I have more sympathy for him than I do for Theoll."

"And I," agreed Vered, "but it is difficult to join a band of rebels when all they seem to do is waylay honest travelers and rob them."

Vered glanced over at Lorens. The wizard-king's head lolled forward, bobbing as his horse walked. Since he had reduced the rebel band to ash blowing away in the breeze, he had not spoken. Vered worried that the strain of casting such a potent spell had burned out Lorens' brain. His blue eyes stayed open as he rode, but no intelligence shone through. Vered had not liked Lorens much, but for Alarice he would tolerate the heir to the throne of Porotane.

Now he only felt pity for him.

"Find a way in?" he asked of Birtle Santon.

"We must. Getting through the lines might prove easy, even with him in such a condition." Santon's critical gaze appraised Lorens' physical set and judged the young man wanting. "But getting into the castle will prove even more difficult."

"Who under siege would let in scragglylooking travelers such as us, eh?" said Vered.

"We might enter under a flag of truce."

"More likely they would fill us with arrows or pour burning amber on our heads. No, Santon, my good friend, stealth will win us entry quicker than honesty."

"I leave that to you, Vered. You always were the . . . craftier."

"You chose your word well. I do not tolerate being called a thief and a liar."

"Even if those are truer descriptions?" taunted Santon.

"You never complained before. In fact, you always joined in. For the adventure, you said."

"Only for the adventure. You keep life from becoming too tedious."

Vered subsided and studied the dispersal of Gaemock's rebel troops. No matter how much he thought Dews Gaemock an unrepentant ruffian and thief, Vered had to acknowledge the man's tactical ability. With a handful of troops, Gaemock prevented easy entry—and exit.

"Twilight," he decided aloud. "We try when the sun begins to set. Shadows dance then and make less clear a man's intentions."

"And thoughts turn to a warm supper and a night's sleep," finished Santon. "I agree to that, but how do we enter the castle once past Gaemock's lines?"

"Alarice mentioned a postern gate. I think the key of glass is the one she used for entry. If we

cross the River Ty and go directly for the western
wall of the castle, do you think we can find it?"

"The wall is long and her description was
vague." Santon stared directly at the castle, but
Vered saw the moisture beading in the corners of
the man's eyes at the mention of the Glass Warrior.
Santon had cared deeply for Alarice, and still
mourned.

"There is one last matter to consider," said
Vered. "When we enter the castle, what then?"

Santon looked again at Lorens. He shook his
head and indicated that he had no idea. They
might succeed, only to find they presented a brain-
less husk as king of Porotane.

They rode slowly well behind Gaemock's battle lines. Occasional arrows arched from the castle
battlements, but always fell short of the lines.
Vered estimated that the royal archers intentional-
ly fired short by a hundred yards—and that
Gaemock's men stayed back twice that for safety.
The antagonists played a deadly game, daring,
taunting, moving, always challenging. He had to
be certain that Lorens stayed beyond the range of
both sides until the young king consolidated power
within the castle.

Vered snorted. With Lorens in this trance, it
might all go for naught.

But they could only try.

"It's later than I intended," said Vered.

"The patrols could not be hastened along their
routes," said Santon. "We have done well avoiding
Gaemock's rebels."

"Half-dragging *him* is slowing us," complained Vered. Lorens sat docilely, staring into

their cooking fire. He had eaten with deliberate mechanical jaw movements, showing neither approval nor disdain for their simple repast. When Lorens moved, he moved only in a straight line. To dodge and hide or to change his direction required considerable effort on the parts of Vered and Santon.

"We wouldn't have gotten this far if he hadn't stopped the rebels," Santon pointed out.

"Better to have died out there than to be caught between Gaemock and Theoll." Vered grumbled under his breath, then said, "That's not so. We still live. We can finish what we started."

"For Alarice," Santon said quietly.

"And for ourselves. We've never been quitters. We need not begin now."

The dusk cloaked the River Ty in soft light and a buzzing cloud of insects. Bats swooped low to gorge themselves on their aerial meals, and the water rippled as fish surfaced to dine. Vered spent a considerable time swatting at the bugs trying to suck his blood. He cursed constantly as they forded a tributary to the river.

Halfway across, they sighted a sentry on the bank in front of them.

"Gaemock's?" Vered asked Santon.

"Without a doubt." Santon lifted his good arm and waved. He called out, "Hello! Ready for the shift change?"

Vered saw the sentry's confusion. He might have several hours remaining on his watch before relief came. But he dared hope and did not shout warnings to other sentries. He stood and waited for them to ride up on the muddy banks.

"You come from the main camp?" the sentry asked.

Vered felt sorry for the youngling. Hardly fifteen summers had passed since this one's birth. He had not yet had time to learn suspicion. Vered only hoped that it would not prove necessary to end the young guard's life before he could learn.

"From the other side," said Santon, his gruff, military bearing quelling any fears on the sentry's part. "You are Grogan's brother, aren't you?" Santon tipped his head to one side. Before the youth could answer, Santon said, "By all the saints, he's not the one!"

The sentry's confusion mounted. He had forgotten totally about passwords or security. "What do you mean? I have no brothers. No living brothers," he added sadly.

Santon cursed volubly. "They sent us to the wrong post. For that, give praise to the saints. Grogan died this afternoon, an arrow in his gullet."

The youth relaxed even more. "I don't even know this Grogan."

"An officer in the main camp."

Whether Santon had said too much and given them away or the youth's wits had returned and he realized that proper procedure had not been followed, Vered couldn't say. The expression altered on the boy's face. Before he could issue the challenge, Vered slipped his foot free of his stirrup cup, gauged the distance, and kicked hard. The toe of his boot crashed into the youth's head, knocking him back. The guard staggered and fell flat on his back, arms outstretched.

"He looks comfortable," observed Vered. "Just as if he's sleeping."

Santon fingered his battle-ax, then relaxed, his decision made. "We can reach the castle walls before he regains his senses. He won't even mention this little foray."

"Not unless he wants the hide stripped off his back by his officer's whips. Stupidity is never appreciated, whether the army be rebel or royal."

The trio rode on into the gathering night. By Santon's estimate, it lacked only an hour before midnight when they reached the castle wall. Most of the growth had been stripped away from the walls to give better vision, but they found an ill-traveled path that led them through a patch of trees and past a tangle of shrubs.

"There," said Vered. "I feel it in my bones."

Santon craned his neck back and studied the battlements above, seeking evidence of a trap. He saw nothing unusual. Shrugging, he silently indicated that Vered should investigate.

Vered slipped through the bushes, thorns tearing away clothing and skin. He winced but kept on. He could not contain his cry of happiness when he found the hidden door.

"Santon, hurry! I have it!"

The bushes rustled and Santon pushed through, leading Lorens. The young man had not regained a hint of his senses. For a moment, Vered considered whether they should continue or not. They might survive well outside the castle. Within the walls, they would be on unfamiliar ground, surrounded by enemies intent on slaying any intruder.

Should Baron Theoll find that their charge was Prince Lorens, their lives would end swiftly.

"We go in," decided Vered.

"Where else?" Santon shoved Lorens forward. For a fleeting instant, it seemed as if he emerged from his daze. The consciousness fled as quickly as it appeared.

Vered fumbled at his pouch and withdrew the glass key that had been Alarice's, fitted it into the lock, and turned. The lock snapped open easily. Vered lifted the latch and shouldered the door open. A dark corridor led through the wall. He pulled Lorens after him. Santon closed the door and said softly, "Lead the way, Vered."

"But it's as dark as a whale's gut!"

"Just pretend you're seeking out a married woman's boudoir and you want to avoid her husband."

"That I can do," said Vered. "I've done it enough times before."

"But how many times were successful?"

"All," Vered answered.

"All save this time," came a booming voice magnified by the narrow corridor walls. A torch flared, momentarily blinding Vered and Santon. "Do not reach for your weapons."

They stood in the shoulder-wide passageway, blinded and unable to retreat.

CHAPTER TWENTY

Vered tried to pull out his sword, but even the short length of the glass weapon proved too long for the narrow corridor. Behind him Lorens bumped against his elbow and Santon bellowed for them to retreat.

"Wait," Vered said. His eyes adjusted to the flickering light of the torch held by the man blocking their path. "Who are you?" Vered asked. He had detected no animosity in the man's original challenge.

"I, good sirs, am Harhar, Duke Freow's jester. Would you hear an amusing story?" Harhar spun about; bells tinkled lightly with his every movement. "Or would you prefer a dirty limerick?"

Harhar launched himself straight into the air, twisted nimbly, and landed on his head. Vered took an involuntary step forward to aid the dark-haired man. He stopped when he saw that Harhar had cunningly turned at the last possible instant and had rolled safely.

"Does that bring a smile to your lips? Or should I do something more?"

"How did you happen to be in this corridor?" demanded Birtle Santon. "Are you guarding the entryway?"

"Guard? Me?" Harhar laughed uproariously. "The baron would never trust me with such a role. Even that fount of kindness, Archbishop Nosto, ignores me. But I help Duke Freow."

"How?"

"I make him laugh. I have brought him back repeatedly from the edge of his grave with my jokes." Harhar pulled his legs up tightly against his chest and hugged his knees, his rattle by his side. The torch fell from his grip and landed on the floor. Vered scooped it up and peered at the jester. Harhar cried.

"What's wrong?"

"Duke Freow has died. Even my amusing capers could not save him."

"When? When did he die?"

"Early this morning, just before sunrise. He left me. He left us all."

"Has Theoll crowned himself ruler of Porotane?" Vered's sharp question brought the jester's wide, dark eyes up.

"An odd question. Who else? The Lady Johanna was unable to sleep with enough nobles to insure her ascendancy, though I am sure she got many in the castle to rise to her schemes."

"Just what we need," grumbled Santon. "A jester and a gossip."

"Who is this with you? He speaks little. Is he depressed? May I amuse him?"

"We need to get out of this corridor," said Vered. "A small room where we could go? Do you know of one, jester?"

"Harhar will show you! I know every room in the castle. I do!" The jester somersaulted off, heels kicking in the air with every rotation. He stopped, spun, and kicked open a door. The dusty room he rolled into served Vered's purposes well.

"Where does this door lead?" asked Santon, pressing his ear against a heavy panel. "There is a rhythmic hollow sound outside. Guards patrolling?"

"Verily, yes, that. But they are so easily distracted. That is how I came to this secret passage."

"Tell us about it," said Vered. He moved Lorens around and shoved the wizard-king into a chair. Some small flickering of interest shone behind those blue eyes, but Lorens did not speak.

"I saw you from above. From the battlements. I practice my jokes nightly to keep the guards amused. I happened to lean out to relieve myself when I saw you."

"May the saints be praised. We were quick enough to miss the yellow rain," said Santon. To Vered, he said, "I like this less and less. If Theoll has gained power, we are doomed. And if the likes of this crackbrained jester watch us entering, what chance do we have? All in the castle may know of our presence."

Vered nodded. He hated to admit defeat, but all that Santon said paralleled his own thoughts.

"Is he in need of cheering?" asked Harhar. He danced about in front of Lorens. "Who is he?"

"Quiet, fool," snapped Santon.

"Let him do his best—or worst," said Vered. "It can't hurt." He stared at Lorens. The young man had never recovered from casting the spell. He had said that Patrin had not allowed him to use the more potent spells. Had the casting somehow affected his mind? Or had it merely drained him? It mattered little to Vered. With Lorens in this condition, he could not challenge Theoll for the throne. Who would believe this mute, glassy-eyed man was the true heir?

"What are we going to do?" asked Santon.

Vered had no answer. "The jester does as good a job as we've done with Lorens."

"How do we prove him to be of the royal blood?" Santon slammed his fist against a table and exclaimed, "Damn you, Alarice! Why did you put such a burden on us?"

The jester turned and stared at him curiously, then returned to his capering.

"Santon," said Vered. "We agree that there is no hope with Lorens in his present condition. What do you think would happen if we put the Demon Crown upon his brow?"

"All it could do is kill him. At the moment, that might be preferable to this damnable uncertainty."

"Demon Crown?" croaked Harhar. "You have the Demon Crown? You know the Glass Warrior?"

"She is dead," Santon said with more than a hint of bitterness in his voice. "And yes, we have the crown. Get it, Vered. Put it on Lorens."

"Lorens?" cried the jester. "This is one of the royal twins? But how can this be?"

"The Glass Warrior entrusted us with returning Lorens to Porotane and seeing that he ascended the throne," said Vered. He carefully drew the Demon Crown from its velvet bag. The box within glowed brilliantly with the green from the Demon Crown. Vered flipped open the lid and moved as close to Lorens as he could get. He had to push the curious jester back.

"Is it safe for you to handle it?" asked Santon.

"For a moment. I cannot but wonder who in the family tree gave me the drop of royal blood."

"Start naming the outcasts," grumbled Santon.

Vered moved quickly. He picked up the crown and hastily transfered it to Lorens' head. The young wizard stiffened as the effect of the crown's magics worked on his brain. He smiled almost benignly.

"I am home," he said in a soft voice. "I have returned to my home!"

Lorens rose and turned slowly. His eyes focused past the cobweb-ridden stone walls in the small storage room. He used the powers of the Demon Crown to see *beyond*.

"Truly, he *is* King Lorens!" cried Harhar.

"It is our belief," said Vered. "At least, he's come out of his trance."

"Trance?" asked Lorens. "Yes, I was in a trance. The strain of casting the spell proved more than I had anticipated. But the Demon Crown gives power."

"It also demands a price for it," said Vered. But Lorens did not hear. He pushed past Santon and went into the corridor.

"Wait, Lorens, you dare not let Theoll learn of your presence." Vered's warning went unheeded. Lorens walked confidently past the patrolling guards. Vered and Santon exchanged glances. Vered smiled and shrugged, then hurried after Lorens. It seemed safer to be with the wizard-king than to be left behind.

Vered heard Harhar cackling to himself as they raced along the stony corridors, went up spiral staircases, and eventually emerged in the main audience chamber.

"Now there'll be trouble," whispered Santon. "Theoll is on the throne."

They stopped just inside the massive wooden doors of the chamber and watched. Vered looked around, trying to find the best escape route when Theoll ordered Lorens killed for his impertinence.

"What is this? We are discussing affairs of state!" bellowed Theoll from the throne.

"You discuss Gaemock's forces knocking at the castle gates," Lorens said with great confidence. "You ignore the ten other rebel bands, not aligned with Dews Gaemock, who march toward the castle. You should turn them against Gaemock. That would lift his siege."

"Who is this?" cried Theoll. "Guards! Remove this fool!"

Lorens walked slowly up the steps to the throne. Each step he took caused the Demon Crown to glow more brightly. By the time he reached the top step, no one in the room could look directly at Lorens. The wizard-king reached out, plucked Theoll from the throne, and cast him down the steps. Lorens turned and seated himself. The glow moderated; Lorens wore a shimmering curtain of light born in the Demon Crown.

"I am Lorens, son of Lamost. The Demon Crown is mine by right and by birth. I claim it—and the kingdom of Porotane."

"At least he no longer speaks of himself as a commoner," said Santon.

"How much else of Patrin's spurious education will he deny?" Vered wondered aloud. "He seems able to fend for himself."

"The Demon Crown has done that for him," said Santon.

"More," croaked Harhar. "It takes more to rule." The jester's eyes were wide at the sight of the wizard-king on the throne.

"Well said, fool," agreed Santon. "And we have no idea if he is capable."

"Baron Theoll," came Lorens' rumbling voice. "Order Captain Squann to attack Gaemock's main force immediately."

"What? That is suicidal!" Theoll pulled himself up to his full height. "You can't walk in and declare yourself king. You—"

Archbishop Nosto took Theoll by the elbow and spun the smaller man around. The two talked for several minutes, their argument heated. All the while, Lorens sat on the throne, his concentration elsewhere.

When Nosto made the final gesture of dismissal to Theoll, the cleric called out, "The Church supports King Lorens, true heir and wearer of Kalob's gift!"

"Send messengers immediately," said Lorens. "The fighting will be over in days if the other rebel bands learn that the true king has ascended the throne."

"It can't be that easy," muttered Santon.

Lorens turned toward Birtle Santon and shouted, "Yes, Santon, it is. I know what lies in their hearts and minds. The Demon Crown allows me that, just as I see and hear all that happens nearby."

"He couldn't have heard me," protested Santon.

"Not with his ears," agreed Vered. "You cannot know the power of the Demon Crown unless you've sampled it yourself. He *hears*. He *sees*."

"I am king of Porotane!" shouted Lorens.

Those assembled in the room fell to one knee and bowed their heads. Vered followed their lead, but from one corner of his eye he saw that Baron Theoll's obeisance to the new king came slower than that of the others. To most, Lorens might be king. But not to the diminutive baron.

"The burial should have been more," observed Santon. "After all, Freow ruled Porotane for twenty years."

"Only as regent," said Vered. "But I agree. It was as if Lorens denied all connection with those who have come before." Vered wondered if Lorens knew that the dead duke had not been his uncle, had been nothing more than an opportunistic pretender. Even if he did, Vered puzzled over why the young king did not acknowledge Freow's contribution for so many years.

The wars might have been worse.

"There," said Santon, nudging Vered in the ribs. "There're the first representatives from the rebel bands."

"Only three? Lorens spoke of ten."

"A start," said Santon.

Vered watched as the three marched across the vast expanse between the chamber door and the foot of the steps leading to the throne. Harhar cavorted and rolled about at one side of the throne, oblivious to the pomp and ceremony of the occasion. For the first time in two decades, rebels met to discuss a truce.

"At last we meet in the flesh," Lorens said in a voice an octave deeper than usual. Vered noted how the young king had grown in stature while wearing the Demon Crown; it affected his voice, also.

"We have never met, even in spirit," declared one rebel leader.

"Not so, Tuvonne. I have visited your secret councils and listened to your schemes. You do not bargain in good faith, not when your soldiers march against the castle under the banner of truce." Lorens gestured to the guards lining the walls of the immense audience chamber.

"Wait, stop!" cried Tuvonne. "You violate the terms of the truce!"

"You violated them before entering." The rest of Lorens' words died in the whistle of arrows flying. Tuvonne screamed as a dozen—more—pierced his flesh.

"Uh, King Lorens," ventured another rebel.

"You declare allegiance to me, Belmorgan? Or do you allow yourself to be seduced by Tember of Farreach's sister, Oturra?" Lorens pointed to another rebel.

"No, my king, no!" protested Belmorgan. The man fell to his knee and cried, "I am ecstatic that one of the true royal blood again sits on the throne."

"Good. Then divert your troops against those of Tuvonne. Destroy that traitor's force totally."

"Your Majesty!"

"Destroy them and you will become First Duke of Porotane. And," Lorens said, sarcasm coloring his words, "if you still want her, Oturra will be your consort."

"You are most generous, Majesty."

"Only to those who serve me well." Lorens turned his attention to the remaining rebel leader.

"You, Tember of Farreach, have one chance only of declaring allegiance to the throne of Porotane. How say you? Loyalty to me or death?"

Tember dropped and pledged his unswerving loyalty to King Lorens of Porotane.

"The others who refused to attend. I know the most intimate details of their battle plans, of their lives. In your service to the throne, this information will be given you. None dare oppose the one who wears the Demon Crown!"

Blazing green swathed his body as Lorens stood and shoved a shaking fist into the air.

Lorens swirled around and vanished through a door immediately behind the throne. Harhar followed Belmorgan and Tember from the chamber, shaking a rattle at them and making lewd comments about Tember's sister and Belmorgan's mistress. The men strained to keep their blades firmly in sheath. But Harhar's intimate knowledge of Oturra's affairs stayed them. The jester could have learned such matters only from King Lorens —and the Demon Crown.

"The countryside is more awash in blood now than it was when Freow lived," said Santon. "There seems no end to the double-dealing and merciless battles."

The two men walked to the battlements. Some distance away Theoll spoke in guarded tones with Captain Squann. Squann's arm rode high in a sling and bloody bandages attested to his wound sustained in battle for the new king.

"What do they discuss?" wondered Santon.

Vered did not even glance in the baron's direction. "Plots to overthrow Lorens. Theoll is not the kind to take defeat easily. He has been on the throne, however briefly, and tasted the heady wine of kingly power."

"Power," snorted Santon. "What power can mere men bring to bear against the Demon Crown? Lorens sees and hears everything, no matter where in the kingdom."

"There," said Vered, pointing. "See how the troops line up along the River Ty? A good tactic. Gaemock must either retreat or sustain massive damage to his flank."

"The siege was ill-conceived."

"He had no choice after Duke Freow died." Vered smiled weakly. "Dews Gaemock might have been king if we had not returned with Lorens. Theoll's iron grip would have spawned more dissension within the castle than twenty years of civil war had."

"Nosto could have controlled them with his Inquisition," countered Santon.

"But the Inquisitor is not totally under Theoll's power. Not yet. Archbishop Nosto works for his own ends. He might even believe in what he is doing."

"The saints help us all, if that be true," said Santon. "Forty-three have been put to the Question and died just since we've been in the castle."

"Forty-three in only nine days," mused Vered. "Bloody times. Look! Gaemock retreats, as I thought."

"Even with Belmorgan and Tember supporting Lorens' soldiers, they cannot score a clean victory over Gaemock. See how he slips away to the north?"

"The Uvain Plateau is a difficult spot to hide in," said Vered. "Especially when Lorens magically spies on everyone." A shudder raced up his spine. He fell silent and lost himself in thought.

"Did we do right?" asked Santon. "Bringing Lorens back? Even if it was what Alarice wanted, did we do the proper thing for Porotane?"

"The civil war comes to an end," said Vered. "More death must precede peace, but it comes. Lorens slowly unites the scattered rebel bands— or annihilates them."

"Gaemock's followers are too loyal. He will not be denied the throne."

Vered said nothing to this. He agreed. Had fate turned in different ways, he might have been a supporter of Dews Gaemock, rebel and thief though the man was.

"We know so little about Lorens."

"He works swiftly to consolidate his rule," said Santon.

"But he kills when a better, if slower, way would be through negotiation. He knows the innermost secrets of everyone confronting him. He could use that rather than force of arms. There's been so much killing. Too much."

"He changes, even as we watch."

Both Santon and Vered jumped in surprise at the newcomer. Vered turned to see the court jester behind them. They had been so engrossed in their discussion that neither had heard Harhar approach.

"What are you saying, fool?" demanded Santon.

Harhar shrugged and cut a caper. "He turns cruel. The Demon Crown does it to him. It might do it to anyone enduring its magics night and day."

"He never removes it?" asked Vered, startled at this revelation. He remembered the way it had affected Lorens when he had donned the crown for the first time.

"Never. And he changes, always he changes. Who's to say that this is bad? Or good? Not I, not I!" Harhar jumped to the battlements and started walking on his hands along the precipice.

"Porotane will be at peace one day soon," said Santon. "That is good."

"Good," echoed Vered. "Yes, I suppose it is. It is what Alarice sought for the kingdom."

"The Glass Warrior!" called Harhar. "Such beauty, such courage. Yes, yes, it is what she sought for Porotane. But is it all that she sought?"

For that neither Vered nor Birtle Santon had an answer.

THE BEST IN SCIENCE FICTION

- ☐ 53125-6 DRAGON'S GOLD by Piers Anthony and Robert E. Margroff $3.95
- ☐ 53126-4 Canada $4.95

- ☐ 53103-5 SHADE OF THE TREE by Piers Anthony $3.95
- ☐ 53104-3 Canada $4.95

- ☐ 53172-8 BEYOND HEAVEN'S RIVER by Greg Bear $2.95
- ☐ 53173-6 Canada $3.95

- ☐ 53206-6 VOYAGERS II: THE ALIEN WITHIN by Ben Bova $3.50
- ☐ 53207-4 Canada $4.50

- ☐ 53257-0 SPEAKER FOR THE DEAD by Orson Scott Card $3.95
- ☐ 53258-9 Canada $4.95

- ☐ 53308-9 THE SHADOW DANCERS: $3.95
- ☐ 53309-7 G.O.D. INC. NO. 2 by Jack L. Chalker Canada $4.95

- ☐ 54620-2 THE FALLING WOMAN by Pat Murphy $3.95
- ☐ 54621-0 Canada $4.95

- ☐ 55237-7 THE PLANET ON THE TABLE by Kim Stanley Robinson $3.50
- ☐ 55238-5 Canada $4.50

- ☐ 55327-6 BESERKER BASE by Fred Saberhagen, Anderson, Bryant, Donaldson, Niven, Willis, Velazny $3.95
- ☐ 55328-4 Canada $4.95

- ☐ 55796-4 HARDWIRED by Walter Jon Williams $3.50
- ☐ 55797-2 Canada $4.50

Buy them at your local bookstore or use this handy coupon:
Clip and mail this page with your order.

Publishers Book and Audio Mailing Service
P.O. Box 120159, Staten Island, NY 10312-0004

Please send me the book(s) I have checked above. I am enclosing $_____
(please add $1.25 for the first book, and $.25 for each additional book to
cover postage and handling. Send check or money order only—no CODs.)

Name _____

Address _____

City _____ State/Zip _____

Please allow six weeks for delivery. Prices subject to change without notice.

POUL ANDERSON
WINNER OF 7 HUGOS AND 3 NEBULAS

THE BEST IN FANTASY

PHILIP JOSÉ FARMER